WEIRDSCAPES

AN OTHERWORLDLY ANTHOLOGY

Naomi Artemi

Leah Erickson

Anthony C. Ermi

Augusto Luiz Facchini

Odin Meadows

Tom Ray

Bendix Ross

Kyle Thompson

E.N. Welsh

INK ALCHEMY
BOOKS

AN INK ALCHEMY BOOKS ORIGINAL

Compilation copyright © 2025 by Ink Alchemy Books

All rights reserved. Published in the United States
by Ink Alchemy Books, New York.

Trade Paperback ISBN: 979-8-9906798-5-6
eBook ISBN: 979-8-9906798-6-3

Library of Congress Control Number: 2025912000

Cover Art by Lix North
lixnorth.com

For Amber,
a gem of a friend.
—NAOMI ARTEMI

For my husband,
and daughter.
—LEAH ERICKSON

To my beautiful wife,
Mary Elizabeth Coker Ray.
—TOM RAY

For me, because on reflection,
that's what this was.
—KYLE THOMPSON

For Mom, who fears the bugs
but loves the slugs.
—E.N. WELSH

CONTENTS

EDITOR'S FOREWORD

Welcome to *Weirdscapes*, Dear Reader.

Speculative fiction has a long tradition of giving us a portal to bizarre realities, which despite their heightened nature, give us a mirror in which to examine ourselves more clearly. These fantasies guide us to deeper truths by taking us by the hand and pulling us through spaces and times which might only nominally resemble our own.

This collection leans into that history, each tale allowing us to step through a door that crosses the threshold from the mundane to the strange. Alternate dimensions, different planets, post-apocalypses, human metamorphoses, and lands of the dead are all here for you to wander. By taking us on these journeys through the unreal, these stories give us a chance to examine deeper questions: Why does human connection so often sit in close proximity to hatred and violence? How are we meant to just let each other go after spending our whole lives fostering joy with our loved ones? Who are we if our entire lives are founded on mistruths–or when we learn that our understanding of the world was completely wrong?

What is it about this distance from our own reality that helps us process these questions? It seems that the further we stray from reality, the closer we get to some sense of the truth of things.

Perhaps it's no wonder that we gravitate to stories that deal with the macabre and twisted as a means of understanding ourselves and our world. Our biggest questions seem most pressing when our own world has taken a turn for the bizarre. In the past decade, we've all collectively dealt with a global pandemic, political and economic instability, wars, and a world run by folks who seem to have a tenuous relationship with truth and the people they're leading. Our own world seems less recognizable each year.

Our minds might even use fantasy as a means of self-defense, so that we might process reality more completely from a position of cognitive safety. In the midst of the pandemic, my body turned on me in a big way. Over the course of a summer and fall, my life changed dramatically. I could barely eat at the risk of suffering the worst pain I have ever experienced. I lost eighty pounds in just a few months. I did not recognize myself or my life. When I finally got a diagnosis, I learned that my issues all stemmed from a medical problem I'd thought had been completely resolved (when you've been unequivocally told that a problematic organ has been removed years prior, only to find it is still very much inside you and literally wasting away, it's a shock).

I ended up taking many trips to the surreal while resolving a health crisis in the midst of a global pandemic. Multiple ER trips in excruciating pain led to quite a few doses of "the good stuff." Visual hallucinations became a regular part of my life as doctors tried to treat my symptoms in a world with hospitals stuffed full of those falling victim to a virus barely anyone understood. The pain medications helped, but the hallucinations (even the landscape painting on the wall of my hospital room that danced and swirled in a most unsettling fashion) allowed me an escape from that version of myself that I no longer recognized. They gave my brain space to wonder why all this was happening and to hunt for the parts of my world that I could still recognize (like the love, care, and tenderness of my partner, Kim, who very much was going through this with me).

Finally, diagnosis in hand, I was given a solution by my (new) doctors. I needed surgery, but prior surgeries and scar tissue were liable to increase the complexity of the operation. We anticipated difficulties and a tough recovery. Scheduling such treatments takes time under the best circumstances, which we certainly weren't in. I had weeks to mentally prepare and sink fully into all of the anxieties that come along with big medical news.

The surgery came and went and when I woke up from anesthesia, I was given the hardest truth of the whole ordeal. After months of illness and weeks of dreading a complex surgery and lengthy recovery, I woke up and was told, "Everything went perfectly. There was a lot of scar tissue to fight through, but the surgeon managed to work around it and you were only under for a few hours." Not just that, but I could return home *that very day*.

It was ludicrous. It was impossible. My mind chose to drift into fantasy while it processed this new reality again. I was convinced for months that I was living in an extremely vivid dream. I was not recovering (and eventually, recovered). Surely, I must still be under the knife and everything I was experiencing was some kind of wild hallucination. Things were suddenly going so much better than they had the previous year of my life, that it could only be fiction.

I spent months in this weirdscape, wondering how and when I might suddenly wake up and start my real recovery. These flights of fancy gave me time to understand how my view of the world had changed. How I had changed. How my life had changed. While it was (and still is) a bit scary to have felt so deluded, as I write this story out, I find myself grateful to my mind for protecting itself and providing me a lens, no matter how strange, by which I could examine reality from a new angle.

This is what fiction does. I hope the stories contained herein give you that same opportunity: a chance to look at life's questions and your own perceptions from the relative safety of a book. While many of these tales might wander into the dark and macabre, it is my hope that you will find enjoyment, solace, and a deeper understanding of our world within.

Before I turn you loose to explore all of the alternate dimensions, alien worlds, and delusions present on the following pages, I want to take a moment to thank Naomi Artemi. Without her dedication and drive neither Ink Alchemy Books nor any of the anthologies released so far by this wonderful independent imprint would exist. I am so grateful that she handed me this theme and trusted me with the curation of this collection.

Now, allow your mind to wander as you join each of these authors who've seen fit to share their wildest and strangest hallucinations with the world.

Embrace the weird,
Kyle Thompson

NOW HERE WE SEE A WRETCHED THING

E.N. WELSH

Now here we see a wretched thing: Rancid and ruined—a cottage of collapse held aloft by soggy planks, held together by the sludge of many, embedded into this fetid mountain of waste. When winds whip, slithering stale 'tween garbage heaps, the dwelling creaks and moans and shrieks its tones in promise of inevitable, catastrophic structural failure. The little treasures housed within, reeking and writhing, rattle in putrid, misshapen mounds. This effluvial environment is uninhabitable, but not without inhabitants. Look—there is movement in the dankest corner. Beneath a stinking pile of string and frayed fabric, it stirs: A wretch, rousing.

Now here we see a rotten thing: Repulsive and emaciated, hairless and haggard, what flesh persists pallid and peeling. It has eight teeth left, all pocked with black tar the same as its gums. Its eyes hold little light and its mind holds little thought. Burrows dot its freakish form, some boring deep into lumpy, discolored organs, and it is called Flea Mattress. Bedding for the bedbugs and the bleeder mites, ticks, fleas and mosquitoes nesting on and within common ground. A home for the larva and the maggot, when the surrounding refuse becomes too repugnant for roosting. Their love for Flea Mattress is conditional, and the purest thing it will ever know.

It is morning, or it is about to be. Even underground there is a clear delineation between night and dawn, but internal time-keeping allows for a certain, uncertain precision. Flea Mattress has a busy day ahead of it, and can scarce afford to wait for first light's signal. It extricates an unwelcome centipede from its nostril and feels about the moldy floor for a rusty latch. There is purpose in this creature and its movements, and soon it is rewarded. From a hidden compartment, nestled securely, it plucks a wooden bucket, and hugs it lovingly. Precious skin had been spent to secure so valuable a vessel, and precious little remained: A small flap, whole and healthy, tucked beneath the chin and overlooked by some miracle. Care was taken to safeguard this skin; care was taken to safeguard this bucket, and to venture far with either poses substantial risk—but a special day demands special exceptions. Believing itself equipped for the trials ahead, the creature slunks out of the dwelling and into the wasting world.

Now here we see a timely thing: Three gargantuan orbs open above, spilling down amber light through cracks in the vast false sky. The eyes of a hairy red beast, long blind but still searching, searching; morning has arrived in the cavern. Aided by this illumination, Flea Mattress weaves its diminutive form through the labyrinth of sewage and drek and whatever rot's wrought, the path well-trod but amorphous. Some shifting of sludge or dislodging of guck warps the way and demands detour, but the process, the *path*, remains stagnant. This creature has no fear of becoming lost, but remains vigilant for the lost that may come upon it. Indeed, one such stray haunts the wider avenues ahead, an odious curse to passerby and general decency.

Now here we see a tragic thing: A bottom-feeder, despondent and begging, life worthless and claimed. It hunts daily for shavings and castoffs, its own skin spent long prior. It is called Something Sharp, and soon it will be murdered. It is aware. It is frightened. It is all too often ignored. Not yet a ghost but discarded by the living, it clings to dark thoughts of hope and one more day. Flea Mattress recognizes this desperation, and protectively cradles its chin skin and bucket as it hurries past. Its destination is near, and the source of Something Sharp's woes: A grand cathedral, loathsome and resplendent, fashioned of wattle and dirt and detritus and large bleached bones and mud and miserable labor and columns of a pitch black stone. Banners of fresh flesh and dried hide festoon the facade, advertising ill business conducted within. After a pause and two false starts to steel its nerves, Flea Mattress enters.

Now here we see a failing thing: The Graftwerk, a great patchwork, an always-yet-to-hatch work. With each scrap of skin tithed, with each debt of flesh collected, it grows closer to a perfection it can never reach. Adding others to itself layer by layer in a disgusting jigsaw of such majesty no mortal mind can comprehend, it expands and expands a grim, grimey shadow across the denizens of the depths. It is doomed, dying, and will outlive all it touches. From this throne all worth is determined, depleted, and denied, as the turgid Graftwerk swells colossal. Flanking it are two brutish enforcers, wielding cruel curved flaying implements to sate the gluttonous appetite of their immobile master. Flea Mattress is glad to be the morning's first petitioner; no time spent here is time spent well. It approaches the Graftwerk's imposing desk and looks up expectantly at the stitched fleshy thing. Wordlessly, a feeding pass is granted. Gracious to the point of obsequiousness, it accepts this earned gift and departs. Something Sharp watches from a nearby perch, boiling with envy.

Now here we see a steady thing: Flea Mattress trudges onward 'til beneath its feet the pollution gives way to cracked clay, 'til beneath its feet cracked clay gives way to spongy moss that shrieks when tread upon. Tangles of roots and all manner of bottom dweller lurk below the still waters of the bog, waiting to ambush the unwary, hidden from sight by dense afflicted foliage and an oily film that clings to the surface. Flea Mattress navigates all obstacles with practiced ease. One moist and muggy hike later, with new bugs nesting within, its destination comes into view: A large dead mushroom, dried and hollowed into a dwelling. Crossing the threshold, it is welcomed by a familiar obscenity.

Now here we see a wicked thing: Fungus protruding from various clumped pustules and laying claim to infected, infested patches of raw and open flesh. Stipes surround sinew, mycelium margin muscle, caps consume crown. Twisted limbs reflect a twisted interior. Spoiled from sole to soul and confusing canniness for virtue, it is called Rash Colony, and calls Flea Mattress its "girlfriend." This term is alien and likely holds little meaning. The creatures embrace, exchanging pestilence.

"Girlfriend! Long we wait for us together again. Pleasant see you, yes, pleasant for we. Good morning? *Great* morning?" Spores sputter from between elongated teeth with each utterance. Flea

Mattress beams, its own fractured teeth assembling into what could charitably be called a smile.

"Great morning! Feeding pass! Grub day!" It displays its bucket and pass proudly, expecting Rash Colony to rejoice. Instead, the vulgar creature sighs with practiced drama.

"Ah, how lucky girlfriend is! Not we, no no no, bad fortunes. Graftwerk make us drum, but we too hungry to drum! Graftwerk demand deal today, but we busy drumming! Miss last grub day too, we starve, we is! No time deal, no time eat! We wilts . . ." It slumps theatrically, torn eyelids drooping. Before Flea Mattress can extend a consoling hand, Rash Colony rights itself with alarming speed, a devilish twinkle in its sunken sockets. It has come up with an idea—just now—an idea it has rehearsed all week. "What if girlfriend drums? We deal, we feed, grow strong again. Give pass to we, we make good use."

Flea Mattress stiffens, unsure of what it's hearing and unwilling to accept what it's sure of. Rash Colony asks favors of it often—upon every visit—but never before such a violation. It recoils.

"No, no. Earn feed. My feed. Earned."

"We no take feed, we no take," Rash Colony coos. "We share. We go feed, bring bucket, give bucket to girlfriend. We will safekeep, yes? Fill full-brim and share our share, yes! We promise-promise, so no worry!" Flea Mattress remains hesitant, but this promise-promise lowers its guard. Rash Colony snatches the bucket and feeding pass before further protest can be mustered. "Girlfriend work hard, girlfriend rewarded. Trust us. Good eating, trust us. Move now quick, move now fast! Far walk to drumming ground. We talk to Graftwerk, we catch up. Quick!"

Now here we see a puzzled thing: Flea Mattress is ushered out the doorway, unsure of what's transpired. It knows it has a task, one it did not have before. It knows it lacks a bucket, which it paid dearly to acquire. So too it lacks a feeding pass, earned through worthy effort. Of all the things this thing now lacks, time is chief among them. The ritual site is far, but the drum far farther. A walk, a hike, a climb, a clambering. Flea Mattress has no time to think, only to act. There is only ever the time to act.

Now here we see a sacred thing: The remains of a god—or something of the sort—buried by soil and time until it pressed itself fused with the cavern's ceiling. Toxic to the tongue and inimitably vile, these qualities afford it a dead immortality, and an ecological niche. Flea Mattress stands precarious upon scaffolding, before a massive drum, built elaborately and haphazardly into the dead god's spine. It had at least one heart before its demise. With this drum, the beating would continue. Flea Mattress hefts two mallets with great effort. Below, a small crowd coagulates in anticipation.

Ba-bum. Ba-bum. Ba-bum. Ba-bum.

What was silenced stirs anew.

Ba-bum. Ba-bum. Ba-bum. Ba-bum.

New sounds arise from all around.

Ba-bum. Ba-bum. Ba-bum. Ba-bum.

Something moves within the walls.

Now here we see a joyous thing: Grubs of grand size emerge from tunnel networks, called by the bloodless beating of a dead dinner bell. Swarming the gargantuan corpse, they dig in. Messy eaters with multitudinous mouths, they rend and tear and gnash and gnaw. They alone can stomach the noxious deity. They alone purify what has putrefied. Their excretions—solid, liquid, and whatever falls between—cascade from various orifices in blessed rain upon the eager congregation: The dead god's toxic flesh, recycled into vital nutrients. The fortunate carry buckets, but most simply cup their hands and raise their open mouths in supplication. Flea Mattress attempts to scan the crowd for Rash Colony, but must refocus on the drumming. The rhythm is precise, or precise enough for a creature without any. Failure would not be tolerated, least of all by itself; on this holy day alone fresh feasting could be had, and Flea Mattress refused to disappoint. The adoring crowd delights in the transubstantiation, dancing and singing and ingesting and eating and licking and devouring and slurping and consuming and guzzling and the ritual goes on for hours.

Now here we see a tired thing: As finally the grubs retreat into their hollows, Flea Mattress slumps to the hard ground, exhausted. It lays still for a time, hoping to regain energy or faculties in any measure. It cannot feel its arms, though it can feel a burning where they ought to be. It cannot feel its legs, which is worrisome, as they are needed. The trek back to Rash Colony will be arduous, but thoughts of a bucket full-brim with ambrosia empowers Flea Mattress to stand, to stumble, to struggle. Shuffling down scaffolding, past pollution and cracked clay and moss that shrieks when tread upon. It does not feel the eyes upon it, or rather, it does not feel more than usual. It does not realize it is being followed, or rather, it mistakes the dread for what is always present. It enters the dwelling of Rash Colony, oblivious.

Now here we see a savage thing: Rash Colony sucks its mildewed fingers for any residual sustenance, too preoccupied to notice Flea Mattress's arrival. Too preoccupied to formulate excuses. Too preoccupied to conceal its crime. The bucket is in some dismal corner where it was haphazardly discarded. It is empty, licked clean. Marring the bottom, there is a hole. Screams tear Rash Colony from its blissful haze.

"Lie! Lie!" Flea Mattress cries, jumping and pointing and voice rising in distress. "No bucket full-brim! No bucket any-brim! You promise-promise! Lie!"

Caught unprepared, Rash Colony struggles at first to find placative words; when they manifest, however, each drips with a sweet and caustic venom.

"No lie girlfriend, no lie we say! Mistake made in hunger— we were so very hungry! Yes, from much tired, many fear, most excitement! Before grub, talked to Graftwerk, bargain struck, we struck, we did. New home for us, for girlfriend, us and we, sharing together."

This stems the mounting hysteria of Flea Mattress. Imagination begins to blossom, distracting from betrayal. Together with Rash Colony? No more oppressive hikes just to see a friendly face? Sharing, no more borrowing and failed returning? But no, there has been a lesson in today, in all days prior and pickled. Some thesis on trust and belief. Its eyes narrow.

"Bargain. What price?"

Rash Colony beams, its crooked teeth assembling into what could charitably be called a smile.

"Girlfriend skin!"

Vomit rising. Sharp and shallow breaths. Vision cloudy, ringing in gnawed ears. Leaking. Flea Mattress is on the brink of collapse.

"My skin!? No! No, my skin!" It covers all it has with all it can, curling tightly into a ball of spindly limbs. Rash Colony attempts to reassert control.

"Is only small flap, girlfriend! Big bargain, small-small price, small-small price. We never ask too much, yes? We only ask what fair . . ."

These vinegar words do nothing. An egg hatches in Flea Mattress's cheek, releasing several maggots.

"My skin. Why? Why my skin? My. Not you! Never you!" Every favor ever asked of it worms about its feeble recollection. Every suffering endured for promise-promised rewards that it can not recall receiving. Furious, it storms out of the dwelling, Rash Colony close behind. "My skin! My bucket! My skin! My bucket! My—"

There is a sudden, tearing violation. Something Sharp has darted past, and now it darts away, *away*, astray, off into elsewhere and afar. Flea Mattress feels a coldness, a certainty, and gropes frantically beneath its chin, desperate to feel a security it knows cannot be found. Not here. It breaks into a gallop, propelled on all fours, leaving behind Rash Colony and whatever impure words are being shouted in its wake. Something Sharp is escaping with its precious skin, *its* precious skin. The terrain is cruel, but Flea Mattress has experience. It gains upon the thief, and gains, until Something Sharp is tackled, pinned against the broad rooty base of a tainted tree.

"Give back! Give back! My skin! My bucket! Give back!"

It shakes at every exclamation. Tears and drool and snot dangle in thick strands. Something Sharp feels about for egress, and finds one. Flea Mattress feels something blunt against its chest, and a terrible emptiness. It lurches away from Something Sharp, which now holds a bloody stone. Temperature plummets. Breathing has become an ordeal; it looks down to see a bloody crater. Flea

Mattress probes numbly at the new cavity; each intrusion begets pathetic spittles of dark essence. It has yet to process the pain, but it begins to process the fear. Another strike lands, crashing into its skull. Flea Mattress topples to the boggy ground, sinking slightly into the muck. Something wet begins to fill its mouth, and something wet begins oozing from its head. Something Sharp drops its weapon with a gooey *splorch*, chittering what may be an apology before scuttling from the scene. Flea Mattress remains, and remains, though it can't be certain of this. Left is right, up is down, and down is also right. It doesn't understand where it is, or why. No, it is forming a why now, collecting stimuli to form an image. Foul taste, clammy cold, wrongness. It understands a hurt, or the idea of hurting. It understands a loss, or many, or perhaps a single, continuous instance. It understands a distance, or a relation to one: Its precious skin is moving farther and further away.

Flea Mattress rises from the mire, dripping, dripping, recalling what it means to see and feel and be. What it takes to see and feel and be. It forces a hand into the hole in its chest, digging. Filth-laden digits brush briefly against a faintly beating heart. Close. There is a purpose in this creature and its movements, and soon it is rewarded. Its hand wraps about a rib, its teeth clench against gums, and force is applied. It's with a pull, it's with a snap; eyes bulge in disbelief at what's been freed, and what pains it took to extract. The break is unclean, jagged—precisely as intended. This is a specialized tool; Flea Mattress is proud of what it is, but has no time to waste. Its precious skin is moving farther and further away.

Something Sharp scrambles through the marsh, moss shrieking beneath each blundering footfall. It clutches stolen salvation tightly in its grubby mitts, and this will cost it dearly. A gnarled root catches it by the ankle, and with no free hands to break the fall it plunges headfirst into the bog. Flailing and splashing, motivated by a pure panic, it fails to free itself from the suction of the mud and the tangle of the roots and the grasping of the tentacles. Its head surfaces, sputtering, a brief gift of clarity: It must focus if it wants to survive. Yet a cacophony distracts, an unmistakable wailing that draws closer, and closer. It redoubles its efforts, concentrating on what is necessary, pushing down the terror that serves only as anchor. Out, out, out—yes! The swamp releases its hold. It is free, it is free, please let it be free. Too late—Flea Mattress is upon it. Something sharp pierces Something Sharp, and green blood mixes with oily film. Something sharp pierces Something Sharp, and its shrill cries harmonize with the shrieking moss. Something sharp pierces Something Sharp, and its pathetic attempts to resist grant it nothing. Flea Mattress stabs again, and again, and again, each attack violently imprecise. Its body provided a weapon. Its body is a weapon. If only it realized sooner. Then it would not be afraid. Then it would not be destitute. Then it would not be here. Its own screams join the chorus. It stabs Something Sharp for each injury. It stabs Something Sharp for each indignity. It stabs. It stabs. It stabs. This continues longer than necessary.

Now here we see a drastic thing: Something Sharp lies dead, limbs curling over its pincushioned torso. Flea Mattress stands triumphant, miserable, gulping painful lungfuls of tainted air. A throbbing in its chest is understood but ignored. Only one thing holds meaning anymore. It rummages through the mud for its prize, anxiety mounting. Where is it? Where is it!? There! In the mandibles of a toe-biter. Flea Mattress yanks the flap free, and holds it close and dear. Upon examination, it has not emerged unscathed. Soaked in muck and peppered with small bites and scratches: A precious thing we see now stained. Would this ugly bauble suffice? Secure a future with Rash Colony? Secure a future alone? Earn a moment's rest, a moment's rest? It will have to. Despondent, Flea Mattress takes one shaky step, and then another, and then one more. It staggers 'til beneath its feet shrieking moss gives way to cracked clay, 'til beneath its feet cracked clay gives way to pollution.

Now here we see a wretched thing: Flea Mattress waits in the Graftwerk's queue, breathing laborious, a faint whistling emitting from its ruptured and leaking chest. In its right hand it holds precious skin, value fading rapidly. In its left it holds a shiv of rib, value awaiting appraisal. It has much time to think, and uses none to do so. As the line oozes forward, its movements are automatic and sluggish. There is no urgency; it is the day's final petitioner. Naught matters but the waiting, and the waiting matters not. At last it approaches the lopsided desk; the Graftwerk reaches out expectantly.

"Payment."

Flea Mattress stares blankly at the outstretched hand, then at the impatient collector's hollow eyes. There is no reflection, no connection. It is not alive in a way that can be recognized; it breathes, it covets, but this is the extent. It is constructed of that which lived once, of stitched skin detached from owner through flaying or less obvious violence. Flea Mattress cannot see its own skin in the ragged patchwork, but knows it must be part of it. Some beautiful graft, graded for its purity, now dully indistinguishable in the moldering mass. A small sacrifice to maintain a life detestable; a wound that festers and spreads its spoiling and will never, ever, heal. Rot atop rotten foundations, in a rotten hole and a rotten whole. Something hatches inside Flea Mattress, and its grip tightens.

ORPHAN

AUGUSTO LUIZ FACCHINI

Most of all it was the image of the cadaver that haunted him, the body lying still as though frozen in time, the skin stretched so tightly over the skeletal frame, the bones of the hand and shape of the skull visible under the veneer of flesh, eyes still open and mouth agape, giving the impression that in death the corpse still gasped for air in wild confusion. He hoped his father would not look that way anymore when he found him here. He lifted the oars from the ghostly waters and looked behind himself to get his bearings towards the shore, the shift in weight of his movement slightly rocking the little boat. The black shore of Hades stood in the distance stark against the waters of the Styx. Above the land, the air which he could not consider a sky, not in the way he knew a sky to be, was neither dark nor luminous, but rather a strange gloomy lightlessness, and without stars or moon. The ghostly pale of the river's waters stretched out before him, endless and vast in all directions, as silent and still as death. The only sound was his own breathing and the quiet motions of the water displaced by the movements of the boat and the touch of the oars.

Charon had denied him. He had forgotten to bring coins for the ferryman and in any case it was a trespass for the living to pass through the gates of Taenarum. The ragged man had only shook his head in silence at Orphan's pleas, pushed the ferry away from the shore with his long, crooked oar, and disappeared into the mist, the ghoulish green light of his lantern soon fading into the bleak nothing. He wandered along the cavernous shore of the river until among weeds and thick brambles he found the rowboat, caked with old dirt and crawling with strange insects. Still, the hull was without breach and the oars, though swollen and warped with the weight of years of water, were still serviceable. And so it was that Orphan resolved to row himself across the Styx.

Presently, he set himself back to rowing. Forward and back, forward and back. He pulled the oars with ease and watched as the water rippled in widening rings that extended out across the pallid plain. He could feel no progress towards land and yet he continued, resolute. The river seemed endless and despite his labors, the shore seemed ever distant. Nonetheless, he rowed.

§

In the days that followed after his father died, he helped his mother sort through the old things that had belonged to him. They sat on the floor of the walk-in closet in the bathroom and folded dusty shirts and put them in boxes upon which he had written "DONATE" in red sharpie.

"This will fit you," she said, turning a faded blue button-down over in her varicose hands. "You should take it with you."

"I won't have occasion to wear it," he had said, and she nodded as though in acquiescence of a terrible but inevitable truth, and trembled, and he could see her anguish so he embraced her, felt her frail body in his arms as she wept.

"All of these things of him," she sobbed softly. "All of these things. I'll have nothing left."

He clutched her head gently against his shoulder, felt the shuddering of her body as her tears soaked the fabric of his shirt. She was so small and fragile, like a baby bird. He wanted to tell her that it would all be all right in the end, but he could not find the words in himself.

"Ashes!" she sobbed softly. "All I will have left of him are ashes!"

He didn't know what to say.

So he just held her and they wept together.

§

I'll bring him back, he had decided then. Then everything will be right again, as it used to be. I'll go into the underworld and bring him back. The crooked places will be made straight and the rough places will be made plain. I'll bring him back. And so he was there, in the empty void of the Styx, rowing endlessly to a shore he could never approach. His face burned with tears and even though the raft felt weightless, his hands were sore from his grip on the oars. He gritted his teeth and rowed faster. The water splashed around him, and he thrashed furiously, futile. He turned and saw that black shore, unyielding, no closer. He doubled over in the seat of the boat and screamed. He screamed and screamed and heard his voice echo in the emptiness around him until the screaming in him died to pitiful sobbing and he sank his face into both his hands and wept, shuddering. The Styx remained indifferent, a stoic and placid expanse. The little boat rocked in rhythm with his lonely lamentation, and everywhere around him the lusterless nowhere was stillness and silence. He did not know how long he remained there, in that eerie realm between the world of the living and the world of the dead. Perhaps it was a few minutes, perhaps hours, perhaps years had gone by. In that timeless space, it was impossible to know for sure.

He must have fallen asleep. He awoke to a tugging at his clothes, a sharp scratching against his skin. Something was tearing into him. He startled awake, and saw a fluttering of feathers around him. The boat had somehow found its way to the black shore, and its prow was wedged solidly into the bleak ground. There were three haggard figures prowling near him.

"This one still has meat on his bones," cackled one of the creatures. It was like a bony and bug-eyed old woman, witch-like in countenance, with the black and lice-ridden wings and legs of a buzzard. She perched on the edge of the little boat and twisted her head at an angle inconceivable by the logic of anatomy, peered at him cruelly, the wicked smile stretched across her face showing rows of sharp teeth rotten yellow and black. Her wasted breasts sagged limply from her skeletal frame, and her hair, like damp seaweed, hung in ragged strips which clung to her leathery and wart-covered flesh. The stench was miserable, like putrid offal, and roiled his guts with the threat of vomiting. The other two, just as vile, crawled around on the land just outside the boundary of his vessel. Swiftly, he grabbed one of the oars and thrust it at the creature on the boat. She fluttered back a pace.

"Get away from me!" he shouted.

"Still too much fight in him," crowed one of the crones, circling the boat like a predator.

"We can just wait a little while longer," said another, "he won't last."

"Get away from me," he said, rising unsteady to his feet and shooing them with the oar.

"You're the intruder here," hissed the one on the boat, batting away the paddle of the oar he waved at her face.

"Intruder!" Shrieked another.

"You shouldn't be here!" Snarled the last.

"Where am I? Is this the land of the dead?"

"Almost," said one, slinking away from the boat.

"Yes, almost. The gate is just beyond." The one on the boat pointed to the distance with a long and crooked finger, like the jagged branch of a barren tree. Her fingers terminated in long, sharp fingernails, as black and rotten as her fangs, curled at the tips like talons. "Go if you dare. You won't make it far."

"Why does such a succulent morsel wander here?" The one who spoke was running her claws along his back, licking her lips like a hungry mongrel. He spun around, wide-eyed with terror, and swung the oar at her, but she fluttered away. He stumbled and fell over backward onto the boat. The hags all cackled and beat their wings.

"I'm looking for someone," he said.

They cackled again. Shrieking, they took flight into the dismal ether above.

"You search in vain!"

"There is no one to find here!"

"No one here is anyone anymore!"

Their shrieks reverberated in the air as did the sound of their wings. They cackled madly, and were gone in a flutter.

"You're wrong!" Orphan cried out after them, his face flushed with fury. "Stupid birds! What the hell do you know!" He feebly tried to hurl the oar in his hand, but it only clattered uselessly against the stern of the rowboat. He kicked his feet madly against the hull and beat his fist upon the side rail. He allowed his breathing to escalate to heaving bursts from his lungs and screamed and screamed until his head hurt and his vision blurred with burning tears. At last, when he tired of his raging, with a profound exhalation, he stood himself up again and tried to get his bearings.

The land was soft earth but abysmally black. He felt neither heat nor cold. Wisps of icy smoke rose from soil, bathing the landscape in an ominous fog. He looked further inland, where high upon a distant hill he could make out the imposing shape of a sepulchral structure. The gate the winged hag had spoken of, he ventured to guess. He stepped slowly and deliberately out of the boat, and with some effort dragged it further ashore so it wouldn't drift away.

On he slogged up the hill. The silence of the Styx had been replaced by susurrant whispers that seemed to wash over him from all directions at once. He could not make out the voices or their words, it was all an indistinct murmuring that coursed through the emptiness like the liquid bubbling of a lazy rivulet. His feet sank softly into the black earth with each stride, and though he carried nothing, he felt the weight of a great burden press down upon him, as though the gravity of his own guilt and solitude swelled to palpable heft.

§

He had not known his father in life, not in the way he could say he truly knew anyone. The man had been reserved, often distanced from himself and the rest of the family. Orphan remembered that in the final days, when his father was unwell and bedridden, what sensible things he could manage to say were pleading to return home, away from the polyethylene oxygen tubes and the wires and the beeping machines and the nurses and aides in medical scrubs who turned him and cleaned him each day with irreverence and detached professional efficiency. Is this how he would find his father here? A frail and confused invalid, lost in his own mind and wandering aimlessly among the dead, pleading with desperate eyes, knowing neither where he was nor why he could not return home? This thought alone filled Orphan with terror. He could not bear the weight of what they had to deny his father, that he had been left to die alone in a hospital bed in the middle of the night. The immense weight he felt bearing down upon him seemed to increase a thousandfold. On and on Orphan trekked up the interminable hill, carrying with him the invisible load of all his misgivings.

He had been lost in his own doubts, watching his own footsteps, when he looked up to find he had come upon another also ascending the blighted slope. The figure was wiry, long-limbed, clad in tattered rags that may have once been white but had long turned yellowish brown with age and soiling. A long, bristled beard of ash-grey whiskers did more to cover the body of the wretched man than did the remnants of his clothes. Against a massive stone the elder strained his frame, buckled against it, with knees bent and torso leaning forward, both arms pressed against the boulder, inching up the slope with each heaving stride.

Orphan stared dumbfounded for a moment, watching the slow and deliberate rolling of the stone against the churning black dirt, the furrow on the earth that trailed behind the man and his labor. He then approached, compelled to help, but the old man reproached him with a sharp and reprimanding look. The gaze pierced Orphan, and there was a solemn quality in those dark eyes, under his heavy brow, sunken with long years of sorrow, something deep within them that even all the hardness and misery of life's endless toil could not reach. Without a word, the old man shook his head, and continued his exertion.

"I understand," said Orphan. "This weight we all have to carry alone." Whether the man had heard him Orphan could not be certain for he made no reply. He wept as he watched the venerable man struggle on. There was nothing else to say or do, so he inhaled sharply, wiped his face on the sleeve of his shirt, and resumed his own trek up the hillside.

§

He didn't have the kinds of memories with his father that many of his contemporaries would have shared with theirs. No games of playing catch in the backyard or being taught how to use a shaving razor for the first time. Mostly, he remembered how his father could magically trap cigarette smoke in a glass bottle and seal it with a cork. As a child, Orphan would watch the smoke swirl and twist within the glass, shaping itself into a myriad of dreamlike forms. In his eyes, the swirling vapor could become a horse, an elm, an airplane, a castle.

He remembered sitting in the driver's seat of the family minivan for the first time, and his father teaching him how to change the gears on the manual transmission. "You have to understand,"

Orphan's father had said, "this is a weapon. Do you understand?" They seldom had serious conversations. Yet this time, his father's expression conveyed a reverence for the importance of the matter that demanded seriousness in equal measure. Orphan nodded in acknowledgment then, a teenager so eager to enjoy the measure of independence that came with driving a car, without knowing he would carry that moment in remembrance for the rest of his days. Then he followed his father's directions as he pressed down the clutch and moved the gearshift to the first position.

He remembered how, so many years later, when age, sickness, and pain ravaged his father's body, Orphan sat once again in the driver's seat, this time ferrying his father to a medical appointment with a clinical pain specialist that promised precious little relief from the endless hurting.

"You have to promise me," his father said, in his ill-fitting suit jacket now too big for his shrunken body, as he clutched his walking cane with both his hands, "you will see your mother taken care of when I'm gone."

"Don't talk like that, Dad." Orphan said. "You'll be with us for a very long time yet."

"You have to understand. I don't want her put in a nursing home," he said. "Do you understand?" He was looking at Orphan with that same somber gaze as he did so many years ago, when he taught him how to drive a stick. There was something in the sincerity of his eyes. As if deep within them there remained an essential quality that even all the hardness and misery of the long years of sickness and ruin could not reach.

"I promise," Orphan said. "I will take care of her."

§

When he could no longer see the shores of the Styx in the distance behind him, Orphan came at last to the gate into the land of the dead, where the departed all stood in line waiting for admittance. They were not phantasmal as he had imagined, not translucent, floating, and glowing with ethereal light as he had seen in ghost movies. They were just as solid and real as he, though they had a lusterless pale that shrouded them like shadow, so they were just as colorless as the silent ether above. There were all manner of people, old and young, tall, short, fat, thin, and all kinds in between. He approached them.

"Excuse me, I'm looking for my father." From his shirt pocket, he produced the photograph he had brought with him. It depicted his father as he appeared in the obituary — a professional headshot portrait of him in his days just before retirement that his old job had used on their website. "Have you seen this man? Can you tell me where he is?"

But all of the dead just shook their heads.

A stocky old woman in a floral dress holding a paper sack full of oranges, a thirty-something in a sharp business suit holding a briefcase, a barefoot child in overalls dragging a ragged teddy bear, they all just shook their heads solemnly without so much as a glance at the picture he tried to show them. He went on down the line, pleading with urgency, but none would answer him. Like resigned somnambulists, they only shuffled forward in their queue, without regard for his desperate supplications, a parade of shambling phantoms.

"This door is not for you to pass, mortal." A chorus of voices rumbled to him in triplicate, their resonance like the low growl of thunder. Still clutching in his fingers the polaroid he had been presenting to the dead, Orphan turned to see the one who spoke. Six eyes of shining yellow were trained upon him. The hound was immense in its bulk, its three fearsome heads extending from its singular hulking physique. Serpents writhed all along its spine, and a dragon-like tail whipped back and forth along the ground like a slithering eel. It was sitting on its haunches, seeming neither threatening nor benign. Rather, it regarded him with the same cold indifference as everything else in the underworld thus far had. Next to the creature stood a monolithic black stone arch, towering before him like an obelisk.

When Orphan stared and did not reply, the trio rumbled again. "This threshold is for the dead to pass. And the scent of life still clings to your bones, mortal." The last was accompanied by a perfunctory sniffing from one of the heads.

"Please, I am only searching for someone."

"There is no one here."

"My father," Orphan showed the hound the picture, "has he passed through the gate?"

"No one here is anyone's father, mortal," replied the choir of heads. "Nor are they anyone's mother or son or daughter, nor are they brother or sister, nor are they husbands, wives, uncles, aunts, or distant cousins. No one here is a scholar, a patrician, a poet, a laborer, or a doctor. No one here is anyone anymore. All are just dead."

Orphan sank within himself, dismayed. He watched as the line of the dead continued to promenade through the gate, the multitude extending out far beyond it, to a point in the distance beyond his reckoning.

"But yes," the hound said at last. "The one in your picture did pass through here. It was sometime ago, I remember not when."

"Is there any way I can see him?"

"You do not need my permission. My words to you were counsel, mortal, not a mandate. I do not guard this gate from anyone entering, but I suffer none to leave."

"So I may pass?"

"This is the final door through which we all must pass. Even I, one day, when the last mortal soul has ambled through, must take myself to the land beyond. If you wish to enter sooner rather than later, that decision is yours. But know — you shall not leave again."

Orphan stared for a long time at the gate. The structure was as imposing as it was astonishing, rising above him to a colossal height, the measure of which he could not possibly even estimate. It made Orphan feel insignificant and small.

"All the crooked places will be made straight," he muttered to himself, his voice shallow and trembling. "All the rough places will be made plain."

He closed his eyes and swallowed in his breath. Then he walked on through.

§

The call from the hospital came in the dead hours of night. In the darkened house, Orphan heard his mother cry out, and followed the sound of her shattering heart through the lightless halls to find her wandering aimlessly among the cabinets and family portraits, wailing alone in the dark.

"What do we do?" she begged, "How is it done?"

He didn't understand at first. Then he saw the abject sorrow on her face and understood all at once. But he didn't know how it was done either. As she was in her nightshift, he helped her dress herself and they drove through the deserted streets under the lights of lonely lamps to the hospital.

A nurse at his ward had been waiting to unlock the door and let them in. She whispered her condolences as they entered into the fluorescent light of the corridor, where her colleagues in floral pattern scrubs were pushing carts loaded with the recondite machines used to keep dying old people alive. The door to his hospital room had been left open. They had to draw open the hospital curtains to find him there, in between the plastic bed rails, under the thin standard-issue blanket, still as a memory. Under the sepia light of that dingy and narrow room, the bubbling and hissing of the oxygen machine the only sound, Orphan could almost believe that he was only sleeping. That he would awaken again, startled and confused, moaning haggardly, as he often had when they had come to visit him in these final days. Yet that was only illusion. What was before him was only a cold cadaver. His mother, her face twisted in the colors of anguish and resignation, touched her forehead to the dead man's, clutched his cold, gaunt hand, wept soundlessly. Orphan stood behind her, with his hand on her shoulder, her body trembling quietly under his touch. And there the three of them for a time that seemed eternity remained, in silence, the dead man and his son and his widow, a triptych of the sorrow at the end of life.

§

Beyond the gate the space above the black earth was a cosmic nebula of bluish purple and crumbled statues of onyx black stone stood sentinel along avenues of tomb-grey ash. Stately edifices, accented by monumental columns, appeared as somber as mausoleums. The dead shuffled in their solemn procession along the street towards a great hall in the epicenter of the necropolis, and their haunting whispering filled the air. Orphan walked beside the marching line of the condemned, searching for his father. Still, no one would speak to him or acknowledge his presence. It was as if among the deceased he was the true phantom, invisible and unheard, only a spectator into this strange world. He went along, for how long he did not know, for in that place there was neither light nor shadow, nor did he feel weariness, hunger, or thirst, and the ashen road seemed to continue on and on without end. At last, he came to a crossroad where roads converged, and at the center, upon a stone pedestal, rose a colossal statue of three women conjoined together, each facing a different direction, and their hands held serpents, torches, keys, and other objects Orphan did not recognize. All around the base of the pedestal grew stalks bearing ghostly blossoms of white asphodels.

He gazed up at the idol in wonder. The eyes of the face that towered above him seemed to look down with disdain. With little hope, he held up the photograph as high as his arm could reach, and called out above the din of whispering.

"I'm looking for this person," he bellowed, afraid his voice would not reach the figure's dizzying stature. "Have any of you seen him pass?"

To his astonishment, the statue replied.

"No one here is a person anymore, mortal," spoke one of the stony faces, austere in expression. Her voice was a hollow echo in the dismal quiet. "No one here is a —"

"I know!" He called again. "No one's a father or mother or brother or anything. I've been told already. But I seek this one anyway. Can you help me?"

The statue was silent for a long time. Orphan stared, awaiting a reply, but none came, and the sculpture — if indeed it was a carving of stone — was as unmoving as the grave. So at last, Orphan relented.

"Okay. Thank you anyway," he said and began to slink away, but stopped again when the figure replied.

"Haughty is a mortal who demands answers from the divine," one of the faces said.

"Yet more haughty is a mortal who enters the realm of the dead to seek out one here interred," spoke another.

"Do you believe you alone suffer in the wake of death?" said the third.

"Are you so misguided to think none of the other dead here left behind sorrow in their crossing?" The faces continued speaking in turn, one after the other. Orphan circled the pedestal, observing them from below, as their voices rang out in sequence, permeating the space around him.

"Or is so great your hubris that you believe you alone can undo what no other mortal before you ever has?"

"It's just that everything is wrong now," Orphan called, the pace of his orbit becoming more frantic and erratic. "It's not as it used to be."

"Fool!"

"Arrogant folly!"

"Obstinate disregard!"

The ground seemed to tremble with their accusations, and Orphan stumbled headlong, struggling to maintain his footing. He lurched forward in his circling, flailing his arms to keep from falling.

"What if I trade places with him?" He called, regaining some balance, but now striding with a desperate and unsteady gait as he made his circuit. "Stay here in his stead? Could he go back?"

"Do you dare presume,"

"That none before,"

"Have this same bargain offered?"

"Please," he pleaded. He was now in a mad dash around the trimorphic goliath.

"There is no bargain, mortal!"

"No measure of wealth,"

"No pact or treaty,"

"No service or penance,"

"There must be something!" His legs were vaulting before him, and as the earth shook again, he became tangled in his own limbs, and went sprawling onto the ground.

"NOTHING." The three said the last all at once. This reverberated in shockwaves, rang out like the toll of a bell, shook the foundations of buildings and lingered in the air, a vacuous echo, definitive in its finality. Fallen, Orphan balled up his fist and hammered it into the earth, weeping uselessly into the crook of his own arm. "Nothing . . . nothing . . ." the sound resonated.

§

The funeral home had offered a private viewing just for the family. In a conference room, Orphan sat next to his mother as the man in a tasteful navy suit and green tie clicked through a slideshow of all of the options and their costs. His mother stared vacantly. When he spoke to her, it was as if she could not hear him.

"Do you want the wreath arrangement or the — mom? Mom —"

"What is it?" She said as though she had just been awakened from a stupor.

"We're trying to choose the flower arrangement for the service," Orphan said, pointing to the colorful pictures in the pamphlet the nice man in the tasteful navy suit had given them. Her own copy was clutched absently in her fingers, unopened.

"Just choose whatever ones seem best," she muttered, weakly, and lowered her gaze. Her breaking voice was barely audible over soft piano notes playing from speakers hidden somewhere in the room, among the decorative vases and paintings of sea shores and sunsets.

The very next morning they returned for the viewing, which was to be done before the full service. The funeral home people had put him on a platform, covered him from the mid-breast down with a dark blue blanket, placed his hands over one another so delicately, and closed his eyes and mouth, so that the whole appearance was that of a man at peace. All around were white candles and wreaths of flowers. She collapsed.

She had been weeping beside the cadaver when she buckled down. Her hand remained precariously on the shoulder of the dead man, like a quivering leaf easily tumbled over by the slightest breeze. The rest of her body sank to the floor like a withering blossom. Orphan caught her by the shoulder. He knelt beside her and tried to comfort her with words, but she did not seem to hear him and instead only wept with her head bowed towards the floor. When she finally spoke again her only words were, "Take me away from here."

§

At last Orphan arrived at a crumbling yet grand edifice,

boasting platoons of regal columns aligned rank and file like gargantuan marching soldiers carved of onyx stone, and graven upon each of them in relief were images of people adorned in togas or ancient armor, with sandaled feet, sometimes bearing weapons and shields and at other places carrying urns or harps. The dead all filed into this building through a massive open threshold that yawned open as the mouth of a great fish swallowing them all like tiny plankton. Orphan pushed through the throngs of the dead and entered into the great hall, wherein the multitude congregated in number beyond counting, their gaze fixed trancelike upon an arched threshold beyond which Orphan could see a triumvirate tribunal. All of the murmuring susurrus that permeated the air outside ceased within these walls and the vast chamber was as soundless as a crypt. He wove his way through the assembly, feebly asking for his father, but the dead remained transfixed on the court of judgment beyond the door. The task of finding any particular individual in the endless sea of mesmerized petitioners seemed herculean. Orphan looked at the photograph in his hand, feeling something heavy within him sink and collapse into ruin as though a support bearing a ponderous load had been demolished. He buckled to his knees and bowed his head in defeat. He knelt there and wept as the host of spirits moved slowly around him, and when he had no tears left anymore, he simply remained idle, his heart as vacuous as the infinite quiet around him. The inkling of thought that he should get up again and persist in his endeavors extinguished inside him like the feeble flame of a match doused in darkness. Sorrow enveloped him like a funeral shroud and there he remained, surrounded by countless souls, yet irrevocably alone.

There were so many congregants gathered that at first he did not notice the one figure among the crowd who moved with intention towards him. But unlike the shades around him who no longer bore the color and trappings of life, she was vibrant and vigorous. Where she walked, bursts of bright flowers bloomed at the touch of her feet, and motes of golden light hovered about her like tiny faeries.

"You need not await judgment here among the dead, mortal," she spoke brightly, her voice resounding like notes of harp string in the austere silence. "At least not for a little time yet."

Orphan, on his knees like a crumpled up piece of refuse long forgotten, looked up and admired her through his bleary vision. She was wearing a sprightly green dress, adorned with brilliant golden flowers, and her sable dark hair cascaded in tresses about her shoulders. In one hand, she absently twirled a long stalk of wheat. She peered down at him with glistening emerald eyes.

"It doesn't matter anymore," Orphan stammered and wiped his wet face on the palms of both his hands. "I can't leave anyway, and I can't find the person I came here looking for."

She knelt down beside him, and gently laid a hand upon his shoulder. Orphan felt a pulse of warmth course through him at her touch. She was smiling at him, softly. There was something about the way her eyes washed over him that felt comforting and familiar, like the tune of an old song or the caress of a favored blanket.

"If you're worried about that silly old dog at the gate," she chuckled, "rest assured, I know how to bring him to heel."

Orphan nodded glumly. He looked down at the photograph and then back at her. He tried to speak but all he could manage was unintelligible blubbering.

"There now," she caressed his hair and made a hushing sound.

"It will be all right." She picked up the photograph delicately in her fingers, leaning forward slightly as she did so, and suddenly Orphan could smell flowers and hear birdsong. "Is this the one you're looking for?"

Orphan nodded, sniffling. He felt like a disconsolate child, unable to articulate anything of substance, only pathetic whimpering.

"We can find him together, come." She rose to her feet and took his hand in hers with a featherlike touch. Orphan felt a rush of warmth radiate through him, filling him with something that felt like golden light. Unsteady, he stood again. She smiled once more, and with his hand still in hers, she guided him through the throng, gliding swiftly and with gentle ease though this way and that, like the dancing wisp of a dandelion carried in the kiss of a spring zephyr. Orphan followed, entranced by the sound of her merry laughter and the radiant luminance she wore about her.

"Look, see," she said at last and pointed and Orphan could see among the multitude a feeble figure in an ill-fitting suit jacket and matching trousers that sagged on his gaunt frame. There was no mistaking the slump of the shoulders, the arch of the spine, the bewildered visage. Orphan was looking at his father.

He parted from his guide and went to him.

"Dad," he called. "Dad, it's me, Dad!"

He stood before his father and looked into his disoriented eyes. Grasping the old man by the shoulders, Orphan regarded him with great trepidation.

"Dad, it's me, your son," he said and he threw his arms around him. The old man did not return the embrace, but rather stood there, motionless like a mannequin. "Dad, I'm here."

The old man made no response.

"I've come to bring you back home," Orphan continued. "I'm sorry I took so long, Dad. But I'm here now. We can go home." He embraced the old man again and wept bitterly. "I'm sorry," he cried into the old man's shoulder. "I'm sorry I couldn't bring you home when you were in the hospital. I know you wanted to come home, but I couldn't bring you then."

He pulled away and looked upon the old man's countenance. His father only stared blankly, as all the other dead, without any sign of recognition or understanding.

"Dad . . . ?" Orphan said, and placed his hand on his father's brow. "Dad, can you hear me?"

Nothing.

"Dad, please," Orphan pleaded. He felt a swell of desperation surge in him. He looked around, though he knew not what for. "Dad, listen to me. Dad — Dad, look at me!" He put his hands on each side of his father's face. He tried desperately to capture the attention of those vacant eyes. "Please, Dad, you have to come home."

He threw his arms around the old man, felt how fragile he was, even in this place.

"Please, Dad," Orphan said through a burst of tears. "It's time to come home. Mom misses you, Dad. I don't know how to help her. I don't. We don't know — I don't know how to do things without you. Please. You have to, Dad. I'm sorry. I'm sorry I failed you, okay? I'm sorry I wasn't a good son. I'm so —"

The bitter weeping overcame him and he clutched his father tightly to him, and sobbed with great consternation. When at last the anguish in him abated and he regained himself, he again looked upon his father's face. The distinct features stood out to him. In the wrinkles that beset the corners of his eyes, the lines of his furrowed brow, the curve of the old man's jaw, Orphan could see all of the hardship and toil that the years of living had worn upon him. He could see the weariness, the longing, the weight of duty and love.

"All the crooked places will be made straight," he muttered softly, barely a whisper. "All the rough places will be made plain."

At last Orphan saw — there was a tiny spark in the glassy desolation of his father's eyes. The man was looking at him very intently. There was something in the intensity of this gaze that Orphan recognized. It took him a moment, but then all at once he saw it and knew completely: it was that same deep sincerity with which his father had looked at him so many years ago. That special something that all the long sadness of life could never touch. His dad was still in there. He was there.

"I understand," said Orphan with a solemn nod. "This weight we all have to carry alone."

He stepped away and watched as the specter passed him, along the rest of the procession, through the archway.

He felt the woman's warm hand once again on his shoulder. He watched without speaking for a time, then knelt down briefly to pick up the photograph of his father's portrait — he must have dropped it during the exchange. He nodded with acquiescence. He looked at the woman in the green dress standing behind him. There was a tender, merciful radiance of warmth emanating from her, which reminded Orphan of lying down on the soft grass of a sunlit meadow.

"Are you ready to go?" she asked simply.

Orphan nodded slowly.

§

When he at last came again to the riverbank on the side of the world of the living, he dragged the little rowboat ashore and left it on the rocky embankment where he had found it among the brambles and leaves. It was day and the sun was rising, rose and gold in the eastern sky. Orphan trudged up the muddy shore, through the thistles and brambles, away from the riverside. When he reached the road, he brushed the dirt from his clothes and with a last look at the misty waters of the Styx, he began his trek homeward. In his hand — he had gathered them for his mother — he carried a small clutch of white asphodels.

RABBIT FLESH

ANTHONY C. ERMI

I

Nitroglycerin. Phial. Rabbit flesh tightly bound around, soft, pliable. Footsteps traveled down shafts, echoing, echoing through spraying corridors silent and destitute, stripped of all things valuable. Stone; only stone remained. Chaoxiang breathed heavy, but not too heavy, for he could not let his hands shake. He could not let them quiver. But his fingers tensed, his spine trembled, beads of sweat came down his forehead as he walked. Thick as sludge, the air was; thick as mud, thick as the layers of stone that surrounded him, rock, rock, rock. Miles of the stuff. He couldn't help but think about it. It was human nature.

The little wrap of rabbit-skin, the volatile, the deadly bundle, slickened with his perspiration. Drenched in fear, drenched in sweat, and the walk was endless, through a void with only a dim lantern to guide. Nitroglycerin. Just a shake, just a disturbance, the slightest touch, could . . . unthinkable. It had happened to others, but he could not consider it. He was different, he was not them. He had crossed the sea. He had crossed the world. He had come with nothing on his back but his own skin. He was not them.

The tunnel ended and the lantern shined on collapsed rock piled in the center of the way. He did not know the types, but there were different colors: reds, maroons, near black shades; different consistencies too, some porous and powdery, some that split sheer and straight. Rocks all the same. All more than enough to kill when dropped from a few feet up. All sound enough to trap, to enclose, to suffocate. Tiptoeing, he approached as if the boulders might hear, might jump out at him for trespassing, might collapse all over again.

Chaoxiang placed his package between a crease of the shattered rock, careful, hands like air, hands like tides, hands like pillows and cotton and rabbit flesh. Hands like rabbit flesh, soft and delicate. The bundle slipped into the crease, and he slid it as far as he could without jostling it; his breath did not move from his lungs all the while. And despite himself, despite it all, he pushed it a little more and shimmied it with two fingers like he did when his keys fell between the couch cushions, felt the little cork stopper at the top of the phial through the pouch. Nitroglycerin. After a little wiggle of the fingers, after his knuckles scraped raw against the stone, it moved no more and was snug. He exhaled a little, the only sound in the shaft.

With the tips of his thumb and pointer finger, he peeled away a flap of the rabbit-skin wrapping, saw the dead veins still imprinted in the sides of the inner part, red roads, red corridors sprawling all ways. Flesh like stone, but soft, and he unfurled the other flap, and saw the little spool of twine he kept inside. The fuse. It unwound like any other string, like he might knit a sweater of it if he knew how, and he held the little wooden ends of the spool as he rose, legs like clouds, like cushions, legs like rabbit flesh, and began to back away slowly. He stooped and picked his lantern up as he went, and the sweat stopped running somewhat: nitroglycerin. It might make it all worse, might kill all survivors if they yet lived behind those boulders. But they would know to back away. They knew it would happen, that someone, eventually, would come. They were human, after all. Smart, capable, ingenious. They would find a way to survive, and they would stay as far away as possible from the blockage. Ingenious. Nitroglycerin.

§

The others crowded around the end of the fuse and watched as Chaoxiang opened up his lantern and placed the twine to it. A spark lit the end, and began to move, serpentine, bouncing over rocks and pebbles and divots into the darkness. All bated their breath, all twenty men, and all watched as the light disappeared down the slope, down into the mine, and they waited there in silence for what felt like several unceasing minutes. California sunshine beat down on their exposed necks. And the time passed, and passed, and they stood there before the yawning black—and then it was not black anymore. A rush of air, what little must have remained down so deep, came out, and the faintest red flash, reflections upon reflections, came ricocheting upwards, carrying with it a dreadful rumble as of distant storms. And then all was silent, and dark again.

Someone nodded and stepped forward, carrying a lantern and

a little cage. The sulfur-colored bird inside chittered nervously, flapped its wings as it clung futile to the bars. Chaoxiang watched as the man started down, and as the others went along, one at a time. One at a time. He was the last, sitting next to the burnt away ashes of the fuse. Futile.

§

The detonation had worked as well as it might. The shattered rocks that once had sat piled nice and impenetrable in the way of any would-be rescuers had been effectively powdered or blasted in one of the two possible directions anything could go. A great hole yawned in the ceiling of the tunnel, and the ruins of the beams sat clear to see, uncovered by the blast of . . . nitroglycerin. The group waited, soundless, standing all with cotton legs at this place, some looking up at the space from which so much had fallen, others at the many-colored rock fragments, others at the still-standing supports, judging whether those had been weakened by the initial cave-in or the subsequent detonation. But again, someone went forward, another someone, a different someone, yet an individual. One among the others. Just one. And the man with the bird followed close behind, into the new gap.

Nobody waited inside. It had just been too long. Five days, but there had been no air. Maybe if there had been some ventilation, they might have made it—but no air at all. The area beyond the boulders was small, frighteningly small, claw-someone's-eyes-out-if-they-tried-to-put-you-there small. Maybe ten, fifteen feet across. Maybe thirty, forty feet in length. Chaoxiang had lived in smaller apartments, but it was not the same down there. Rocks and rocks, and darkness, and no air. They had died in seconds, not minutes, not hours, not days. Instant asphyxiation, likely.

No, that was wrong. There hadn't been *no* air. There had been *bad* air. Bloodstains beneath their eyes, beneath their noses, stuck cannibal-grim all over their teeth. Hands on throats, hands over mouths, muscles still tensed, still rigid, still yearning to convulse but incapable, incapable of everything but leaning rigid against the walls or lying motionless on the ground evermore. Five days. And before them, around them—all ten bodies—were the cages, the cages, the cages with their captives, dead too. They hadn't helped a bit. They hadn't done a thing. Maybe, he thought, after the rocks fell and after the initial screams and cries for help had subsided, the birds had squawked and squawked their warnings, danced their little dying dances, and maybe they died first to show what awaited the others: but the miners could do nothing. Caged much the same. Human ingenuity. Rock, rock, all around, all above, before, behind, miles and miles. Where the tunnel caved in, only a few feet of the stuff had lain. A few feet, a million miles, a billion—it made no difference. Impenetrable. They had no nitroglycerin. It would have blown them all to hell if they had—it mattered not.

Chaoxiang picked up one of the cages and rattled it around a little, watched the stiff ball of rigid feathers inside bounce around the bars—bars not miles, not feet, not even inches thick. A millimeter or an inch or a foot or a mile. It was all useless. Carefully he placed the cage down with his human dignity, and he placed it down with full knowledge of his human superiority. And there, as he put it to the floor, he saw something else in a divot in the stone: a little, tiny, miniscule sliver of matter, of soft and pliable *something*, that just maybe, might have been a piece of burned and shredded rabbit flesh. Across the chamber he heard the rattling of cages as the birds began to dance, to squawk, to play their useless part. Human ingenuity.

II

If the sun rose before they caught anything, they would not make it through the day. Even the tiniest salamander would be enough to tide things over for a bit, maybe a little rodent—the horizon burned blood red. The baleful sun hung like death above the garrote horizon.

They did not catch anything, and like thunder, like rolling and terrible peals of inner thunder, came unto all of them the realization that today would mark the end of the human race. The things from the sky and the things from the ground would remain indefinitely, but humanity—two-legged, two eyed, sun-vulnerable, wingless humanity—would be gone. Their great monuments of steel and stone would continue to corrode and crumble until even they, the time-worn fossils of civilization, would vanish, another page turned in the ever-expanding tome of time. When fire and brimstone reign, the soft burn first.

Concretized nuts and seeds, bones leftover from meals consumed months ago, leaves of trees that had not seen growth in years. Huddled in the sweet and comforting darkness of their cave, as the fire of the dying sun raged outside, the last men and women ate and wept together, they slapped the stone beneath them, they hastily scrawled pleas upon the walls in their own blood: calls to higher powers—powers higher than higher powers—to intervene, to bless them just this once with some bounty, some lamb that they could gut and spill. The Gods would come today, and they would reach their hands into the mouth of the cave no different than one does a rabbit hole, pluck them out one at a time and judge, and deliberate among themselves in their olden tongue, and deliver their divine will.

The day crawled, and the humans stamped their feet in the dirt and paced to and fro, argued among one another, screamed about what could have been done different, about where they should have searched instead, under which stones and within which holes. But now the sun had risen, and it was far too late for anything else to be done. Yes, they all agreed that much: that to go out now would be to invite a death perhaps more gruesome than the one to be dealt by the Gods, and one, at the very least, less honorable and sacred. They all agreed on this, yes. They would die with honor, not to the Forces outside, but to the justice dealt out, the justice they deserved. All agreed, yes, fine and well, and they stopped writing their pleas and crying their tears.

But one did not agree, and did not stamp his feet, or argue, or any of the rest. Crimson runoff from the fingerpaint dripped onto his forehead as he sat, thinking. He was Sam. Sam also did not agree that the best alternative to going outside would be to stay in the little cave and grumble and weep and wait for death to come; for an honorable death and a death dealt by the Forces were death all the same. Honor meant little when there was no one left to do the honoring. A strange one, that Sam.

While the others began another argument about how exactly they should go about submitting to the Gods, which directions and how violently they should squirm when the mighty and omnipotent hands reached into the cave, into the comfort of the dark—Sam went out into the sun with his spear.

He did not go out to the valley where they hunted in the night; though he did not agree with the others about most things, they still had the same base of human knowledge he did. It was a risk to be out in the sunlight. An act of stupidity. Through the thick leather shawl he had wrapped around his head he could already feel the blaze, the cell-splitting burn: just to look around he needed to squint, look away frequently from the more reflective boulders and flats of rock upon the slope. The things, the Beasts, that might be watching him as he wandered under the sun that spawned them did not have the same issue. Their skin and eyes hadn't the same sensitivity his did. They flew down, hidden in the gleam of the sun, scorched what they wished, left without a bite of their kill. Fire and light and heat did not need to eat. Icarus would only need to walk out his front door these days. Lions and tigers and bears (and light and Mists and Gods and Beasts), oh my!

He strode up the hill under the ruins of the Steeltree, fanning out its half-dome canopy wide around and blotting the sun, sending a partly-shattered but still thoroughly relieving shadow across Sam's face and most of the hilltop. Here he sheltered and looked over the opposite side of the hill, down over layers of cliffs and what amounted to pastoral highlands of seething green fields, some of the only places untouched by the decay. Beneath, the Strange Mists had already begun to rise, and the valley below was swathed in a mixture of frothing whites and swirling bits of earthy light, so potently bright that his eyes stung and ran when he looked away. He could smell the stuff too, though it still coalesced so far below: the sulfureous, rotten stench, the coppery metallic lace. Poor, sweet Maxine had succumbed to it a month before, having not escaped the lowlands before daylight. Poor Maxine, he thought. Beautiful, young Maxine. She had seen the burn on the horizon, the signal red, and still she said that she needed to keep on looking, that the next rock would hide enough centipedes for the week, or even something larger, like a toad. Human arrogance. Poor Maxine, he thought, remembering her dying dance, her spasms upon the ground, the blood that ran from every orifice. There above the valley in which she let herself die, Sam shed a tear, even as he schemed to use the same Strange Mists that choked her to his own advantage.

The animals would leave the valleys and rise the hills as the Mists came up the more, as the sun rose higher. And he would strike them then, for their instincts told them the places the Mists would not reach: high and overshadowed caves like the one his group lived within, or ledges above the land. The high pastures. It seemed, by way of his human logic, a sound and quite well-decided plan. But the Strange Mists began to swirl up higher, and higher, and nothing came. Noontime neared, and still, not the slightest movement.

So, Sam went down, and the heat and brightness struck him like a fist—like a hundred smoldering fists upon every inch of exposed skin—as he left the shadow of the Steeltree, the great skyward-pointing disk, its purpose, its companions, its recipients long forgotten. Satellites fall like rain throughout the long years. Orbital stations crumble to space dust and dissipate. Radio waves fan out in infinite directions, and in the expanse of deep cosmos, lose themselves in the blank spaces never blessed by the music of the spheres.

He went down slowly, with a strip of fabric wrapped around his nose and mouth as if that would do anything to quell the toxins still steaming up from nowhere, from out of the deepest deeps of the world as the surface warmed and warmed, as the sun reached its terminus and beamed straight down, suffusing into the air all the maleficent leftover chemicals and poisons stagnant in the ground as once wells of freshwater were buried. On the ledge above the white infinity radiating in sunlight, snaking tendrils of the Mists reached up at Sam, but they could not reach high enough yet, and would not for another hour or more. Other hills, lower hills, sat like islands in a frothing sea, and he squinted to see if maybe anything moved on those: but it was far too bright now, and he could only look for instants. Useless instants, anyway, for theirs was the last mountain anywhere with life. This was known. This was agreed. They had seen the others go out one by one, the glows of their caves extinguished with the mighty comings and goings of the Gods, by the hot fangs of the Sun Beasts as they came down on wings of alabaster fire. Sam and the others had tried to tune out the screams, tried to think only of where they would hunt for their next sacrifice.

Nothing came. He picked up his pace, readied his spear for the first chance he might get, dove into the tangle of overlapping stones and ground-vines that made up the eastern side of the Last Mountain, not an island, but a tower floating tentatively above the surging tides of oncoming death fog.

Thirty minutes passed of shambling and stumbling search over and under flat stones, in bushes burned bare by ultraviolet, in dry and dead caves where nothing had lived for centuries, over the scorch-mark footprints of the Beasts. He did not hear the clamp of hooves he had hoped for, nor the fluttering of any wings. Nothing.

An hour passed. White fangs of vapor rose higher to his side as the Strange Mists crept nearer. In hollows moist with slime and in fields of crackling grass he crawled on hands-and-knees, peering in places that he would never think to look by night. The sun burned down on him, but only him, and the leather stung against his skin as hot as anything he had ever felt.

An hour and thirty minutes. He could smell it thick in the air, wafting deadly and inevitably nearer up cliffsides and over places that he thought it would never reach. It came like a wave, like a glacier sliding upwards, like a monstrous slime mold searching desperately with cilia and pseudo-arms to find its next nutrition, its next victim. He had already left behind the pleasant fields he looked upon from the Steeltree and walked now over a dead and dying landscape of ruined plant stalks, never entirely decayed.

Two hours. Oxidizing copper. Smashed rotten eggs. The decaying carcasses of a thousand lives. The smell lived, the smell moved, the smell penetrated him and made his head go light.

Two hours and thirty minutes.

Three hours.

And then—fortune took pity. Over the edge of the cliff, straddled by wisps of the horrible Mists, a flash of living white light dashed by and away, further into tangles of dying undergrowth drying in the sun, waiting to be reborn when the moisture and chill of night returned. As if before he had been dead, Sam's blood ran quick through his veins as he saw this, his heart skipped a beat, or two, or three, or more. And he ran. Maybe, just maybe, he could save everyone. The entire world.

Sam chased the rabbit over and under and all around without ever getting a clear chance to launch his spear or throw one of the nets he carried in his sling. Too fast, too erratic, too small. Over boulders and around, down slopes and up: his two human legs were hopelessly outmatched. A rabbit's brain is wired entirely for flight. It lives to run, to flee, to escape. He lived to chase, but hadn't the infinite generations of development to push this into his innate faculties; what he used in his pursuit was only personal prowess and fitness, and it did not amount to much. His breath came heavy, came labored, came desperate, and he sent forth his spear in a hopeless final attempt to catch the critter in stride, but the weapon landed a foot or two beyond the warren the rabbit dove into. Sliding to a halt upon his knees, he pounded the ground as the others did in the cave, as they likely still did now as the dreaded time grew nearer. The sun beat down. He stamped his foot over the hole, paced around in circles, screamed out over the bubbling valley, cursed himself, his lineage, the Gods, the rest of humanity: and it did make him feel a little better, all things considered. But it did not draw out the rabbit.

The Mist came nearer, and he felt it in his chest, in his lungs, in each helpless cell that burned inside, surrendering itself to toxin, to death, attacked on two sides. It did not feel good to give up and die, he realized after a few minutes of huffing down the rancid air, watching the shroud of vapor come upward and peer into other holes all around the lower sections of the ledge. He got to his hands and knees, plucked his spear from the soil and grabbed it near the point. With the edge, he began to dig around the periphery of the hole, breaking up harder clumps of soil before scooping it out with his hands. While he did this he began to cough, and a new burning came to his eyes distinct from the one the sun made. He had time, but not much. It would do . . . maybe. It would have to do.

He reached his arm all the way into the newly-expanded and

unearthed rabbit hole, and kept reaching and reaching until he felt certain that his arm might pop off, until his whole side and cheek were pressed against the soil, so that he could watch as the arms of Mist came over the edge of the nearest rise and slowly approached, passing over things and killing them indiscriminate: grasses, mushrooms, insects too small to be of any sacrificial use. He felt his hand enter an open place, barely his fingertips. Something moved around in there, just out of reach. He was just out of reach of the Mists.

Like mad, he pulled out his hand and dug, and dug, throwing soil and stones backward into the approaching death. And he went in again, and felt a little bit closer. The Mists lapped at his heels. Out again, and he dug more, and more, and more. This time he felt fur, and he felt teeth, and he felt little tiny claws scratching over his fingers and gnawing into his wrists. The rabbits fought hard, tooth and nail, and they drew some blood; but negligible. They could hurt him as much as he could hurt the Mists. He was a mountain, he was a monster, he was the sun shining in the sky: something they could not hope to quell, something they could not even conceive. Vapor wrapped around his ankles, tugging, pleading for him to give it up and die. He thought about it well, considered the proposal, but declined.

Out from the warren popped the first of the rabbits he could gain a firm hold on, pulled back from the comfort of darkness and into the palm of harsh and all-encompassing brightness, back into the land of death and of things it could not hope to understand. Fear danced in its black and stupid eyes, and it tried for a moment to squirm free, chirping and chirping at him to be let go. But he squeezed all the harder for every amount of effort the thing tried.

He squeezed all the harder, and it ceased to move. It only looked on in horror, a horror all the more complete because Sam left it without the knowledge of why it should fear at all. He did not bare any teeth, he did not coil about it like a snake, did not take it in talons like a hawk: but it knew it would soon die all the same. It knew that much. It knew the thing that held it, held its life, was something it could not hope to combat, to evade. He was a mountain, he was a monster, he was the Mist creeping up the hill. His human superiority won over.

As he snapped the rabbit's little neck, as the spark left its stupid, ignorant little eyes, Sam muttered a prayer; not to absolve himself or anything otherwise, but because it seemed like the right thing to do. The little creature pissed him off. To look at him like that . . . to plead with him like that . . . such a pitiful creature. He hoped it would be enough to save the world.

§

Beyond the Steeltree to the north, on a promontory overlooking the Vault of the Gods, lay the black and blue altar, the pit of life that he must spill blood upon. The place at which he must declare his subservience, the subservience of all his people while they squabbled and argued incessantly, their words still ringing out from the near southeast as he stood there. What was it now? From what he gathered from the loudest shouts, it sounded like someone had bumped into another, who then backed into another, and around and around, this spawning an omnidirectional confrontation in which everyone besides oneself became an enemy—even if they had not hit anyone directly, *that bastard did something, and I will find out what!* someone yelled.

Sam had to fight off his human tendency for confrontation

even as he stood there; he wanted to run back to the cave and shout for them all to *shut the hell up and get on with their dying if they were content to die.* But he didn't. His stupid human need to be the savior . . . it consumed him from the moment he saw the fires of dawn break on the horizon that morning, had eaten through him all until he crept out the cave. He would save everyone, and he would do it alone. Man needed nobody else. Just himself. The alpha and the omega of the Earth, the ruler that never truly died, always crawled back out from his destruction like a cockroach. All else existed to serve him, and the Gods had made the world that way. This was known, yes. Sam agreed with that. Nothing contrived by nature could be stronger than man—for man had taken nature out back and put it down with a swift shot to the head.

But an odd feeling came over Sam as he stood there. A feeling that he had not felt before. As he placed the carcass of the little white rabbit upon the stone, as he pulled from his bag the knife with which he would split and skin and drain the critter, as he looked out over the brilliant sea of undulating incandescence, even beneath sunlight a thousand times brighter and hotter than what was comfortable, through layers and layers of protective leather and cloth, he felt a heat behind him. He felt eyes burning, feet smoldering, breath wafting deadly as the Mist below. He had lost himself in his taste of success so thoroughly that his shield of caution—whatever remained of it during this fool's errand—flaked away like skin from a sunburn and left him alone in the eternal eye of daylight.

The creature was spawned of the sun. When the sun first began to engorge, they had come down from the sky. It had no flesh, no blood, and it could not be sacrificed. But it could kill. Without a doubt it could. It bared fangs of solar energy there as Sam turned, drew his spear. The weapon would not do much, but the obsidian point at the end could reflect much of the creature's harshest rays, buy him a razor thin chance. Its mouth was like fire, its wings like thrashing solar flares spraying out and trickling down, bleeding into the very stone below. It looked for a moment at Sam, eyes no different than the sun above, before it leapt upon him.

He thrust, he dove, and the obsidian worked to make the beast hesitant, if nothing else. When he swung his sweeping strikes or prodded and poked from afar, it backed off a little, reeled on its pulsating hind legs, kept wits about it the whole while. *Wits.* Didn't only humans have *wits*? The rabbit did not—it had nothing behind those lightless button eyes. But this thing, the Sun Beast, most dreaded of all human-hunters unleashed from the stars in the earliest Dying Days, was not the same: its eyes were all aglow, nothing but light. Knowledge burned there, awareness, conscious desires that Sam could not name, could only feel, wordless, but present.

He swung his obsidian desperately, trying to suck as much of the light from the monster as he could: but it would not stop the beast. It would not kill it. Only night could do that, still afar off, sitting without urge behind several hours of unrestricted sunlight. The fray had begun just minutes before and already Sam's muscles ached, he felt himself slowing, hesitating the same as the beast did. And he knew the beast could sense that. It had not been *hesitating* at all: it had used its accursed wits, waited him out, knew that he would tire himself long before he could land a good blow. Fear had made Sam foolish, allowed the thing, the animal, the *beast* to outwit him. A human. Outwitted.

So, Sam did all he could think to do in what might be his last moment: raised the spear to his shoulder, made as if he would try one last desperate strike, shouted and took a step—all before he turned and brought the tip of the spear down straight into the rabbit, obliterating most of the little thing, but letting its blood pour into the divots of the stone, through the cracks, down into the tunnels and passages below that would lead beneath the Vault of the Gods.

Into Sam's left leg sank the million billion gamma beam teeth of the Sun Beast, and he felt the layers of leather ripple away in the heat and radiation; then it went deeper, deeper, deeper and reached *his* flesh, and a million billion points of searing agony melted through his skin. And he shouted, and shouted as it gnawed, and tired, and moved on to the other leg, and peeled away layers and layers, causing sunburn that melted, that incinerated, that cancerized as it sheared away, crisping flesh as it dug. Over and over Sam felt the oncoming dark of unconsciousness peering up at him through the pain, but still he shredded away at the rabbit before him through bloodshot eyes, mangling every chunk of flesh, juicing the dead thing as one might an orange. And then, as he prepared to die, like an eclipse had passed over, the Sun Beast stopped, and the pain subsided somewhat. The creature lifted off him, spread its plasmatic wings, turned, and ran off before taking flight and soaring into fading rays of sunlight. It was clear why. For a moment, in the brightness of its eyes before it went, Sam saw fear. Lion eats tiger eats bear eats man.

He sprung up—or would have, if his legs still worked. Truly, he crawled his way back over to the wreckage of the rabbit, as he had slipped away in another lapse of awareness, and began to dissect all he could in earnest, squeezing to get all the fluid out he could. Meat popped like bubbles, gushing out red. The ground shook all the while, as he bathed the top of the altar crimson and orange, as the pure white of the stupid rabbit dyed maroon.

Idiot rabbit, he thought as he peeled and bled the thing, *did you think your hole would be deep enough? Did you think it would save you? The Beasts might not have reached it, but I did. The Mists might not have reached it, but I did. I did. I am the Beasts. I am the Mists. I am your God. I am the sun shining in the sky.*

Did it think that, though? Did it? Or was it acceptance that led the rabbit there? Blind instinct? Did it know somehow in its tiny, walnut brain, that it would end up this way if a human came? Or did it identify a threat and run the only place it associated with safety?

Stupid rabbit.

The Gods then came out of their Vault. The ground shook only from the opening of the door: when the Gods stepped, they stepped silent over vales and over forests. The Mists clouded thick around their titan legs, and they pushed through heedless, two of them. One went south, the other came right toward Sam, silent and sublime, a world moving noiseless through cosmos. It stopped just before the altar, knelt to reach eye level, and all the cursed world disappeared behind its gargantuan head.

Sam met its eyes, and he did not look away. He could not. Never had he seen one up close, a God; never had he seen their eyes, the eyes that swam with nameless emotions and wordless wonders, shines that came from nowhere but the God's own splendid and multitudinous thoughts. The shine was not like that of the Sun Beast, for that had been an indistinct brightness; the light permitted to enter the hallowed eye of the God was calculated, condensed, purified energy, vaporlike and pure.

The waves of the God's brain rolled over him then, and the thing spoke, but it spoke in a language that had no syllables. But the brainwaves let Sam hear, and understand, and it said something like this:

Human, you are failed. Humans, you did not sacrifice. We ask but for one kill, and you fail. You hide away and wait to die. Why is this so?

"I have sacrificed this creature," said Sam, his nerves so shattered that somehow he was able not only to speak clearly, but to *protest*. "We did not fail. I went out, and I got the rabbit. It is not much, but I got it, and I drained it."

More slices of emotion and nameless thoughts went over the eyes of the God, contorting into shapes, almost expressions all their own, and it seemed to laugh with its brainwaves.

You did fail. You killed this rabbit today, but the sacrifice was required the night before. Human, you are failed.

Screams erupted from the south. The other God reached its hand into the cave.

But, said the God, *you did show bravery at the last in going out by day when the others conceded, and I applaud you for that. Your fellows failed more detestably than you, but honorable failure is failure all the same. Our pact has been sundered.*

The screams came again, nearer, and Sam turned to look—his gaze was torn away before he could, his brain no more than that of an obedient dog, the God holding some invisible treat to make him sit nicely at attention.

Look not at their fate. Care not what becomes of them. Death is death is death, and that is all you helpless things know, all you would know if not for us. What? Your kind spent an infinity foraging through the savannahs and fighting over rotting kills. Who did you think brought you the flame, the field, the great bombs that ruined this world? Surely you did not think you had done it all yourselves, no? Which one of you found that 'Last Mountain' in which you live? Was it old Farner, who went out to relieve himself and had his head engulfed by a 'Sun Beast,' as you call them? Was it Obelea, slipped off a cliff and fell a thousand feet because the midnight dew made the stone a little too slick? Was it 'poor Maxine'? Oh, send off that dread, it hurts me just touching it. This is what your species is for now.

The God laughed then, and its brainwaves rolled all across the world, a shockwave, a psychic earthquake. Sam did not speak again. Ever again.

The God used some of its appendages to lift a cage to the edge of the promontory, the size of Sam, thimble-like to the God. The screams stopped as the other deity passed by behind, blood dripping from its enclosed fists. Great red globules, large enough to drown in, tree-thick fingers failing to keep them in. Squeezing, squeezing, crushing. Then the world lurched, and the other God disappeared from sight as Sam's two eyes locked with the many of the one before him. Light swam there, made shapes of friend and foe, future and past, hypnotic angles and senseless creations. His human mind, the ultimate weapon, the thing that conquered all the world, reached out into the stars: it surrendered, and bowed.

Do not look away. Step inside the cage. Step inside now. Don't worry, your wounds are healed. Good. This will be the end of our discussion. Thank you for your past devotion. I will take you now to see eternity in motion. Hop along, little rabbit.

§

Down, and down, and down, and down, and down. Indescribably deep. Unfathomably deep. Through the great gate in the mountain, the Vault of the Gods, whose tunnels go endless and sprawling veinlike through deeps of limestone, further slates and diorites, and deeper, to layers of rock never discovered and never named because they had not existed yet in the times when humanity went around categorizing all its subjects, placing them in boxes of form, of shape, of composition, of purpose: all meaningless now, the words and the ideas they contained all long buried. Deeper, past ruins of civilizations never known and never found, through caves of crystals that glowed with light still held fast from the first wan beams that issued flickering from the young sun, soon to consume this sorrowful planet. Down, and down, and down, and down, and down.

Light gave way after some time, but the God still walked straight. The clattering of the chain on which Sam's cage hung rattled forever down the corridors into abysses never considered by man. They passed through chambers wider than the valley above, where Sam's breath echoed out in shade as loud as a drum, and places tight and compact where no sound stirred at all, and many of these, and many of those, and many other things besides as they went ever downwards. Down, and down, and down, until they stopped.

Sam could see here, from a faint phosphorescent glow about the walls, and it was surely a room of titan size, fit for the titan inhabitants who strode around here and there in the darkness. The one who captured him spoke out when they arrived in slow rolling, booming words of thunder, phonetic jumbles and rhythms without sense. And out of the dark came the same sounds, the same claps of thunder and the same drivel of speech that Sam could never hope to replicate, never hope to understand. He was little. He was foolish. The wordless words resonated around in his skull, in his chest, and he imagined they were all mocking him.

The God placed his cage on a rack among many others, and he screamed for a while, and whimpered—but the others did not, and soon he joined them in silence. Gods passed by at whiles and threw crumbs and morsels wayward at the cages, and Sam kicked them over the edge and watched them fall. The Gods sprayed water that pooled in the center of the cage, and he used it only to wash the tears and grime from his face. And days passed. Hunger and thirst fought with his human stubbornness, with his fear, and he looked out in the darkness over the others as they scrambled to eat what they could, drink every drop. And soon he joined them.

One-by-one the cages went away, as Gods grabbed them and left, and one-by-one the people went silent unto their deaths. The others did not lament for them, they did not lament for themselves; all was quiet in the room, all waited for their turn.

Sam began to eat the food on all fours, lapped the water up off the floor like an animal. He *was* an animal. He was a beast. He was a beef cow, a chicken lined for slaughter, he was a thing ready to be used and discarded. The hand would come and there would be no action he could ever do to even make it think twice about what it would do with him. He was not an afterthought. He was not a thought. One does not speculate upon the feelings of the axe before they swing, or the intelligence of the tree they will smite; they are no more, no less, than nothing.

He could slip through the bars of the cage, he found one day.

They were wide, made of a metal malleable enough to bend. He could leap through, scale down the rock, down a titan leg, run along the infinite corridors. But every time he considered it, every time he wanted to, around again came food and water sprayed like fertilizer upon him. The fall would kill him. The Mists would reach him. The shaft was too deep, the rock too thick. The Gods would stomp him out. He was an ant, a creature, a rabbit on the run. He could find a divot, he could find a hole that seemed but a crack to the Gods, but it would be pointless, it would be fighting against the sky, or the ground, or the sun. He was a little man. A little thing. A stupid thing whose eyes held not the brightness of those above. Always as they passed, as they sprayed, he watched those eyes, opening and closing in rhythm with some universal hymn that he could not detect, shining their hypnotic light around and around and around. They would see him before he saw himself if he tried to run. Their eyes, their eyes knew of things, of things he had never come close to. That *mankind* had never imagined. They knew of elements and of formulae that we could never speculate. They knew of histories that we considered fantasies. They knew, they knew, and they knew because *they* were capable, and *we* were not. The ant queen rules her colony and does not seek conquest against the house she dug her hole before, stays and fights her battles in the lawn where she belongs. So long man ruled their colony, long enough that they forgot about the lawn, about the house, about the greater things that lived inside. Humanity died and the Gods survived because *they* were better suited, and *they* won the rat race from the darkness, living to themselves and doing whatever it is they do. Because they do not need us. They do not need anything. They are beyond it all. Sam was an accessory, a trinket, a bobble, a tool that might come in handy. Not a life-or-death thing, not something they would go out of their way for. The blood from the sacrifices, the blood of all of humanity's endless labor, drained into a bucket and the Gods sprayed it at the cages to conserve water for themselves. They did not give him water. He was not worthy of water. His lips and beard were coated and stuck all red, as fur does when a mouse cannibalizes another, drawn mad from running their mazes back and forth and back and forth, and *he* had nowhere to run. He was not given the simple dopamine hits of a maze, the occasional morsel of sweaty cheese; he got scraps of flesh from something or other, uncooked, gamey, beginning to rot, and he ate it because he did not get to choose anymore. He did not cling to life. It clung to him. A caged dog will not starve itself, a whipped and beaten and kicked dog will not try to die. It will eat what it is given, and it will bark like a good boy when its owner comes back from work and kicks it smack in the ribs all over again. He barked and barked and barked when the Gods came by, and he smiled when they sprayed him with the blood and with the chunks of flesh, the flesh whose origin he did not dare speculate. Food was food was food. Death was death was death. Holes of rabbits, squirming, stupid, idiot, mindless, lightless rabbits. Fucking and eating and dying and fucking, and nothing more, nothing more, because they could not think of anything more. Where did the Gods go out there in the dark? Down further, further than far, what did they do? It did not matter. He wanted to fuck and to eat and to die and nothing more. He was nameless, he was loveless, he chirped sometimes to the others beside him and sometimes they chirped back, and sometimes he stamped his feet in resurgent anger, but the anger passed, and he waited in the dark for his next meal, and for drink, and for the next cage in line to come off the rack, to file away into the darkness and not return. Where did the cages go? Why did they bother keeping them? Stupid, mindless, hopeless animals.

And then they came for him after endless cycles of meal, of sleep, of drink. The eye of eternity looked through his cage and saw something new, saw a blood-soaked maneater, a thing lower than low. With a rattle of a chain, each link the size of a house, the God took him up and bore him out, and the nameless man watched as the other cages receded into gloom. And into gloom he went, though he could still see all the while. Into another descent, deep and deep and deep, down they went, and the corridor sloped and sloped. The God smiled with its mouth of suckers, flickered its antennae, its antennae that with each flash and pulse sent electric shocks up and down the thing that once was Sam's body, blurred his mind and calmed his fear. With eyes of post-spectral radiance, the God looked at things in the dim light in passing, looked all around, but he, the thing that once had been Sam, saw little anymore aside from the God who held his life by chains. But he could see the Mists. When they came, after hours, they curled out of cracks in the floor, twisted like tentacles around the bases of the walls, luminescent and reeking. The God hung him lower, and it felt like the planet fell out of orbit as the cage dropped. Soundless the deity strode ever downward as the thing in the cage vomited up blood, not his own, and the mist curled up, and up, and up, and up, tickling with impressions of doom and reminders of his helplessness, of his stupidity, his inferiority.

The God spoke in that old tongue and began to sing low notes that burst through the corridor like airwaves from an explosion.

Sam's head shook, his heart shook, his throat and lungs burned with the Mists. And soon they curled up and around the bottom of the cage, reaching in with hands of smoke to grasp him, to kill him, to show that there was something less considerate than the Gods. But it did not reach him yet. They went down, and down, and down. It must have been early evening, for had it been day the Mists would have consumed all air in the tunnels and gone out into the land, but it still waited around the bottom, choking the passage full of reek and toxin. But the God seemed not to worry. It seemed not to notice. Why did the God take him? Why did they go into the Mists? Stupid rabbit, don't think, just eat, just fuck, just die.

They came to a place where the Mists lay somewhat dormant, and again he could breathe clear. This room expanded all the ways he could see in all directions, held up by columns like the trunks of great trees, like the fingers of the Gods, like the bars of some titanic cage. Lights hung on these columns, dull and flickering, and shined across the misty floor, hundreds, hundreds of feet below from where he hung. Sam looked up to the face of the God and saw it bright in the light, and it turned to him. In the many eyes, behind the light, lacing it, there was understanding, there was a sympathy: the same sympathy one feels when crushing a spider that should not be where it is, that if some better alternative existed, the unfortunate spider would not meet its fate. But the glow of the eyes, the swirling light, it did not dim. The great God would not find that other option, it would not even look; it was not worth the energy, and the thing in the cage *could* find itself a use if it knew its place, if it strung its web in the corner and caught the houseflies like it was meant to.

There were other Gods in this chamber, and they each held their own cage, their own human. Across the floor rusted other cages, empty or holding naught but bones, cracked, trampled on, forgotten. Shards and splinters, femurs and skulls; fed on by maggots the Gods could never hope to see, so small. The other Gods took their cages and went down into dark shafts where came the deep and dull ring of mining, of excavation, of the expansion of these corridors. Sam's God found a tool for this job hanging from a rack upon one of the columns, another tool it would use and throw away.

Down and down and down and . . . hours passed as they went through not complete, but deep and terrible, darkness. Shafts went every which way, and the walls grew warm with geothermal heat. Magma broiled beyond the walls in places, open to air, popping and smoldering in others, and the Strange Mists curled low around the ground. The God swung the cage as a schoolgirl might her backpack, and the nameless creature inside grasped to the bars to keep from being flung out. Why did he grasp? Why did he persist? He could not find the words, the comparison—but he realized then, after all, that he was not a rabbit. He was lesser.

Rabbits can be pets, rabbits can be loved. Rabbits can be something to coddle, something to play with. He was only a warning. He was only a canary, one that would chirp, one that would cry out if the Mists grew too thick, too potent, too high. He was a clock that would tell the coming of day, tell the God to go up and up and up again. Loud, loud for his size, he would chirp and chirp, and sputter, and die, and be left there to decay. Sacrifices in vain made outside: eating of the carrot, gatherings around the bird feeder. Caves of comfortable darkness would be snuffed, and snuffed, and the vault would open and open, and the Mists would come and come. Canary. Canary. Clang went the axe on rock, on masonry from the ages of conception, of the great genesis. Clang. Clang. Chirp. Chirp. Choking. Clang, on an asteroid that caused an olden extinction. Clang, clang, clang, crack. Chipping away, the walls came down as the great God who ripped him from his warren, from his nest, smashed the world, smashed the remnants, smashed the old things that did not matter anymore. It did not matter anymore. The Mists curled. His throat burned as with napalm, but he did not know what that even was. Clang, clang, through buried crypts of dead kings and queens, crack, crack, crack, crumble. Spasms, pain, chirp: chirp, went the canary, went the rabbit, went the stupid thing, went the helpless thing, the nameless thing: chirp, chirp, he filled with toxin. He flapped his wings and stomped his useless paws, and finally the God looked over, and it looked at him with its eighty eyes of wonder, and it smiled with its heavenly, gorgeous, unbelievable eyes, thanked him, and left away. It placed the cage on the ground all delicate, not to hurt the little thing inside. Amen.

Enwrapped by the Mists, swathed as with cotton, with clouds, with the down of millions of dead and dying birds. Enwrapped, enwrapped as with soft rabbit flesh. Chirp, chirp, chirp went the canary, the stupid thing, the lightless thing, the thing that did not, could not know the mind of the God who snapped its stupid little helpless neck. Chirp, spasm, chirp, spasm, cough, chirp, dead. Death is death is death. Man is man is man is beast. What a gift! What a gift! Hallelujah!

OVERLAPPING

ODIN MEADOWS

Zeph crashed into the couch with a gleam in his eyes that could only mean mischief. Grinning ear to ear, he pulled a little baggie out of his pocket and flicked the two purple pills inside. His boyfriend August feigned a stare of stern disapproval but soon, a smile broke across his face. It was their weekend off. They had time to retreat for a while.

"It's less like a trip and more of an adventure. At least, that's what Dan said," Zeph explained as he placed the tablet under his tongue, wincing from the bitterness.

"What is that even supposed to mean? Is that his new tagline or something?" August's face scrunched up as he popped the pill in his mouth.

"No. I don't think so." Zeph leaned back into the cushions. "He's no marketer. He just said it's weird, kind of like ket but different. It's supposed to take you somewhere else, but like . . ." His voice faded out into a whisper as his eyes glazed over and his head lulled to the side before collapsing on the couch.

August started to say something, but the words got caught in his mouth, and the world blurred around him. His head hung heavy on his shoulders and suddenly, it was difficult to hold himself upright. He slumped into the recliner as vivid colors streaked across his vision, crashing into the walls.

Tiny lines split into hairs that slowly constructed the outline of a door, then a wall. Frozen in place, his heart thumped in his chest as a dilapidated hallway materialized around him. A feeling like electric menthol tingled over his skin. Every muscle was clenched. His throat squeezed shut while his lungs banged against his ribcage, pleading for air. The final details solidified and then, whatever had a hold on him released its grasp, allowing him to finally pick himself off the floor.

"Zeph?" August called out after sucking in a long breath. His heartbeat was returning to normal, but a creeping sort of dread wound up his spine. It was dark, but just enough light drifted through the corridor to see where he was going. There seemed to be no source. A flat coat of dim light covered everything, leaving no shadows.

The hall stretched into the distance, gradually disappearing into a fog of darkness. He could see maybe ten feet in either direction. The paint on the walls was chipped and cracked, several tiles were broken along the floor, and few of the doors that were peppered along the walls hung broken off their hinges, opening up to nothing but an even deeper, cooler darkness.

Sticking to the at least somewhat visible hallways, August picked a direction and began walking. He'd bump into the occasional ninety-degree turn or forking path but despite walking for hours, it never felt like he was nearing an exit. His mouth was dry. His feet were tired. He could have been walking in circles for all he knew; everything looked the same. It was dusty and broken down everywhere he looked, and he couldn't shake the thought that he'd end up withered, dead, and flaking away just like the wallpaper.

The halls were quiet, mostly. He could hear himself breathe. Each footstep echoed down the hall towards oblivion. Here and there, however, he began to hear little noises: a scratch, a tap, a knock. At first, he assumed it was his mind playing tricks. Something would rasp against the wall and despite seeing no signs of life, he'd tell himself it was a bug or a mouse. Then, something knocked twice in quick succession. He could no longer deny it was the sound of someone tapping their fingers against the other side of the wall, approaching one of the open doors tap by tap.

August sprinted past the dark void. Refusing to meet whatever it was, refusing to look back, he turned a corner and froze.

Just down the hall, leaning out of one of the open doors was a gaunt face with dark holes for eyes. He turned around and ran in the other direction.

Something banged against the wall right next to August. He jumped, but kept running. The bangs only continued. Following him through the corridors as he ran, the banging on the walls soon filled the hallways with a cacophony of hollow duds.

August came to a dead end. The banging became even louder, surrounding him entirely. He sank to his knees, covered his ears, and cried in the fetal position for what felt like hours.

"Are you okay?" A hand touched his shoulder, and August

jerked his head up to see Zeph, a worried look strewn across his face. He yanked Zeph into a tight hug as his cries died down. "Bad trip?"

"Yeah," August moaned, "That was . . . I don't know. I was stuck in a hallway. There was no end. I couldn't find an exit and . . . There were like people . . . but not people. There was something on the other side of the walls. They wouldn't stop."

"Shhh," Zeph rubbed August's back, "It just took me to a weird ass forest. It was pretty chill." He kissed the top of August's head. "I'm sorry it wasn't fun for you. Dan said you can sometimes hallucinate others, but I guess I assumed they'd be peaceful." He let out a dry laugh and August nodded his head. It was dark. He checked the time. Almost 2AM.

"Yeah, I guess not." August forced a chuckle and wiped the tears from under his eyes. "I think I just need some rest."

§

The next weekend, Zeph came home from work with another set of pills. He pulled the baggie out with a sheepish grin, and August's eyes widened in fear.

"Again?" he asked. Zeph sort of shrugged his shoulders and nodded.

"I had fun last time . . ." His eyes fell to the floor. "It's okay if you don't want me to do it."

"No. It's fine." August took a deep breath. "I just don't think I will be partaking this round. I'm good. This ones not for me, I don't think. I'll stick to weed for the night." He laughed, but Zeph bit his lip. "Really, it's fine."

"Okay." Zeph finally smiled, for real. "I'm going to go get comfy," he said, placing the tablet under his tongue. He kissed

August on the cheek and curled up on the couch. Within moments he was transported to some metaphysical forest, and August was alone in a quiet living room.

Zeph remained in that position until well after the sun went down. His breaths were deep but consistent. August tried to speak to him a few times, but Zeph never reacted. Lost in his world, his eyes darted back and forth underneath his eyelids. August spent the evening watching TV. Not long after midnight, Zeph shot up from the couch. August jumped in his seat, but Zeph's eyes were lit up with excitement.

"That was crazy!" He spun around until he saw August and ran up to him, grabbing him by the arms. "I don't even know how to begin to explain. I continued like right where I left off. I got to *really* explore this time. It was crazy. There was so much weird shit. I saw the other-people too. I tried to speak to them, but they kept running off into the bushes."

He spoke like electricity coursed through his veins as he explained the mysterious runes he discovered in the forest. August did his best to keep a smile on his face but as Zeph laid out his theories on the meanings of the strange symbols, an uneasy feeling gnawed at the back of his mind.

§

The following weekend, Zeph took the other pill. He asked August first, but he didn't feel like he could say no. Zeph had already bought the pill, and he wasn't going to take it, so he tried not to think too much into it. Zeph sank into the couch, explored the depths of the forest for hours, and came back to reality later that night. It still made August uneasy, but he was thankful for it to be over. He didn't expect Zeph to show up the next weekend with a baggie of at least fifty pills.

"What the fuck?" August hissed through his teeth, trying his best to stifle his knee-jerk reaction. "I didn't think you were going to buy more."

"Oh." Zeph grinned, but his eyes looked guilty. "I'm sorry."

"Why did you get so many?" August shook his head.

"Dan cut me a good deal." He shrugged. "It's cheaper to buy in bulk."

"No shit. That's how *all* drugs work.' August rubbed his temples. "So, is this becoming your new lifestyle? Is this just like your thing now?"

"No." Zeph scratched the back of his head. "It's not like that. I'm not hurting anybody. Why does it matter?"

"It doesn't . . . not really." August sighed. He hated to hurt Zeph's feelings, but it still worried him. The occasional nightmare of the endless hallway continued to haunt him. "I just don't want to lose you. It's not like I'll be able to go in after you if you get lost in there. Besides, I get lonely when you're off on your *adventures*."

"Don't worry." Zeph kissed August on the cheek. "I've got a plan for that," he said with a wink and placed another tablet under his tongue. He sank back into the couch, drifted away. August's chest flooded with dread.

§

After a few months of weekly adventures, August got used to the routine. He spent most Saturday evenings alone, watching over Zeph as he disappeared for hours. One night, however, in the middle of his weekly excursion, while August was streaming some cheesy movie, Zeph began to stir much earlier than normal.

"August?" he moaned. August paused the movie and walked

over. Zeph's eyes were wide open and darting around the room. "August?" he asked again.

"I'm here." he responded, and Zeph's eyes shot straight towards him.

"I did it." His eyes stared with an intensity that made August uncomfortable, never blinking, almost bulging.

"Did what?" His voice was shaky.

"It's crazy." Zeph spoke in quick, whispery bursts. "I found myself. I found me. In here. I found them both. I'm now both. I'm both."

"What do you mean?" August sat next to him on the couch. His eyes kept darting in random directions but every few seconds, he would meet August's eyes.

"I'm overlapping." Zeph's voice flattened into a monotonous drone as he concentrated on his words. "I followed the runes. They brought me to a room deep in the forest, and I found myself. I saw myself curled up on the couch. I lay down in the same position, and it took a while, but I can now overlap. I can see both. I can see the forest. I can see you. It's all happening at the same time."

"That's great," August said through a forced smile. Zeph nodded along, too out of it to notice the apprehension in his voice.

"Yes. I'm so excited. I wonder . . ." he trailed off, moving his head in circles as he looked around the room. "Can I . . ." He wiggled his leg and then laughed. "I can."

His eyes somehow widened even further as he flung his leg off the side of the couch, almost kicking August in the face. It took a couple attempts, but he was finally able to get himself into a sitting position. He patted around on the cushion until he found August's hand, then clenched it tight.

"What are you doing?" August asked, but Zeph was too focused to answer. With wobbly legs, he stood up, stumbled a few steps, and almost fell but caught himself. Pacing around the room like he was on stilts, he laughed like a mad scientist. A pit formed in August's stomach.

"This changes everything," Zeph said with a gleam in his eyes.

§

It did. It changed everything. After a few "practice rounds," Zeph started taking the pills daily. In some ways, things were better. August no longer spent his Saturdays alone, but it created a new kind of loneliness. Zeph was always present, but he was never fully there.

Sometimes, mid conversation, Zeph slipped into a trance and stared off into the distance, distracted by the overlap. August tried not to take it personal, but it felt like he was losing more and more of him every day to that wretched place.

At first, it wasn't that bad. Zeph was energetic and excited, proudly referring to himself as an "overlapper" and boasting about his adventures. He told August stories of encounters with the other people, explained to him the secrets of the runes, and described the strange flora that populated the forest in his mind. Sometimes, it was beautiful and entertaining; he loved the way it made Zeph's eyes light up. Other times, it frightened him.

August held his tongue until he woke up in the middle of the night to an empty bed.

"Zeph," he called out, but there was no response.

Still half asleep, August jumped out of bed to search for him.

He found Zeph standing in front of the wall at the end of their hallway, staring into the beige wallpaper, lost inside a trance.

"Zeph?" What's going on?" His voice trembled.

"Can you see it?" He asked in a whisper. August followed Zeph's gaze to nothing but an empty wall."

"No. Do *you* see something?"

Zeph nodded his head.

"It's like a long hallway. There's a dim light at the end of it. I can see that there's a wall, but it looks like I can just . . ." He moved his hand forward, but his fingertips passed through the wall like it was a mirage.

"Stop!" August grabbed his shoulder and yanked him back with enough force to send them both crashing into the floor. Zeph shrieked. His eyes darted around the hallway before landing on August who pulled him into a hug. He held Zeph's sobbing body tight as they trembled in each other's arms. "It's okay," August whispered. The wall loomed over them like something conscious, something malicious.

He had to get Zeph away.

He stood up, dragged Zeph into the bathroom down the hall, and turned on the warm water. Hanging onto August's shoulder for support, Zeph climbed into the tub. He held a tight grip on August's leg as August massages his shoulders with a lavender body wash, running his fingers gently through Zeph's hair. He couldn't help but notice how thin Zeph had become, the indentations on his ribs clearly visible.

"Are you okay?"

Zeph looked up at him with a trembling lip and shook his head.

"I'm scared." His voice broke. "Everything has become dark. The forest, it's all warping into something . . . I don't know. At first, the messages in the runes felt like breakthroughs. It was almost therapeutic, but now . . . they only reveal dark secrets. The other-people won't stop following me, telling me nasty things. Sometimes it's hard to tell the difference between what's real and what's the overlap. Sometimes, I see a person staring at me, and it takes me a while before I realize nobody else can see them." He buried his face in his arms. "I don't know what to do."

"It's okay." August rinsed the suds off his back and kissed him on the forehead. "Maybe it's time to take a break for a while?" he suggested. Zeph was vulnerable, trembling in the bathwater, holding back tears. August didn't want to break him.

"Yeah." Zeph nodded his head. "I'd like that. I think I've had enough adventure." He offered a wry laugh, but the smile quickly fell away.

August helped him step out of the bath and wrapped him in a towel. Zeph rested his head on August's chest as he helped him dry off. They both knew there was something irrevocable about what happened. But they were together. For the moment, it was all that mattered.

§

For a few weeks, August assumed things had returned to normal. Zeph stopped taking the drug, seemed close to his usual self. August had almost stopped thinking of it entirely until, over a plate of eggs and toast, Zeph admitted he could still see the overlap.

"I don't know why. I can just see it. It's not as bright. It's different, but it's still there. It's always there." He stared at the kitchen table with haunted eyes. August tried to comfort him, but his muscles remained tense.

There wasn't anything August could do. Zeph only forfeited details through bits and pieces, revealing by the end of breakfast that the other-people were still following him.

"They won't leave me alone," he said, looking at the floor.

August held onto hope that the drug would work through his system, returning everything to normal, but Zeph only got worse. August even floated the idea of rehab or a three-day stay, but Zeph refused, saying it wouldn't matter. They'd follow him anyway. August was already considering seeking intervention when he came from work to Zeph walking in circles through the house, darting his eyes in every direction, mumbling to himself.

"What's going on?" Zeph continued to pace around the living room, stuck in a trance.

"Zeph!" August yelled. "What's wrong?"

"They're trying to hurt me." His eyes were bloodshot. His pupils were large black discs. His cheeks were puffy and wet.

"They can't hurt you." August tried to reassure him but he still wouldn't stop pacing.

"You don't know that." Zeph spewed the words like an accusation, making another lap around the coffee table, where there was a bag of purple pills next to a smear of lilac residue on the glass.

"I do. I do know that." August grabbed him by the shoulders. "Come. Sit down. Take some deep breaths. It's okay."

Zeph shrugged away from August's hands and continued pacing, darting his eyes between August and something unseen, circling the living-room rug before he finally collapsed into the couch and clung to August, breaking down into sobs that wracked his chest like a violent storm.

"It hurts," he cried, clenching his teeth.

"It's okay. They can't hurt you." He ran his fingers through Zeph's hair, rubbing his back gently. "Why don't we go somewhere? We can get some help."

"No. No no no no no." Zeph's body writhed and jerked under August's arms. Panting, groaning, and struggling to catch his breath, Zeph dug his fingers into August's back, squeezing, grasping.

"It's okay." August whispered.

"No!" He pushed August away and stood up. "It hurts." A bright red gash blooded across his chest, just beginning to bleed through his blue t-shirt. He turned to run away, revealing a back full of leaking cuts.

"Zeph!" August called out, but he wasn't sure if Zeph could hear him. Zeph darted around the room, then bolted towards the hallway. "Where are you going?" Zeph yelled, running after him, chasing him to the end of the hall.

"I'm sorry." Zeph's voice trembled. "I'll come back. I promise. I'll find my way back."

"What do you mean? What—" Zeph pulled him into a kiss, holding the back of August's head, holding him so tight it hurt. Zeph's tears rolled off onto August's cheeks. August clung to him tight, but Zeph pried himself away.

"I'll find my way back to you," he said in a broken voice and kissed August on the forehead. He gave a shaky smile and a thumbs up, then stepped through the wall like nothing was there.

August slapped the wall, but it was solid.

Zeph was gone.

August crumpled into a ball on the floor, a sniveling mess. Beyond his muffled whimpers, it was quiet. The silence buzzed in his ears.

It didn't feel real. Zeph was gone and he couldn't chase after him or follow. He kept rubbing the wall with his fingers, punched it with his fist until his knuckles were raw, but it didn't budge.

Refusing to let go of hope that Zeph would return, August spent the night alone in the empty hallway, curled up in the fetal position.

At some point, the combination of sleep deprivation and grief was enough to convince August to grab the baggie of pills from the living room. He sat back down in front of the end of the hallway and swallowed a pill, then another, and another.

He pushed against the wall. Spindles of light loomed across his vision, weaved through his body and back outwards. His bones felt like vibrating chunks of ice, but he kept pushing, and pushing, and eventually, his hand sank in, just a bit, but enough for proof of concept. August ate pills with one hand and pushed with the other until his vision became a whirlwind of color, and he passed completely through the wall as if there was nothing there.

THE FAMILY ON THE STEPS

TOM RAY

When six-year-old Millie Hardin came to wake up her little brother Mac, she found him already awake. "Who were those people?" he said.

"What people?"

"Those people who were just here. A man and woman and a boy and a girl."

"Where were they? Here in your bedroom?"

"Yes. Going up steps."

"You saw them in a dream." Millie often had to explain things to Mac, he being only four years old.

"What's a dream?"

"That's when you see things when you're asleep, but they're not really there. Your mind sees them, they're inside your head. Come on, Mama's putting breakfast on the table."

After breakfast Daddy left for downtown in his new Model

A Ford. School being out for the summer, nine-year-old Walter went out to play with neighborhood boys. Ruby, the housekeeper, cleaned off the table and did the dishes. Millie played school in the living room with Mac. "I'll show you how to act when you go to the first grade."

They played school until lunchtime. After lunch, Walter played catch with Mac until Mama came out and said, "You need to rest, Mac. Come on in."

"I want to play more with Walter."

His brother said, "We'll play another time, pal. You better go in and rest like Mama says. I have to go play with the fellows."

Millie saw Mac's face redden and saw how he clenched his mouth shut to keep from crying. When Mac cried, Walter would frown and tell him to grow up. Daddy would call him a baby for crying and tell him to be a big boy. Mac made Millie proud when he went into the house with Mama, holding back his tears. Mama washed his hands and face with a washcloth, before taking off his shoes and putting him to bed.

§

He saw those people again. They must be a family, a man and a woman with children, like Daddy and Mama and Walter and Millie and him.

These strange people walked up steps. His bedroom had no steps, but now from his bed he saw steps, leading up to the door of a house. He remembered what Millie told him, so this must be a dream. The people wore regular clothes, the man in a suit and tie, the woman and girl in dresses, the boy in knee pants and a long-sleeved shirt and sweater without sleeves. But they looked different from other people, gray in color but clear like glass, the center of their eyes white.

They scared him, but they smiled and talked to each other. The girl looked back at him as they climbed, and she said, "Look! Who's that?"

They all stopped and turned to look at Mac.

The father said, "Well, hello, young man, where did you come from?"

When Mac remained silent, the mother said, "Maybe he can't talk."

The girl, taller than Millie, but still a kid, came down the stairs and stood over Mac. "What's your name?"

"Mac," he said. Her odd look still scared him, but up close she looked more like a regular person.

"Where do you live, Mac?"

The girl's question confused him. "I live here. This is my room."

The boy and the two adults laughed, but the girl remained serious. "We should take him inside. He's confused and we need to protect him until we can find his parents."

"You're right, honey," the mother said. "We shouldn't laugh. Yes, let's get him inside and find out where his people are."

They resumed climbing the stairs, the girl leading Mac by the hand. They still scared him a little, but as they climbed higher they looked more real, no longer gray, and their eyes were normal. The girl had blonde hair like Millie, and blue eyes, the boy brown hair and eyes like Walter. Both parents also had brown hair and eyes, the father with a ruddy complexion while the mother had pale skin.

Double doors, taller than the doors in Mac's house, stood at the top of the stairs. Looking down the stairs he no longer saw his bedroom. For the first time he saw the house that the stairs led to, a house longer and taller than his house or any house on Linwood Street. Opening the door, the father led them down a long corridor with a high ceiling, to another door opening onto a covered porch. Bigger even than the porch on the front of Mac's house, this back porch ran along the entire width of the huge house.

From the porch he saw green countryside running to blue mountains in the far distance. Halfway to the mountains stood a cluster of shops and houses. In the rest of the countryside an occasional house or barn appeared. They all sat on chairs lined up on the porch. Mac sat on a smaller chair that the mother explained had been for the boy, named Pylwol, and the girl, Sagef, when they were little. He liked having a special size chair, more comfortable for him to sit in.

"Where is your mother, Mac?" the mother said.

"In the kitchen."

The man and woman looked at each other for a second, until the woman said, "His mother must be visiting Hilda or one of the girls. I'll take him down. Are you hungry, Mac? Would you like something to eat?"

"Yes."

She led him along corridors and downstairs. "Do you remember this, Mac?"

"No."

"Hmm. I wonder how you got out to the street in front of the house."

They came into a large room with stoves, sinks, and tables. Three women worked, one at the sink and two at tables preparing food.

Smiling, the mother said, "Hello, ladies. Who's looking for a little boy named Mac?"

The three women looked up with startled expressions. The heavier, older woman said, "What was that, ma'am?" Her look of surprise shifted to one of irritation as she looked down at Mac, standing next to the mother.

"This little boy, Mac, was in front of the house. He's a little confused. He said his mother was in the kitchen. Has anyone been visiting here this morning?"

"No, ma'am," the older woman said. Turning to the other two, she said, "Have you girls seen this little boy before?"

They both shook their heads. Mac became afraid. He had meant the kitchen at home and had no idea where this kitchen and this house were.

"Not this kitchen," he said.

The mother looked down at him. "Oh, I see. So you came here from someplace else. Do know where you live?"

"In my house."

"Where is that?"

"Where my room is."

The mother smiled again. "We're not going to get very far this way. Let's get you something to eat like I promised, then we'll try to figure out how to get you back home."

He felt better. The woman understood he meant a different kitchen than this one. And she said she'd find a way to get him back home.

"Let's start with some juice," the mother said. "Hilda, pour him a glass of mango cream."

Hilda took a jug from the ice box and poured a pinkish-orange creamy liquid into a glass. She handed it to Mac, who took a sip. This creamy drink tasted better than milk or even Coke. He took a gulp of it, and all the women laughed.

"We'd better get him something solid," said the mother. "If all he has is mango cream he'll get a little runny, if you know what I mean. Hilda, set out some cookies. Slow down a little, Mac. Just take little sips."

The mother sat him on a stool high enough for him to reach the top of the table. He did as she said, taking sips rather than gulps. The cookies Hilda gave him tasted better than Mama's, and he loved Mama's cookies.

Meanwhile the mother cranked the phone on the wall. "No, we have no idea," she was saying into the phone. "The nearest neighbor is a quarter of a mile away, and I'm sure they have no children this age. Anybody close by would be calling around to find him if they had lost a child, don't you think?"

Mac became worried again. The woman had no idea of how he could get back home, nor did the person on the phone.

After hanging up the phone the mother said, "Oh, you finished everything. Good. Do you need to go to the bathroom?"

"Yes."

"Right through here," she said, and she took him to a hallway from the kitchen and showed him the bathroom.

When he came out of the bathroom she said, "Did you use it?"

"Yes."

"Did you wash your hands?"

"Yes." Mama had taught him to wash his hands after using the bathroom.

"Good boy, Mac. Let's go back to the balcony."

Back on the front porch the mother said, "Mac didn't come from our kitchen. Hilda and the girls haven't seen him before. I called the police and they suggested maybe we should go back to where we found him, or I should say where he found us, and see if we can re-trace his steps."

That worried Mac, and he hoped the mother would show him how to re-trace steps. Now they all walked back to the door leading to the outside steps. Once they stood at the top of the steps the father said, "Remember this place, Mac?"

"Yes."

"Do you remember how you got here?"

"I climbed these steps from my room."

"And where is your room?"

"At the bottom of the steps."

The man frowned, but then smiled and said, "OK, let's go to the bottom of the steps."

Looking up the street Mac saw a house, farther away than the houses near his home. In the other direction he saw another house, also a long distance away. As they started down the steps he began to see a room, gray in color. Blurry at first, the further down the steps they went, the clearer it became. At the bottom of the steps he found himself in the room. He turned to tell them that this was the wrong room, but the steps and the people were gone.

The room now had a normal color, and it had windows on two walls like in his and Millie's room. But it had only one bed, a big bed like Mama and Daddy slept in, rather than the two smaller beds he and Millie slept in. Brighter than his and Millie's room, this room had a vanity with a mirror.

A woman with skin dark like Ruby's sat at the vanity. Dressed in pants like a man, but a top like women wore, she rubbed something on her face. She stopped as she saw Mac in the mirror. "Where did you come from?" she said in a loud, scared voice.

"There," he said, pointing to where the stairs stood before, but had now disappeared.

"Next door?" she said. "From the Watsons'?"

"No. I don't know."

The woman got up and went to the open door of the room. "Mama! Mama! Come here!"

He wondered if the woman meant his Mama, but he knew other people called their mother mama.

A woman's angry voice came from outside of the room. "What are you shouting about?"

He heard heavy footsteps approaching and another woman, older and heavier than the first one, appeared.

"What are you—" and the older woman stopped and stared at Mac. Her face looked mad, and he felt his throat tighten and his eyes fill up with tears. He fought to be a big boy, but a sob came from his throat and the tears flowed.

The woman's face softened into a smile. She bent to pick Mac up. "It's all right, baby, nobody's going to hurt you." When she stood clasping him in her arms, Mac put his arms around her neck without thinking. "That's it, baby," she said, "Go ahead and cry. You just got a little lost, didn't you?"

"Yes."

"That's right." She laughed. "Where'd he come from, Tamla?" the woman said to the younger woman, in a sterner voice than she used in talking to Mac.

"The Watsons.'"

"What would he be doing over there?"

"I don't know. I asked him where he came from, and he pointed that way."

"I'll call Cynthia and see what's going on. You better go on to class."

She carried Mac through the house into the kitchen. Sitting on a chair with him still in her lap, she reached into the pocketbook on the table and took out something. She pushed buttons on it and put it to her ear.

"Cynthia? This is Geneva. Are you missing a little boy? He's real little, maybe three or four years old, and just turned up in Tamla's bedroom. She asked him where he was from, and he pointed toward your direction. He's probably disoriented." Then in a quiet voice, "The thing is, he's white."

Another pause and Geneva laughed, and talked some more, and finally said, "I don't know, we'll figure it out. Don't say anything to anybody about this, OK?"

Tamla came into the kitchen wearing a jacket and carrying books. "Is Cynthia coming over to pick him up?"

"She doesn't know anything about it. Could this have anything to do with Kevin?"

"No! He doesn't have any kids around his place. I told you, he's never been married."

"I'm just asking. I can't understand where this kid has come from. Can you think of any other explanation?"

"How about the Leonards?"

"That's a good idea. Maybe a grandchild visiting. I'll give them a call."

Tamla poured coffee into a mug. "Do you need me to do anything? I'm going to be late to class, but if you need me to do anything…"

"No, you go on. I'll call the Leonards."

Tamla spooned sugar into her coffee from a bowl on the table and put a lid on the mug. "OK, Mama." She went out the back door of the kitchen.

"Let me set you on this chair, baby," Geneva said. After pouring herself a cup of coffee and putting milk and sugar in it, she said, "What's your name?"

"Mac."

"What's your last name, Mac?" After he sat silent for a few seconds she said, "Do you know your last name?"

"No."

"OK. That's fine." She took the thing out of her pocketbook again. First she talked to someone called Heather and told her she'd be coming in late that day. Next she talked to somebody she called "Mrs. Leonard."

"This is Geneva Tarver down the street. Yes, that's right. How are you today?" Geneva's face matched the smile in her voice. She listened briefly before saying, "I have a stupid question. Are you missing a little boy, a grandson maybe?" Pause. Her smiled faded. "Ma'am, I'm sorry to bother you, and I'm not trying to be funny. This child is white and is too small to tell me his name or where his parents are. I thought I'd just call you as a courtesy, since you're the only household on the block which he might conceivably belong to. That's all I'm doing." Another pause as Geneva looked madder and madder. Then, "Yes, ma'am, I am very familiar with Child Protective Services. A very dear friend of mine from church is head of that office. I just thought if this little boy was yours it would be better to get him back to you without getting the city involved. I was just trying to be a good neighbor. I'm sorry I did."

She pushed a button on the device and set it down on the table, scowling. When she looked at Mac she smiled again and picked him. "Oh, darlin', don't look scared. I'm not mad at you. Some old white women are rude, aren't they? That's not your fault. Don't worry, we'll find your mama."

Geneva used the device she held to her ear and called someone named Ruth at a place called Child Protective Services. After talking to Ruth, Geneva set the device down and said, "I just thought, you must be hungry. Would you like something to eat?"

"Yes." The juice and cookies had filled him up, but he felt hungry again.

"How about a banana?"

"Yes."

She gave him a banana from a bowl on the counter and poured him a glass of milk. "How about some cereal? You like Cheerios?"

He stared at her.

"Let's try this, what does your mom usually fix you for breakfast?"

"Sausage and eggs and biscuits and gravy."

Geneva laughed. "Must be a stay-at-home mom. No working mom can cook like that."

She put the bowl of cereal in front of him. It took him a few tries to figure out how to eat without spilling the Cheerios off the spoon, but he finally managed it.

After he finished the cereal she said, "You want to watch TV?"

Again, he stared without answering. "I'll take that for a 'yes'.

Let's go into the living room."

§

After Mac lay down for his nap Millie spread a blanket under the elm tree in the back yard. Taking a needle and thread, a small piece of cloth, and her doll, she practiced what Mama had been teaching her about sewing.

Ruby called from the back porch, breaking Millie's concentration on the dress she was trying to make for her doll. "Millie, honey, is Mac with you?"

"No! He's taking his nap in the bedroom."

She had just pulled the thread out of the cloth in frustration when she looked up to see Mama standing over her. "Have you seen Mac?"

"No. I told Ruby already. He's taking his nap," she spoke crossly.

"No, he's not. I laid him down an hour ago. I just now looked in on him. Are you sure you haven't seen him?" Now Mama spoke sharply.

"I'm sure."

Mama turned to Ruby, standing behind her. "Check the shed again, then the basement and the attic. I'm going to get Walter and we'll search the neighborhood."

Millie felt tears come to her eyes. She had never heard Mama speak in a frightened voice like this.

§

Two uniformed officers canvassed the neighborhood while a plain clothes detective talked to the Hardins in the living room. The detective, an old man, spoke in a rough voice, like he had gravel in his throat. His fat stomach, double chin, and bald head repulsed Millie.

After questioning Daddy, Mama, and Walter, he said to Millie, "Can you think of anybody who might have come around today, sweetheart?"

"Mac said he saw some people."

The room became quiet. Daddy said, "What people? When did he say that?"

"This morning when I woke him up. He said, 'Who were those people?' He said a man and woman and two children. It was a dream."

The detective said, "Who was it? Some of the neighbors?"

"No. It was a dream." Now Millie regretted mentioning the dream.

"Where did he see them?"

"In our bedroom. On the stairs."

"Let me look at that bedroom," the detective said.

In the bedroom he said, "I don't see any stairs."

Mama said, "There aren't any stairs. She said it was a dream."

"Could he have seen them outside on your front steps?" The policeman looked at Millie as he spoke.

"It was in a dream."

"Probably nothing. Let's go back into the living room and think about this some more."

After they all sat down in the living room the policeman said, "Has Mac ever wandered off before?"

Mama said, "No, never."

"Let's think some more about strangers. Since he dreamed about a family, maybe he's seen them in the past few days. Are you sure you haven't seen any strangers in a group like that, Gypsies, maybe." They all said "no."

"What we'll do now is, my men will keep going through the neighborhood talking to everybody who may have seen Mac. Meanwhile, I'm going back to the station house to make some inquiries by phone. Don't you folks worry. We'll find your boy."

After he left, Ruby finished preparing supper and went home. The Hardins sat at the kitchen table ignoring the meatloaf, mashed potatoes, and peas before them.

Millie and Walter stayed up past their bedtime, listening with their parents to the living room radio. "Rudy Vallee's Fleischmann Yeast Hour" came on, followed by "Death Valley Days." Millie tried to pay attention to the shows but kept thinking about Mac. When the "Fred Waring Show" started, both children went to bed. Daddy and Mama remained in the living room, he holding her in his arms. Millie cried herself to sleep, alone in the bedroom she shared with Mac.

§

Mildred Connelly, Judge Connelly's widow and a lawyer herself, watched morning network news on TV as she sipped her breakfast coffee. When they began reporting on the war in Bosnia she switched to the channel broadcasting local news. The newscaster said, "Finally, Knoxville police are asking the public's help in finding the family of a little boy who turned up at a home in the two hundred block of Linwood Street last Thursday."

The mention of Linwood Street caught her ear. She lived at 202 Linwood on the east side of town over sixty years before. Her family lived there when her younger brother Malcolm, who they called Mac, disappeared.

The announcer went on. "He's estimated to be four years old, and says his name is Mac. He doesn't know his last name or where he lives. He appears to be in good health and is intelligent. Given his age, however, he's unable to tell authorities about his family. If you have any information about him, please call . . ."

The child in the video looked exactly the way Mildred remembered Mac. The name and the location where he appeared seemed to rule out coincidence. Hurrying to her office, she phoned Child Protective Services.

§

Mildred knocked on the door of a ranch-style house in a middle-class suburb on the west side of town, far from her childhood home on Linwood. A heavy-set woman with graying hair and glasses answered the door. The woman smiled. "Are you Mrs. Connelly?"

"Yes. And you're Mrs. Wright?"

"Yeah. Ruth told me you'd be coming over. So you think you may know Mac?"

"I don't think I know him, but he may be a relative of mine."

"Come on in. He's a sweet little guy."

In the living room a baby sat in a play pen and a young boy and girl sat on the floor watching TV.

Without waiting for Mrs. Wright, Mildred went to the boy. "Malcolm?"

He said, "Mama?" and looked up at her. His face darkened when he saw Mildred.

"No, honey. Your mama's not here. Does she call you Malcolm sometimes?"

"Yes."

"And does your daddy call you Malcolm?"

"Yes."

"What does your sister call you?"

"Mac."

"What's her name?"

"Millie."

"Did Mama ever call her something besides Millie?"

He thought for a moment before saying, "Mildred."

"Do you have a brother?"

"Walter."

"Where did you go when you took your nap?"

"I went with those people up those steps. They lived in a big house with a big porch."

She smiled in order to relax him. "That's interesting, Mac. How long did you stay with them?"

"Just a little while."

"I see. So you took your nap, and saw those people, and visited them, then went back to your bedroom."

"I didn't come back to my bedroom. It was that other bedroom."

"I see. Well, stay here a little longer with Mrs. Wright, and we'll find your family."

"I want Mama." His face reddened, and she saw him fighting back tears like her brother had done.

She got down on her knees and took the boy in her arms. "I know, honey. We'll fix everything. We'll take care of you." As she heard him sob she fought back her own tears. After struggling to her feet, she said good-bye to Mac and Mrs. Wright. She cried sitting in her car before starting the engine and driving to Child Protective Services.

§

During the time Mac stayed with Mrs. Wright, the old woman who'd called him Malcolm visited him every day, all day long. She talked to him to learn about where he had disappeared to, and to prepare him for the future.

"Do you remember your grandma?"

"No."

"You can call me 'Grandma,'" she said. "I'm not her, but you can call me that."

"OK," he said, wanting to please the old lady.

"Good. You saw people in your bedroom, didn't you?"

"Yes."

"And you went somewhere with them?"

When he remained silent, Grandma said, "It's OK. I think it's brave of you to go exploring. Tell me about those people."

What she said made him feel better. He told her about the stairs and the big house the strange family lived in, and juice and cookies that tasted so good. Grandma listened closely to him, which he liked because nobody ever listened to him like that. She said things like, "How interesting," and "Isn't that strange?"

§

She practiced family law and knew her age precluded her adopting Mac. Her daughter and son-in-law, Charlene and Jason Wampler, easily qualified. They agreed to adopt him with the understanding that she would take responsibility for raising him.

DNA testing confirmed a close relationship with the child. Mildred concocted a story of Mac being the grandson or great-grandson of her long-lost brother Malcolm. That's the story she sold Charlene and Jason as well as to Child Protective Services and the court.

She moved in with the Wamplers. Their adult children moved out a few years before, leaving two unused bedrooms. She and Mac could be comfortable there.

§

Mildred retired from her practice and devoted all her time to Mac. She taught him shapes and colors and numbers, and even how to read. By the time he entered kindergarten he was ahead of all the kids in his class.

And she talked to him about his life on Linwood Street. She showed him pictures from her photo album, pictures of their parents and Millie and Walter and Mac himself. It had to be their secret, she told him. Other people, kids at school, teachers, even Charlene and Jason (who he called "Mom" and "Dad"), would call Mildred and Mac crazy for believing this strange story.

As he grew older, she shared more of their story with him. His memory of their old life on Linwood dimmed, despite Mildred's efforts to keep it alive. Now his memories were of Mom and Dad and Grandma. So by the time Mildred told him that he would never see Mama and Daddy again, and that she herself was Millie, and that Walter died in World War II, he didn't become upset, only a little sad.

Mildred's making him tell her about that strange family and their world kept that memory alive, especially the delicious juice and cookies. As he grew older he realized the uniqueness of his experience.

In third grade he asked, "Why am I the only one who's ever been to that place, Millie?" (Once she told him she was his sister, he began calling her by her name, rather than "Grandma").

"I don't know, Mac. We have to figure that out."

"Who were those people? They were nice to me, at least as I remember them. I'd like to see them again."

"I don't know who they were. That's another thing we have to figure out."

"How did I get there, and how did I come back?"

"I don't know any of that. When I showed you the pictures of our family on Linwood Street, you said the way we dressed then looked the same as those people. But during the few hours you spent there, years passed in our world. Maybe you were time travelling in some weird way. We'll figure this out some day, but right now I don't have any answers."

She monitored his progress in school. When he finished eighth grade she said, "I've been trying to find what field of study would most likely help us find out how you went away. I'm guessing quantum physics. It's so far out, so counterintuitive, it may have the answer. What do you think?"

"Yeah, that might be the answer." He said that to please Millie, knowing quantum physics only from a perfunctory mention in science class. So Millie and he read up on quantum physics. By his junior year in high school he had surpassed Millie and his teachers' abilities to digest the subject matter. As Millie had hoped, he chose physics as his major in college.

§

By the fourth grade he began suspecting Millie was wrong about some things. Other kids bragged about exciting events in their lives, so why not tell about his big adventure? He started to tell a classmate about the strange people on the stairs, a boy he considered a friend. The supposed friend told other kids. They all made fun of him, called him a liar or weird. After that he kept quiet about the strange family. Having to guard his secret all the time made him feel an outsider.

When Harvard accepted him he looked forward to leaving his hometown. People at Harvard would be different from those in Knoxville.

He became serious about a girl at Harvard he met in freshman English class. After they dated for a while, he started telling her about that strange interlude from his childhood. She laughed as if he were kidding. When he tried to convince her he was telling the truth she said, "God, Malcolm, you have a funny perspective on things." She said it in a way intended to sound joking, but he heard derision in it, too.

"I was just kidding," he said, trying to laugh. "I was trying that out as an idea for a sci-fi story."

"Stick with science, dude. Your creative imagination is too weird."

Sci-fi should be weird, he told himself. Maybe she really meant he was too weird for her. From that experience, he decided to resume following Millie's advice and keep the strange family a secret.

Millie died during his sophomore year in college. Toward the end, she made it clear he had to stay focused on finding the other world regardless of her passing. He missed three days of class for her funeral but otherwise carried on his studies as before.

§

He had wanted a serious relationship with that girl he met his freshman year who called him weird. After what happened with her, however, he avoided closeness with anyone. In order to fit in, he made it a point to attend some social event every week. But he never took more than one drink for fear of blurting out something about his secret. Every conversation resulted in odd looks or awkward laughter from people puzzled by his guarded responses. He preferred one-night stands. Partners in occasional longer relationships always ended the affairs complaining of his aloofness.

He could have lived a normal life if he made a concerted effort to forget about the other world. Instead he chose to pursue that meaning of his odd experience. He had to know where he had gone as a child, and why he was the only one able to go there.

As an undergraduate he impressed his professors with his thorough knowledge of the current literature on quantum physics. He even published papers as an undergraduate. A fellowship came easily to him, as did a tenured professorship, achieving a full professorship at the age of thirty.

Students flocked to his seminars. He threw out ideas for exploration, which his best students turned into major innovations in physics. The many paths he pointed students to held potential explanations for the staircase in his old bedroom. But no definitive explanation emerged.

§

After he gave up on physics as the key, he contacted a realtor in Knoxville and asked to be informed when the house at 202 Linwood came on the market. When it did, he bought it and retired from Harvard. He furnished his and Millie's old bedroom with a bed and a desk. Having exhausted every theory, hypothesis, model, experiment, and simulation imaginable, he concluded he had to go back to the site of his encounter with the strange world and wait for the staircase to re-appear.

For seventeen months he spent most of his waking, and all of his sleeping, moments in the bedroom. He ordered meals through delivery services rather than take time to cook for himself. Doing some research, watching movies, video calling acquaintances, occasionally interacting with neighbors, he worked to keep his mind alert.

He woke one morning lying on his side, facing the opposite wall where the mysterious stairs had appeared decades before. Having expected to see the steps for so long and always being disappointed, he failed to recognize them at first. When the realization came that they had at last appeared, he sat up quickly, swinging around to put his feet on the floor. Doubt for this undertaking gripped him for a moment. His childhood memory of a pleasant home and kind people might have been distorted or missed signs of danger. "Too late to stop now," he thought, as he stripped off his pajamas, half dressed in the business apparel set aside for this moment and grabbed his suitcase.

Standing at the foot of the stairs, he wondered if the translucent first step could support his weight. Then he remembered how the mysterious girl led him up the stairs to her family, stepping on this same translucent tread. He tried it now, and it did indeed support him. Climbing quickly, he finished dressing at the top of the stairs, tying his wingtips, tucking in his shirt, pulling the suspenders over his shoulder, knotting the tie. When he looked down the stairs he saw no bedroom but a street, the same street he saw as a child. As an adult he noticed details that escaped little Mac. The street was brick rather than asphalt, the stairs were marble rather than concrete or wood. While the double doors at the top of the stairs impressed him before because of their height, he now noticed the rich, dark wood, probably mahogany, and the brass fittings freshly polished.

Recognizing the upper-class status of the house, he now appreciated Millie's advice. From his descriptions of the place—the clothing, the old-style telephone on the wall, the ice box in the kitchen—Millie had surmised it was early twentieth-century America, or a world similar to that. "So don't dress casual like people do now, dress like a serious person—suit and tie," she said a few years before she died.

The knocker resonated loudly as he pounded the door. After knocking three times he waited, long enough to wonder if anyone was home, or even if he were at the right house.

When the door opened a young woman in a black dress, white apron, and a white cap said, "Yes, sir?"

"I'm here to inquire about a little boy named Mac. Are you familiar with him?"

Her jaw dropped and her eyes widened. "One moment, please, sir." She slammed the door shut.

When the door opened several minutes later the maid said, "Mr. Kanwerf would like to speak with you, sir." She stepped back to allow him to enter.

"May I leave my suitcase here?" he said, setting the bag on the floor just inside the door.

"Of course, sir," she said, and led him down the long hallway he'd walked down decades before. It looked smaller now.

When they reached the porch he saw the mother and father sitting where they sat when he was four years old. At that first encounter he perceived the couple as old. Now he guessed them to be in their late thirties, which seemed young to him. The man had combed his receding hair back, the woman had piled her curls on top of her head, both people attractive despite showing the beginning of middle-age weight gain—full faces with a hint of double chins.

The man stood. "Good afternoon, sir. I'm sorry, Guty failed to get your name. I'm Sugdat Kanwerf and this is my wife New Lee. I understand you're looking for the child called Mac."

"Good afternoon, Mr. Kanwerf. My name is Malcolm Wampler. I'm sorry if my lack of clarity confused things. Mac is safe and sound. He made it home just fine. I only wanted to come by to thank you for your courtesy to him."

"Really?" Kanwerf looked surprised. "Frankly, we were concerned about the little fellow. Both about the way he suddenly appeared without an adult, and then how he disappeared. I mean, literally, disappeared."

"There's a long story about that. If you have the time, I can explain it to you."

"Why, yes, Mr. Wampler. I'm very interested. Have a seat. Would you care for some refreshment?"

"Mac told me about a delicious drink you served him, an orange drink?"

New Lee said, "Really? That was just mango cream. Wouldn't you like some brandy or sherry or something?"

"No, I would just like to try that mango cream Mac talked about so much."

"Would you like some cookies also? Mac took quite a shine to those."

"Yes ma'am that would be delightful."

After Guty brought the drink and cookies, and Mac enjoyed

tasting each, Sugdat said, "Now what is this story about Mac?"

"First, let me show you this." Mac reached into the inside breast pocket of his jacket and produced a mobile phone. After turning it on he pulled up a video and handed the phone to Mr. Kanwerf, who looked at it in stunned silence. Mac produced another phone and handed it to Mrs. Kanwerf. "See anybody familiar?"

"What is this? It's like a moving picture, but I've never seen a device like this that can show movies in your hand!"

"I'll explain that in a moment. But look at the people in those movies, particularly the child."

Mrs. Kanwerf said, "Why, it's Mac!"

"Exactly. This is a compilation of images taken over the years by Mac's grandmother."

"Who is this child here? Mac's older brother, I suppose."

"No, Mrs. Kanwerf, that is Mac. The beginning of that movie showed Mac only a little older than he was when he visited you. Then you see him a little older still. There! See that? That's Mac at six years old."

"I don't follow you Mr. Wampler." Kanwerf's brow was furrowed. "The child at the beginning of the movie looked like the Mac we saw right here, just a few hours ago. How can you have pictures of him several years older already?"

"I hope it's obvious to you now that I'm a serious person. I take it you've never seen a device like the one you're holding in your hand. In fact it comes from the place I've come from. The problem for me as a scientist—and as a human being, frankly—is, where is this place we are in now, and how does it relate to the place I came from. Does that make sense?"

Both Mr. and Mrs. Kanwerf remained silent, glancing at each other, then staring at Mac.

"Let me begin a little investigation. You speak English, with an accent I would identify as American, or possibly Canadian. Are you American? Or Canadian?"

After a moment of further silence the Kanwerf's laughed. Mr. Kanwerf said, "I have no idea what creatures you just called us. Are these species?"

"No, they're nationalities. And you just answered my first question, my most basic. Now we know I didn't travel here through time, or at least time alone, but through space, from one place to the another, to a world where people speak English like in my world but are not of my world."

Kanwerf said, "But where is your world?"

"I don't know. When I was four years old I saw you and your family mounting the stairs to this house. At the time I was in my bedroom in that different world. I followed you up the stairs. You brought me into your house and I spent a delightful afternoon with you. When I went back outside and down the stairs, I found myself back in my bedroom in that other world. Only during the few hours I spent here, the other world had moved through time at a much higher speed than your world. My parents had moved out of our old house, and new families lived there over the years. I was still four years old, but my sister, who was six when I came into your world, was in her sixties. By chance, she found me when I first arrived back in my native world."

He told them the rest of his story, about being raised by Millie, trying to determine how the two worlds existed, and waiting for their stairway to reappear in the old bedroom.

Kanwerf said, "Well, your device is impressive. Do you have any more evidence of who you are, and where you come from?"

Mac sent Guty to retrieve his suitcase. When she returned, he opened it and withdrew a book. "I wrote this. I hope you can recognize me from the picture on the back flap of the dust cover." He handed it to Kanwerf.

"*An Alternative Quantum Cosmology?* I take it I'm supposed to be impressed by that gibberish."

Mac laughed. "No, Mr. Kanwerf. I've given up trying to impress people with my field of study. Back in my own world most people would react the way you are." He became serious. "But the few specialists who work in this field understand the ideas I put forth in this book, and other books. I've developed new theories about time and space, and my work has led to dozens of discoveries in physics and other disciplines. Unfortunately, despite the success of my work in the eyes of my colleagues, I have failed to discover the thing I set out to discover decades ago: who you are, where you are, and how I came to enter this world of yours."

Kanwerf flipped through the first few pages of the book. "It says here this book was published in Boston, wherever that is."

"In the state of Massachusetts, in the United States of America, on the planet Earth."

"And you can't tell me how to get here from there." Kanwerf continued perusing the book. "It's obviously a bona fide published book. I can see you didn't paste this thing together yourself, Mac. What is your plan now that you're here?"

"Find a place to live, then contact the scientific community here to begin finding out about our two worlds."

"Do you have any money?"

"Just these." He pulled a pouch out of his coat pocket and extracted a large diamond from it. "Does this have any value here? This pouch is full of similar specimens."

Kanwerf took the stone and examined it. "If this is genuine, yes it has a lot of value." He handed it to his wife.

Mrs. Kanwerf said, "It certainly looks genuine. What a beautiful diamond!"

Her husband said, "A client of mine is a jeweler, and may be interested in doing business with you. There may be some issue with provenance, but I think I can find a legal way to finesse that."

"Are you an attorney by any chance?"

"Why would you think that?"

"For one thing, you have a client. And my sister was an attorney, and she often used the word finesse in describing things she had to do for me."

Kanwerf chuckled. "Yes, I am an attorney. Between your little movie gewgaw, your book, and your diamonds, you've convinced me there's something to what you say. Spend tonight with us, and tomorrow we'll start on your quest."

§

The receptionist for Vikopshem University's physics department said that Dr. Rebces had been detained. Dr. Fardaj Jagbrot would meet with Mac instead. She directed Mac to an office down the hall.

As Mac walked down the wooden-floored, dimly-lit corridor he counted the distance from the department head's office to Dr. Jagbrot's office—fifteen doors, the last office on that corridor. The title on the frosted glass of Jagbrot's door matched that distance: *Assistant Professor of Physics*, the lowest level of prof. He rapped on the door. An angry-sounding voice said, "Come in!"

Jagbrot, a thin young man with his slicked-back hair parted in the middle, had no receptionist. He sat behind a desk cluttered with books and papers. The chair in front of the desk and bookcases against the side walls crowded the room.

Mac sat without being invited. "I don't want to waste your time. Let me begin by showing you this." He took out a mobile phone and turned it on to a video of a lecture.

Jagbrot frowned at the phone as Mac handed it to him. "What is this? How does it make sound?"

"That's Professor Lionel Tremaine, a mentor of mine at Harvard, delivering a lecture in his introduction to quantum physics course."

"But what I'm asking about is this thing. How does it produce a moving picture like this, and with sound?" Now Jagbrot laughed. "You've got me, old boy. I've never seen anything like this. Where are you from?"

"This is called a mobile phone. It provides communication, mathematical computations, recording of images and sound, and storage for data. I come from a world you have never heard of, much less seen. I am here because I must confer with scientists in your world to determine where our worlds are in relation to each other, and how I got here. Let me tell you my story." He told Jagbrot the same narrative he'd recited to the Kanwerf's. Following that he showed Jagbrot more videos on the phone: the highway system in Los Angeles, a cricket match in New Delhi, the launch of a space vehicle from French Guiana, an automobile assembly plant in Japan, a rock concert in Kampala.

"Good Fesgeth! How do we get to this world of yours?"

They drafted a research plan.

§

The textbooks, videos, and lesson plans he brought with him became the basis for Vikopshem University's Interworld Institute, headed by Mac himself. After training scientists in quantum physics, the Institute launched research projects to find analytical models beyond existing physics knowledge to explain the two worlds and Mac's travel between them.

After the first hectic weeks of the Institute, Mac resumed the practice from his Harvard days of attending one social function each week. In this new world he enjoyed such events. He no longer had anything to hide. Everyone already knew the story of his bizarre experience and his alien world.

At a cocktail party given by the Kanwerfs he talked with Erimu Dytez, the widow of a professor of literature at the University.

"So what is the significance of the latest findings from the astronomical research?" she asked.

"They've found no galaxies visible from Earth that are also visible from here. The inference is that this world and my old world are in two separate universes."

"How can you travel between universes?"

"That, Eri, is one of the questions we have yet to figure out. And I don't expect that question to be answered during my lifetime."

"Does that mean you'll never return to your world?"

"Yes."

"Oh, Mac, that must make you terribly sad."

"Not at all. The only true friend I had back there was my sister, and she died long before I returned here. The few times I tried to tell people about this world of yours they laughed at me. I had to keep it a secret. I've been more open in my conversation here with you tonight than I was with anybody other than my sister in that old world. As a result, I've enjoyed this conversation more than any I ever had on Earth."

She laughed. "I take that as a compliment."

"You should. Actually, I've enjoyed talking to you more than to anybody else in my entire life. Have dinner with me tomorrow."

She blinked in surprise, then said, "I'd love to."

CHRYSALIS

LEAH ERICKSON

She kept her eyes trained on the sleeve, the narrow white sleeve, on which she had spent hours sewing the beads. The pattern of the beading was one she had used before in her pieces. When people saw it they usually said, *oh, lightening!* or, *tree branches!*

But they never guessed the true inspiration: neurons. Branches of dendrites seen through an electron microscope, like spiky black coral suspended in glowing amber. (Sharon had seen a picture of them in a science magazine while sitting in the dentist waiting room. They never called her name, they had forgotten about her, but she was too shy to say anything. She'd sat staring stolidly at the magazine for about an hour until she quietly ripped the photo out and took it home, where she tacked it onto the inspiration board over her designing desk.)

The dress itself was high-necked, close fitting, made of ecru satin with an overlay of raw silk. The top half of the dress was very structured, but towards the bottom the silk was strategically hand ripped, elegantly ruined. The short train in the back was softly tattered, and the beaded neurons, rendered hugely on the skirt, began to disperse and vanish, as if the beads had come unstrung and were dropping off one by one.

Slowly, reluctantly, Sharon slid her eyes from the sleeve to the face: the bride-to-be was looking straight ahead, into the full-length mirrors. But for a glancing moment her eyes touched upon Sharon's.

"Your work is so unique. I mean, this dress looks like it was dug up from a grave . . . but in a *good* way?" The girl's voice was high and flat, and it echoed in the high-ceilinged front room of the design studio. She was a well-known influencer. A *content creator*, though Sharon still didn't understand what that was. "What are the beads made of?"

And here, Sharon drew a mental blank. Her mind was spluttering, clutching for the word that she couldn't remember . . . why did this keep *happening* to her lately? Was it common for people to lose their memories at sixty-five? She could almost grasp the word, then it would slither away. Her face began to flush pink with embarrassment until the word, on its own bidding, at last fluttered into her brain: "Vertebrae! These beads were created from the vertebrae of deep-sea fish. They have a particular sheen. I custom order them from Shanghai. Because I've found that compared to, say, mother-of-pearl . . ."

"Oh my god, I *knew* you would say something like that!" The girl who, at first seemed humorless and imposing, now clapped her hands delightedly like a child. "You and your sister are so . . . *goth!* Are you twins?"

"Are we . . . no . . ."

"Oh. I guess maybe I just imagined it. Cause how goth would *that* be?"

But she did not wait for an answer. She wandered the showroom, pausing to finger a wispy, transparent dress in a pale blue, hanging by itself on a brass hook on the wall.

"The *silk*. How do you make the silk look like that?"

"I weave the silk myself, from my own silkworms. Then I bury the silk. And exhume it." Sharon always wore a stiff smile when talking to the clients. It was a strain, talking to these young people who seemed so opaque. Their words barbed in irony. She always had the terrible feeling that they were laughing at her.

She and her sister Viv had designed together for forty years, always in this same building with the name of their label, *Esme*, frosted onto the glass of the transom. Forty years! Just the two of them for so long. Rarely interacting with the "outside world." Living a miniature life. But not necessarily an unhappy one, she thought.

Until the Women's Wear Daily article broke them out: *The two mysterious sisters living in genteel eccentricity create works of art; the Esme dress is an imaginative construct, delicate but complex, its textures and trimmings, expressing emotions that are unutterable.*

Now that they were "famous," it was like opening a sealed vacuum chamber, the rush of fresh air causing an explosion. And there seemed to be no going back.

"Oh. Well, no one else does work like yours. It's art, really. Truly one of a kind. You and your sister are *hot*. I just saw one of your dresses on that new singer. Liliana Vex? You know, that *sadgirl* singer. Everyone thinks she's *mood*, all tragic poet aesthetic and all, but I think she's a fake . . . They say that she's *striking* but I saw her at the Chateau Marmont once and she had a face like a pig fetus. But anyway . . ."

She had arrived at the showroom accompanied by an assistant, a young woman with short brown hair and a small, fixed smile who now moved deftly into action, her movements precise and efficient as ballet. When the arrangements were made, payment tendered, and the dress zipped into a garment bag, they left. The showroom was quiet again. Sharon felt the spark of a headache begin behind her left eye.

Her sister Viv emerged from the back room, from which she had been covertly watching the whole scene. "You know . . . when people say they want something 'unique' and 'exquisite'? Usually, *they don't really mean it*." This she said in a strong declarative voice, then paused a beat, staring into Sharon's eyes as though challenging her to argue. Though her lips were always painted a stark red, her eyes were nakedly raw looking, transparently blue, piercing. Viv had always been, and always would be, the eldest by two years.

Sharon was the first to look away, with a sigh:

"Sometimes I think I don't want to do this anymore, Viv."

"Do what?"

"Well, *this*. Client meetings, sales reps, always having to smile. I'm not even good at it. Sometimes I think I should go back to school."

"And study what, pray tell . . ."

"I don't know. Maybe . . . neurology? A life science. I want to know more about . . . life."

"Life?" Viv looked at her, really *looked* at her, and for just a moment her expression was blown open and vulnerable. Scared.

Then she blinked three times, rapidly, and it was like a curtain came down again, and she said, "You and your ideas. Like when you ran away to Italy in college to work on an archeological dig! To blow dust off of *caveman drawings!* Remember that? Then you got infatuated with a local boy and thought you were in love. Good thing your family reeled you back in, or I don't know what would have happened. At least now we can just laugh at it! Anyway, everything will be okay, you're just tired."

"No I'm not! What's wrong with wanting to do something meaningful for once?" Since she was a girl, she felt she was always waiting for her real life to begin. Waiting for . . . something. Something that was taking years to come to her. Maybe, it never would.

"But Sharon, fashion DOES mean something! I don't always enjoy this work either, but we built Esme together. Mommy and Daddy always dreamed this for us. If . . . you insult Esme, you really are insulting them."

"That is a ridiculous thing to say!" But she felt a flutter of panic in her chest, as though her sister could see inside of her and read her true thoughts. That she hated Esme.

"Well. I can't help but feel like they are watching us, all the time . . ." Viv's voice trailed off fretfully as she cupped her own elbows in her hands, looking away. "I just want to hold everything together. If you ever left me, I don't know what I'd . . . Oh, just never mind. Let's just go home."

Home was up the stairs, the second and third floors of the building, where Sharon and Viv slept in side-by-side bedrooms separated by the thinnest of walls, where they could hear each other's every stir, every snore. The thought of it, for some reason, gave Sharon the panicky feeling of being buried alive.

"Well actually, Viv, I have something I need to do."

"Oh god not *that*."

"It *is* mulberry season."

"I don't know why you have to raise silkworms! All that trouble to spin your own silk, and the weave is always too grainy. The heft . . ."

"I-I'm fascinated by the process." Sharon had a weakness for antiquated arts, like writing calligraphy or making orange rind tea. Especially ones that were laborious and time consuming.

"Those worms are revolting. Like little maggots." Viv's lip lifted into a sneer "And they make *nasty* little sounds. Like clicking or munching, it makes my skin crawl . . ."

"Honestly, Viv . . ."

"They sound like this: *schnick schnick schnik schnick schnick* . . ." Viv now had her eyes wide open and was making little pinchy motions with her fingers. She was smiling now, coming closer, pinching at Sharon. Just as when they were girls, Viv loved to torment her, loved to get under her skin . . .

"Stop it stop it STOP IT! Leave me alone!"

With that, Sharon rushed out the door without her coat into the misty spring afternoon and, before she knew it, she was running, tripping blindly over the cobblestoned sidewalk, her own thoughts a relentless, echoing roar, circling like a vortex, dragging her under. *Losing my mind, losing my memories, where do all the words for things go when they disappear, dead, dead as though they never existed. What's the use in anything, really. Everything disappears, everything dies . . .*

She had made her way to the little gated park at the end of the street, and there she sat, a good ten minutes, before she finally got a hold of herself. Then she closed her eyes, counted to five, and looked up into the branches of the mulberry tree. And there were the baby leaves, glossy dark green and heart-shaped, startling in their newness. She let out a shuddery sigh as she picked a few off, breathing in their fresh, minty smell in her fingers, before she put them into the pocket of her cardigan.

Feeling calmer, she walked back to her building, up the stairs and trough the door into the living room. Entering, Sharon felt that familiar feeling of heaviness. The place was stuffed full their parents' *things*, the dark carved furniture, stained glass lamps, the antique brass telescope, the marble chess set . . . everything had gone to them when their parents died at sea on their around-the-world voyage to celebrate their fortieth wedding anniversary.

They even kept the trunks of their mother's shoes and clothing which had been washed up on a local beach days after the ship-wreck. Their mother's tattered, ruined capes and evening gowns hung in the closet, still smelling brackish, of brine and storm, after all these decades.

Viv was in the kitchen, pouring herself a bourbon. She was quiet and kept her back to Sharon as she opened the refrigerator and removed the large paper Valentine's box of silkworm eggs.

"Those things take up all the space in there. I wanted to make a large dish of Strawberry Fool for dessert but I couldn't because your damn worms were living in there."

"Well I'm taking them out, aren't I? It's hatching time."

"How do you know?"

"I just know."

Viv sipped her bourbon but still would not look at Sharon. She was staring down at a box of water crackers on the counter as though trying to make it ignite with her eyes, but when she spoke it was archly, airily: "Goodness. I should report you to PETA. You're just raising those creatures in order to kill them."

"Viv . . ."

"PETA says those worms have brains and central nervous systems. And endorphins."

"Good god, you were actually researching this?"

"No. No, not really. I mean, everybody knows *that,*" she said stammering defensively.

"Riiiight . . ."

"Well, Sharon, I can't help but be mad. Do you think I don't struggle sometimes? I don't understand young people. Even just talking to these *influencers* makes me feel like I have a head injury! But my god, at least I'm responsible. At least I don't talk about running away."

"But nobody is making you do this, Viv."

"Oh really? What about honor? What about family? You . . . you can be so selfish sometimes. It's ever since you got those goddamn worms. I should asphyxiate them while you sleep."

Sharon felt her face darken with blood. She walked out of the room with the heart-shaped box held tight to her chest, and up the staircase.

"Don't you walk away, I'm your sister! And I know you better than you know yourself!"

§

The fighting got to be such that Sharon moved the silkworm eggs up to a space she cleared in the attic, under the large porthole window. She normally avoided the attic. It smelled of dust and rot. Here were even more of their parents' things, more trunks of clothes, boxes of photos and letters. Most problematic of all was a collection of taxidermied animals. Their grandfather had been a big game hunter. There was a pygmy antelope and a zebra, among others, shoved into one corner with hooved legs sticking up in the air. Sharon wanted to get rid of them, but Viv said, *We can't touch those things, they are chock full of asbestos! Leave them be!*

She had resented being driven into the attic, but after pushing away the junk and making herself at home, she was coming to enjoy the peaceful solitude of it. She placed the eggs inside a large glass aquarium in the warmth of the sun. The eggs were plump and healthy, she could see a dark ring and a clear center in each egg, and it made her heart swell. It could be any time now, but when they hatched, it was usually at dawn.

§

Sharon and Viv didn't speak for two days. But eventually, there was a thawing.

"Guess what?" said Viv to her in the studio one day in a mock stage-whisper, "*Trollop* is coming down to the studio for a visit tomorrow."

"Trollop" was the nickname they had given to the famous actress who was a potential design client. Sharon and Viv had watched a few of her movies and decided that she looked like a horse they had owned when they were children, a gelding that they called Trollop who had perpetually startled blue eyes. So dotty that she had gotten spooked by a goose once and jumped into a lake with both of the girls on her back.

Sharon couldn't help but giggle at this reference to their shared girlhood. "Oh, yes. The *girl*."

"The *girl*. It's all my fault I suppose," Viv rolled her eyes. "I didn't know she was famous! *I* don't go to the movies! If I had *fathomed* this invasion of our privacy I probably would have just said *no!* If I had known it was for that huge awards show I would have . . . Well, the deal might fall through, maybe she will choose someone else. But anyway, there is something you should know about . . ."

"What?"

"This."

Viv flung a newspaper onto the drafting table. It was folded to the "Style" section. There at the top were two photos of Sharon and Viv placed next to each other, with the headline, "Reclusive Sister Design Team Hits It Big." One photo showed Viv walking down the street looking cranky, wearing two pairs of reading glasses, one on her face and another on top of her head that she'd forgotten about. The other showed Sharon on a bench at the park, looking up at the mulberry tree, hair puffed in a messy, staticky cloud, with a look of sad yearning on her smudged face.

Viv picked it up and read aloud in a mocking falsetto voice. "The mysterious heiress sisters have been shortlisted by the actress Amanda Sinclair to possibly design the dress that may well be the most important one of her young career . . ."

"You were the one to say yes to all this, no one held a gun to your head . . ."

"Yes. Well. This would be a great leap, professionally. But irregardless, they have no right to photograph us! The gall of these people . . ."

But that afternoon the sisters sat down for the first time to brainstorm what was to become "the awards gown."

"What are your impressions of this girl? Other than that she looks like the world's stupidest horse when she emotes?" Sharon giggled again.

"Well. She is frail looking. Sylph-like. The sensitive type, as most actors are. Vulnerable. Living in the eye of the storm, she is . . ."

Viv began the line drawings as she spoke, evoking the girl in just a few stark lines of fluid ink. "She appeared in that big movie, the mythological one. Her nomination is for a role in which she plays the goddess Diana. And she does have that body, compact and lithe, you know? I can see her very naturally with a bow and arrow. Wispy. Fleet foot . . ."

Sharon began speaking dreamily. "I'm seeing brambles and heather. I'm smelling wet earth and animal fear. Imagine a diaphanous green, like the shell of a beetle. Short, sheath like, asymmetric. Bound in leather cord . . ."

"I'm feeling plumage . . ."

". . . feathers in a headpiece! And jewelry made from animal teeth. Lots of embellished detail . . ." When the sisters worked together like this, there was no boundary between them. The ideas flowed back and forth, freely, with no need for explanations. It was a wonderful sensation that felt to Sharon like a dive through a clear bracing stream. Or like flying at super speed through a tunnel. "All of the layers of symbols! The girl will be like a walking . . . a walking . . . um, uh . . ."

Here Sharon came to a halt. She could not remember the word that she needed. It was a bookish, heavy word, loaded with history and meaning. Almost, she could feel it drop into her hand. Almost, she could feel it forming on her lips. Oh, this wasn't fair! She slapped her palms over her eyes in frustration.

Viv gently moved her hands away and held them firmly in her own warm ones. "*Palimpsest*," she said quietly, "The word you are looking for is palimpsest."

And it was.

§

The next day, Sharon came down to the showroom, where she was twenty minutes late for the meeting with the actress. She was surprised to find that there was nobody there.

But as she quietly listened, Sharon became aware of a gentle and hesitant conversation, first starting and stopping in spurts, then becoming a steady stream of murmuring and quiet laughter. It was coming from the work room.

Sharon entered to find Viv and a young woman sitting at a drafting table, amongst the sewing machines and sergers, the dress forms and the stacked-up rolls of fabric.

But they never took any clients *there!*

A young woman sat with her back to the door. She was smoking a cigarette, waving it around as she spoke. "Oh, yeah, they're all just like, appropriation is wroooong. Nothing matters more than authen-TIC-ity! What they actually mean is: tell us who you are so *we* can decide what we think of you! It's just bullshit. I hate being famous!"

Viv had her head cocked forward, eyes riveted, nodding. Her cheeks were rosy. She pretended to start, and then said in a bright, false voice, "Oh, look, my sister Sharon is here! Sharon! You must meet Amanda!"

Amanda turned to look at her. She did not look like a movie star at all. Her dark hair did not look as though it had been brushed. And she wore no makeup. Her eyes were pink rimmed and naked, and fixed on Sharon with a childlike directness. She looked young and old at the same time. Beautiful and not beautiful, at the same time . . .

Sharon looked away in confusion, before remembering to speak. "I-I'm pleased to meet you."

"Ya good?" Amanda chuckled, but not meanly.

"It's just, I thought you'd have staff and people here, I was a little surprised . . ."

"Oh, my agent set this up. I prefer to go places on my own. I just tone down my vibe and no one knows it's me." The girl dabbed at her nose with the sleeve of her hoodie.

Viv waved a hand dismissively and said, "Sharon, don't stand there staring like a half-wit. She doesn't bite. We've been talking about such interesting things. Amanda *reads!* She reads Roethke. And she studies world religion, on her own. It's so good to meet someone for once with actual *interests!*" She was speaking in a rush, giddily, completely unlike herself. "And Amanda, speaking of people with interests: my sister Sharon has a very fascinating hobby. Tell Amanda about your silkworms, dear! She raises them herself, you know."

"Really?" Amanda looked at her with frank and open curiosity.

"Well, I just find it interesting. It's a very precise breeding cycle." She knew she sounded stiff and ridiculous, but something about the girl's ease and quiet confidence made her even more self conscious.

"How do you care for them?"

Before she could open her mouth, Viv blurted out, "She totes them around in a sad, soggy old Valentine's box and they are *revolting.* But she is just in *love* with those worms. And she thinks fashion is frivolous."

Sharon cut her eyes at her.

"Anyway, ahem, back to business. I *just* showed Amanda the sketches."

"I thought it was the shit!" the girl said cheerily, butting her cigarette into the lid from a jar of artichoke hearts Viv must have given her. "I don't usually think about clothes that much. I like to walk. I like to move. I like to not even feel the clothes on me, if you know what I mean. So this should be interesting."

Viv was looking at her with rapt attention, nodding slowly, as though the girl was an exotic animal, beautiful but possibly dangerous.

"But something like that might throw them off, you know? I like to confuse people sometimes. I don't want them to know me. I need that . . . barrier. If I'm not known, then I'm not *data.* Protection from information," For a moment she was quiet and pensive, sitting in repose. Then she snapped back to the present, shrugged, and said, "It's a deal. You'll make me and I'll make you. I mean, fashion, it's got it's place. Kind of like ritual. Or religion." She took a little glass vial of white powder from the kangaroo pocket of her hoodie, scooped up a tiny bit onto a spoon in the lid and snorted it up one nostril. "Ritual and religion. Pageantry. When in the end, what else is there? Nothing. Nothing lasts."

"How very inciteful, dear," Viv said in a hushed and reverent voice. "I had never thought of it that way before. It's been so long since I've had intelligent conversation. I swear you are making me feel alive again!"

§

The rest of the afternoon was a frenzy of meetings There was the fall line to prepare, piecework to do. There were orders to take. There were meetings and contracts. Sharon sat in the midst of it all, smiling at the well-wishes and congratulations, but inside she felt anaesthetized. The words echoed hollowly. She just couldn't feel anything.

Her mind kept snagging on the girl, Amanda. The unexpected shock of the girl had given her a kind of vertigo. Why had Viv let her into the workroom? Why was Viv under some sort of spell?

She slowly had a terrible realization: she only knew who she was in her sister's presence. If she didn't have Viv, her very *self* dissolved away like a tissue in water. She was as blank as a dressmaker's dummy.

Sharon all at once felt a choking sensation, as though a pebble was caught in her throat, and she stood up and ran out of a meeting with their new publicist. Ran home. Ran up the flight of stairs to the attic . . .

. . . And what she saw stopped her breath: the glass aquarium was glowing with hot white light from the round porthole window. And tiny, dark, thread-like baby caterpillars were emerging from the eggs. *Oh, my*, she gasped, startled by the beauty of them, so strange and delicate. A marvel, a wonder! Such a frisson of joy she felt, picking each one up with the tip of a watercolor brush, to set it onto a fresh green mulberry leaf. She could feel the firing of neurons in her brain. Nothing else mattered, she was intoxicated. It felt like love. Love that may not always be a choice.

§

The atmosphere in the apartment had changed. The sisters' tenuous truce and sense of goodwill had dissipated, and they moved around each other with stiff formality, each watching the other surreptitiously, as though peeking through venetian blinds. Each jarred by the sense that though they had known each other all their lives, there was much that was *unknown*.

Meanwhile, Amanda was like a princess in exile, ushered in by her fairy godmothers so that they would hide her away in the studio. Viv and the girl sat and drank tea and smoked (Viv had taken up smoking again for the first time in fifteen years.) Sometimes the two women went to a movie or a museum together, but mostly they stayed in to talk and talk and talk. Sometimes about books or world events. But more often the talks turned dreamy and metaphysical:

"Time is an illusion."

"Darling, you're young. Time is inexorable. The march forward. Welcome to the machine."

"Time is a sickness of the mind. Animals don't know time. It's not real, Viv."

"It is the only reality. It will never be stopped or killed. You will see."

Sharon pretended not to hear them and worked on the awards dress, sewing the crystal and bone, parsing the feathers, getting calluses on her fingers. But what she longed for, always, was to be in the attic with the silkworms. They were growing at an astonishing rate, at a stage now that the Japanese called *kego*: hairy babies. Just the thought of them made her go dreamy and mute. Nothing was as sweet and exact as anticipation.

One afternoon, she went up to the attic to steal a peek at her darlings, and was shocked to see her sister standing over the aquarium, looking down inside, holding a large can of Raid with her finger poised on the nozzle button.

"WHAT ARE YOU DOING?!"

Viv's red lipstick was smeared on one side, giving her face an askew look like a clown in a horror movie, and she was wearing a frumpy brown corduroy shirt over her day outfit. She always wore the ugly shirt when she was anxious. "What does it look like I'm doing?"

"TRYING TO KILL MY WORMS?"

"It's for your own good! I'm saving you!"

"Give me that right now you bitch!" There was a moment of tussle as Sharon wrenched the can away.

"Ow, that's my trick elbow!"

"Why, Viv, WHY? Aren't you happy enough right now? With your little movie star friend and your goddamn pretentious gab sessions? Why are you trying to take what *I* have?"

"Sharon, it's not that! Those things *frighten* me!" Viv cast her eyes on the tank, reproachfully. "I can hear them moving. I can hear them through the floorboards. I hear them in my dreams. And it gives me such a bad feeling, and you know I've always been a little bit psychic. Don't ask me to explain it, but they make me feel something terrible will happen. And look, you got even *more* of them! It's twice as many as before!"

It was true, there seemed to be many more than usual, as though they were multiplying. And they were growing rapidly in size, and they writhed with worm-like movements . . .

. . . Activating neurons in Sharon's head. Uncomfortably suggesting death and decay . . .

. . . *my god, what if Viv and I die together, interred in the attic like a couple of asbestos stuffed gazelles.*

Sharon shoved the thought away. Then took her sister's arm and steered her towards the door.

"It is my life, Viv. Only I decide how I live it."

§

She checked her receipts and old emails; she had ordered the eggs from an unfamiliar vendor. But now she couldn't remember what the name of the company was. Her decisions were often scattershot and impulsive, and her record keeping was sloppy at best. She could find nothing.

But she distinctly remembered that the eggs had arrived in a box wrapped in matte black paper, tied up with red twine. And tied to the box was a hanging tag that was stamped with the image of an Art Nouveau moth, and above it in flowery script was the word, TRANSFORMARE. She had thought the packaging a bit quirky, and then put it out of her mind and forgot about it.

But now she wondered . . . had they sent what she had ordered, or sent something different altogether?

Because they were growing into *very* strange looking caterpillars. There were projections, spikes really, sticking out of fire colored tubercles on each segment. And on their heads they seemed to have actual *horns*.

Viv hated the creatures so much that she acquired a pet raven from the back room of a sleezy exotic pet store. Mortimer, she called it. The bird had shrewd, alert eyes, and was allowed to fly free through the rooms. One day Sharon found him in the attic, trying to pick up a caterpillar in its large, curved beak. She chased him with a broom and threw open a window and shooed him out.

That's when she decided to buy an air mattress and move into the attic herself, full time, and the sisters stopped speaking altogether.

There was so much more time now, endless empty days. She could hear the commotion, see the cars coming and going, Amanda schlumping from a chauffeured car for her fittings and long cozy visits with Viv, most likely talking together about her. Mortimer, who had flown back again, hopped around and parroted, "Sharon's gone mad! Sharon's gone mad!" in his strange, piping bird voice.

Alone, the days felt slow and dreamy, and Sharon had taken to picking up the caterpillars, letting them crawl up her arms and over her shoulders. Sometimes she even got bitten by one; they *did* have tiny mouths and teeth. The bites stung, just a little, but the jolt was comforting. It stopped the internal voice that kept repeating itself in her head: *I've wasted my life. I should have broken free years ago, but I was a coward.*

Memories came to her unbidden, playing in her head like images on a flickering movie screen . . .

She had escaped her family, once, at the age of nineteen when she had taken a summer abroad alone. The only time she had lived on her own. She had gone to Valcamonica in northern Italy for an archaeological project, studying prehistoric rock art. She had stayed in a hostel, kept to herself, and was joyfully absorbed in her work studying the carvings in the beautiful grey-purple sandstone. Documenting, tracing the mysterious figures of man, woman, animal, and gods. But then she had met a boy on the site. His name was Nico and he sold sandwiches and cigarettes to the workers. He spoke perfect English. He had long dark eyelashes. His interest in Sharon titillated her, but also made her feel frozen with fear and doubt. With much cajoling, he convinced her to go with him one night to a secret dance party in the ruins of a castle.

Something about the decaying fortress walls and crumbling tower made the past feel entwined with the present; something about being in this new strange place made her know she could be whoever she wanted to be in that moment. She had nothing to hold her back. So she had kissed the boy, gone to a hidden, fenced off area in the grass, and he touched her all over her body, and they stayed up all night, talking of everything. The meaning of life, death, whether there really was a God or eternity . . . She had never talked so much, and so *earnestly,* to anyone in her life. It was colder than they thought it would be, and they slept in each other's arms. She didn't know his last name, and never saw him again, because the next day her parents called her to come home: Viv was in the hospital with appendicitis. And it went unsaid that if Sharon was a good daughter and sister, she would take the first flight home to sit by her bedside . . .

Now, reliving these feelings, Sharon felt a surge of anger at her long-dead parents. At the unfairness of it all. She grabbed a mulberry leaf and popped it into her mouth; she had been doing this recently, compulsively, chewing up that raw acrid greenness, grinding hard with her teeth. She didn't know why, couldn't seem to stop . . .

And she remembered the boy, the stars, and that cold alpine air, the way she had whispered, *I love you* so quietly that he never heard it. Tears leaked from her eyes as she felt all that had been lost to her. The tears made the caterpillars come alert, and they crawled up to tickle her face, to drink those salt tracks. Until they were *all* swarming over her, in hope of a taste. They felt so feathery, squirmy, so strange, that for those moments, she was able to forget her sadness and lay still and give in to the ardent creatures. Those dainty filaments stirring against her skin felt wonderful. It almost felt like love.

§

On the day that the silkworms began to spin their cocoons, Sharon brought out the large bamboo frames, just like she always did. She watched them work, moving their heads in a figure eight pattern, until the cocoons were complete, like fat glossy white eggs. She felt sadness because this was usually the time that she had to kill them, boiling them to death in a pot so that she could tease out the silk threads onto a dowel.

But it seemed something, a million whispering voices that only she could hear, said to her: *Let us live!*

At first she thought it was an auditory hallucination. She blamed it on the stress of working nonstop on the awards dress.

They hand-sewed hems, roughened the fabric with pumice stones, and painstakingly attached the tiny teeth and scales. They assembled the frothy headpiece of blue-green feathers and jade stones. And when the dress was done, the sisters had taken a moment alone to contemplate their work.

"Well. Sister, we've finally done it." Viv spoke softly, conciliatory. "We couldn't have made it without each other."

Sharon turned away uncomfortably. She didn't want Viv to look at her. To guess her secret.

"We finally achieved everything we wanted."

"You mean everything *they* wanted," muttered Sharon.

"Mommy and Daddy you mean? Yes, they had big dreams for us . . ."

"But none of thisth is what I wanted."

"Sharon, why are you talking so funny, with a *lisp*? And what—what is wrong with your skin? Your hands. Your . . . face. Are those . . . welts?"

"Itsth just . . . I'm allergic to the laundry detergent . . ." She tried to pull her sleeves down to hide the worm bites. Tried to ignore the crawling, pin-prick sensations all over her skin; she had a hyperawareness of all bodily sensations that she usually ignored.

Viv grabbed her arm, yanked up the sleeve. "It's those *things*. They did this to you!"

"Leave me alone, Viv!" She tried to sound sure of herself, but she couldn't let her know the truth. That she had been bitten and there were larvae inside her right now, traveling through her veins, her circulation, up to the delicate coils and whirls of her brain. Her very electrical system. Causing her to dream at night of things that were so vivid, so lavish, that her waking hours were dull and muted, hardly mattering at all.

And deep down, she loved it. And she would let the moths be born.

"Sharon? Where are you? You are staring into space!" She waved a hand in front of her face.

"I was justh thinking."

"About what? About those *creatures*? Enough is enough. I'm calling the doctor. I'll have them come and take you away to lock you up if that's what it takes!"

"Itsth my life!" Sharon found that she *was* speaking with a lisp. Her tongue was caught on something. She tried to spit it out as Viv looked on bemusedly. She plucked at her tongue with two fingers. What came out was a strand of silk.

"Oh, well that's nice, that takes the proverbial cake." Viv tried to laugh nonchalantly. But the strand of silk kept coming out, longer and longer. The laugh died away and was replaced with horrified silence when they realized *Sharon was the one spinning silk.*

"Sthay way from me!" Sharon hissed, then ran upstairs to the attic and slammed the door.

§

Bathed in hot white light from the porthole window, she began to forget who she was. She was becoming all sensation. The glossy white egg was hatching, a slit at the top, the slit becoming a dark slice. Something about to emerge. The worms digest themselves, become a soup of raw materials and cell clusters. Die, only to reassemble themselves.

But what will emerge? What is being born? All she knew was that something was being returned to her, something crucial, something without a name that she didn't even realize she had lost. Now the silky white egg was trembling with life, and she closed her eyes in anticipation, *the creature is fighting to break free . . .*

§

Strange, unfamiliar voices, a clamor of footsteps coming up the stairs . . .

"I didn't know what else to do, she has been up there in that attic with the door shut for thirty-six hours, and she had been speaking of harming herself . . ."

A man's voice called, "Sharon? Are you in there? Please open the door we just want to talk! *It could be barricaded, so stand clear . . .*"

When she did not answer they burst in: a policeman, two paramedics, and Viv, trailing behind looking small and frightened . . .

"Good god, what is *this*—"

They couldn't make sense of the scene before them: a female figure standing backlit against the porthole window, surrounded by swarms of moths. Great clouds of them fluttering in the air. They were crawling up the walls, clinging to the arms and shoulders of the woman who seemed to be not repulsed, but delighted and entranced by the creatures.

"Sharon, you are coming with us to the hospital."

"No, I'm not."

"You have a choice; you can go voluntarily, or we'll put a 72 hour hold on you."

§

She chose to go voluntarily. Spent the next day in a tissue-thin hospital gown, speaking to hospital social workers, explaining what happened, that she was not a danger to herself and that her sister, though well meaning, had overreacted. She was careful to sound reasonable, abashed, and contrite. She promised to make an appointment with a recommended counselor. There was some additional paperwork, and she was discharged.

She said what she needed to say, whatever she had to say to look like a good person. Rational. *Sane.* But the entire time she felt a curious sensation, as though she was no longer anchored by gravity. She gripped the arms of her plastic chair for fear that she might float towards the ceiling. She craved bitter green mulberry leaves. She craved the bright light of the portal window . . .

And every time she shut her eyes she saw the *moths*, those beautiful angels with the white iridescent wings tinged with lilac and blue. The coiled proboscis! The large, dazzling compound eyes looking straight into her own, *knowing* her. Witnessing such overwhelming beauty had humbled her, pushed her beyond a point of no return. Causing such a radical and terrifying transformation inside of her, that she couldn't even be angry at what Viv had done to her. She only needed to go back to the attic.

§

When she arrived home by taxi and walked into the front door, Viv looked badly startled.

"What are *you* doing here? They let you go? No one called me!"

Viv then quickly rearranged her face into a forced smile, but there was still a small knife crease between her eyebrows, and she wasn't quite looking at Sharon, but past her.

"Why would they call you? You aren't my keeper. After a full psychological assessment , they found nothing wrong with me and I was discharged. Now if you'll excuse me, I'm going to the attic, I have things to do."

Viv's smile became a bit more strained, and she stepped into Sharon's path: "You can't go up there right now."

"I can and I will!"

"I wouldn't advise it!" she said, grabbing at her sister's arm before Shron brushed her off and began walking briskly up the stairs.

"There are still fumes. It's toxic!" she called feebly to her sister's back.

Sharon opened the door, expecting to be greeted by a shimmering cloud of moths. But there were none. The air was still, the light from the porthole was incandescent and eerie. Empty. No signs of life.

She was too stunned to speak, her brain shifted out of focus.

"I . . . I had the exterminator come. They *said* we can use the room but it was chock full of insecticide only yesterday so I'm not so sure . . ."

Sharon spun around to look at Viv with an expression of fury. Viv cowered and took a step backward and began to stammer: "Well, I-I don't know what else I was expected to do! I thought they would fix you and you would be normal again and we could put this behind us. I thought—"

"You thought WRONG!" There was something bright and clean and pure in her anger. She felt a focus that she had never experienced before. "We will NOT put thisth behind usth. EVER." A long strand of silk was coming strong and fast out of her mouth, wrapping around her tongue.

"You're sick, Sharon! They infected you! You aren't right. You need bloodwork. An infectious disease specialist! You . . . oh my god . . ."

Sharon was levitating, hovering in the air, only a few inches above the floor, only for some fleeting moments. But neither could pretend it hadn't happened.

"You need an exorcist!" Viv whispered and stumbled away in retreat down the stairs.

Sharon savored her anger that seemed to glimmer like a sharp blade. Mortimer the raven fluttered down where he had been hiding in the rafters and in his strange, uncanny voice said, "You're sick, Sharon! You're sick!"

§

In the dark of night, Sharon crept into the studio where the dress was hung, resplendent on a dress form. The dress of dresses, their greatest creation, the frothy headpiece of blue-green feathers and jade stones. Tiny teeth and bits of glass and bone sewn onto the beautiful, diaphanous green silk with a roughened leather cord bound tightly under the bustline and around the hips.

Quickly, before she lost her courage, she took out her box of matches. Her hand was trembling so it took three tries before she struck a flame, and then held it to the bottom hem. Funny, it had been so long since she had seen a fire grow. At first there was just a bit of smoldering, she thought it would simply burn out. Then in the blink of an eye the whole dress was on fire, flames licking hungrily up, all-consuming, and then the headpiece burst into a spectacular corona. There was an odd smell, as of burning hair. And something else under it, the smell of metal or blood.

She felt no regret. The fire made her feel powerful. Invincible. Alive.

Just one bright flare-up and the dress was gone, all that was left was a pile of brittle ash and teeth and vertebrae beads. She alone had done this, she knew. But she had somehow gone beyond language. There was a beautiful humming in her head and her heart and every corpuscle of her body. Her nervous system was like quicksilver, her instincts sharp and precise. Her compound eyes were attuned to every flickering movement. It was as though her vision was panoramic now. The invasion in her blood that she had once feared , she now welcomed. The pinpricks under her skin had given way to the pleasurable pain of the feathers and powdery scales that would emerge. Everything she thought she had lost was here, here, *here*.

She rushed up to the attic so fast that her feet were barely touching the steps, she was gliding, really. By some strange certainty she was drawn to the *corner*, the corner of the room, the tricky slant in the eaves where the sun didn't hit, she could climb right up, she weighed next to nothing now. Language dissolved into animal instinct, she could lash out the silk *at will* and aim it right where she wanted, so that it caressed her body, spinning spinning spinning, she couldn't stop if she wanted to, until soon she was wrapped in the loveliest shimmering gossamer, still so thin she could see right through it, but she had all night, *all night!*

§

Entering the studio in the morning, Viv let out a strangled scream, letting her coffee cup drop to the floor when she saw *it*: a pile of blackened embers that had once been the dress. The scorched mannequin, the scorched black spot on the ceiling . . .

The dress.

She had an overwhelming sense of unreality. As though she had been stunned by a blow to the head. Couldn't see straight. She forced herself to take several deep breaths with her eyes closed, until she could focus, and then time began to rush forward again:

"Sharon!"

She had never yelled so loudly before, the name came out as though wrenched from deep in her soul.

"Sharon!"

She ran up the stairs to the attic, feet pounding.

"Sharon, I don't think I can forgive you, not this time!"

She did not knock, just threw the door open. She did not see her sister anywhere. Was she even here? It occurred to Viv that maybe beneath what she knew of her only sister, maybe much was unknown. Unknowable . . .

Her heart fluttered in apprehension.

"Sharon?" Trying not to let her voice break.

There was an answering sound, barely discernable. Almost like the whine of an insect. A rustling of silk fibers, a gossamer whisper; her eyes lifted up. There was something in the corner of the eves, lost in shadow. Something . . . was up there . . .

Her eyes narrowed in an effort to see it more clearly. Took one hesitant step forward.

Sharon?

OLD LIGHT AND OTHER LIES

KYLE THOMPSON

I'm not really a mirror person. Maybe it's part of maintaining the whole spoiled-rich-girl-student-slash-burn-out story, but probably not. If I went to therapy, I'm sure we'd unpack it, but there's something in me that just doesn't like staring back at myself. It's always felt like looking at the past to me. What you're really seeing are a bunch of scattered photons bouncing off of you, then the glass, then back to your eye, which your brain then takes the time to process into consciousness and eventually, into action and thought. The speed of light might be fast enough we can basically call that instant, but did you know it takes as much as a hundred milliseconds for our brain to accept visual information and then do something about it? That doesn't seem like a lot, but I can tell you after the night I had last night, it's basically an age.

Your brain is a consummate liar. It takes scattered and confused bits of information and does a good enough job at filling in huge gaps in an effort to keep you alive. So yeah, even a quick glance in the mirror feels like getting outdated information at best, outright bullshit invented by the complex inner workings of my least understood organ at worst. Why would I go out of my way to seek that out?

I don't really do makeup and I'm a shower and loose ponytail kinda girl. In covert work, you don't wanna stand out. You want to thread the needle between total schlub and drop-dead stunner. That might seem like a wide gap, but I promise you it's narrower than you'd think.

Despite my best efforts to not pay it any mind, my lying mind parses my own reflection as the door leading into the security queue slides out of my path. I'm maybe five-eight. Dark auburn hair bordering on black. Tired, bloodshot, hazel eyes. And I've failed the whole not-standing out thing today. After a night of no sleep, my ponytail was really leaning into the loose description, and I still had on a slightly oversized black zip-up hoodie with "The Little Dippers" emblazoned in white text on the front that I'd lifted to cover the blood that had soaked into my much more nondescript gray blouse. My slacks were the sort that can look mildly professional and put-together with the right top, but in the wrong context, like say when paired with an overly large black hoodie with some unknown band's name loudly emblazoned across the chest, look more like I was planning to shoplift some chips from an Albert Heijn and do a runner. Whoops. At least I'd washed the blood off my face and hands.

"Name?" inquired the Marine when I reached the front of the line. She was taller than me—probably six foot, with short dirty blond hair done up in a tight bun under her white cap. Her tone was more demanding than instructive.

I matched her confident in-charge demeanor, meeting her dark brown eyes with mine.

"Sam."

"Last name?"

I shook my head, holding her gaze.

She didn't react. They knew to expect me, but she had to double check, "Documents?"

"No," I said confidently.

She nodded now. The name was part of my cover. I've been going by it so long, I'd probably forget to respond to my real name. Sam is easy for me to remember, but tough for everyone else to look up, especially without a last name. Even in Amsterdam, you'll find a whole lot of Sams running around.

The fact that I wasn't going to pass over my passport or anything with no explanation meant that I was probably the person she'd been told to keep an eye out for.

"Everything out of pockets and in the basket. Then, step into the machine, arms above your head. Any weapons or explosives you need to tell me about first?" I think she added that last qualification to the question just for me to let me know she knew exactly who I was.

"Handgun. High right hip. Under my clothes," I replied quietly so as not to alarm the couple in line behind me. People in Europe, even Americans, get jumpy about firearms.

"Keep it there. We'll stop by the security room just inside," her voice was still demanding, but she'd also subtly shifted her volume down a bit.

I dropped my flat key in the white plastic basket alongside

some Euros and pocket change, then proceeded through the backscatter machine. The Marine hit the touch screen a few times, probably turning off any audible alarms since I still had a gun on me, before she ran the scan.

She took a slightly longer than average look at the image that came up, cleared it, punched the screen a few more times, and then grabbed my keys from the X-ray machine's belt.

"Follow me."

We hung a right just inside the consulate proper, leaving behind the glass box of the security checkpoint and entering the beautifully appointed and classical European foyer of the original building, all hardwoods and chandeliers. We weren't there for long though as she guided me into a small whitewashed room, which felt incongruous to the old world opulence we'd just left. Once inside with the door closed, the Marine crossed to a computer resting next to an explosives testing machine.

"Have a seat. Take off your shoes and keep your hands in your lap" she directed, "I'm Staff Sergeant Anderson. I have to check everything out."

There was an extended silence while she tapped away at a keyboard and I kicked off my shoes. You learn to wear clothes that are easy to swap out while on the go when you're at the Farm.

Anderson gave my shoes a thorough look, bend, and a swab, looking for bugs or explosives that weren't there before speaking to me again.

"Stand up. Arms out to the side. I'm going to take your weapon and then pat you down. Understood?" She wasn't asking for permission.

I nodded and she donned new blue nylon gloves.

"On your right hip?"

"Yeah. Under my shirt."

"Holster?"

"Yeah. It's a snap."

"No sudden moves."

"Understood."

Anderson pulled the stolen hoodie up over my stomach. She pulled my blouse from its half tuck and folded the back edge of it into her left hand. She held my clothes in place above the small of my back as she unsnapped the small holster and took possession of my Walther P99Q. I kept my eyes straight forward so as not to make her nervous, like I was obsessing over the gun.

"I've been told to confiscate this. You won't be getting it back," she was not looking for an answer. This was information, not a request.

"Stolen?" she asked as she stashed it in a black pistol case. I was surprised she was in the know enough to ask.

"Yeah."

Apparently it wasn't in her remit to dig any deeper into that because the conversation stopped there. She latched the box after a few moments and positioned it near the computer, where she could see it when she was checking things on the screen.

"I'm going to pat you down now."

I nodded.

Anderson started at my left ankle and worked her way up that leg before doing the other, "Arms back up."

I'd let them drop while she'd stashed the gun.

She worked up over my waist, around my stomach, up under my breasts, along each arm, around my shoulders . . .

A sharp pain, like an especially bad papercut seared along my neck, just below my right ear. All my hair stood on end.

I shuddered and sucked air through my teeth, "What the fuck was that?"

"What?" Anderson asked, stepping back from me. She started peeling off the gloves.

"What did you do to my neck?" I reined in the initial reaction to the pain, making sure I wasn't coming off as aggressive.

"I just finished the pat down. I was checking your shoulders. I didn't do anything to your neck," Anderson was still all business. She was direct, diction clear, and commanding.

I was already in trouble. Now was not the time to make any more. Maybe she'd poked me with a fingernail on accident or something. I rubbed the back of my neck, "I just—it felt like something cut me."

She dropped the gloves in a waste basket, collected the gun case, and opened the door, "Follow me."

She walked out like I'd said nothing at all.

I checked my fingers. No blood. At least she hadn't cut me, whatever she'd done.

Anderson led me to a secure conference room in a small corner of the third floor. There were no windows here and it was locked on both sides with an electronic key reader. She'd swiped a card and held the door open for me.

"There's a bathroom on the left and a fridge in the back. Help yourself to a drink. I don't know who you are meeting with or when, but you can hit 9 on the intercom to reach the guard station. It's all internal. You didn't bring a phone, so I don't have to take it."

She didn't need to tell me to step inside. She let the door drop closed behind me and I heard the electronic lock snap into place.

Not sure how long I'd be waiting, I wandered into the bathroom. Where the conference room proper was all modern teleconferencing equipment and sleek angles, the small restroom was designed to look interwar chic. The fixtures were definitely modern (the fancy Dyson hand dryer shattered the illusion a bit), but the whole thing was meant to look as it probably did a hundred years ago. I locked the door behind me and crossed to the sink.

As much as I hate mirrors, I wanted to see if there was anything on my neck where Anderson had . . . whatever she'd done. Even though the pain was ebbing away, it still stung enough that I couldn't believe I wasn't bleeding.

I turned my head awkwardly and strained my eyes to the edges of their sockets as I pushed and pulled my hair apart to try and hunt for any mark. It turns out, it's pretty difficult to look behind your own ear, mirror or not. I still couldn't feel any wound or blood and from what I could see, it was just my lightly tanned skin and the warm brown-black of my hair . . . until . . . Wait.

There was rusty crimson running rapidly down into my collar. How was it not all over my hands? How did I not see it on Anderson's gloves when she'd pulled them off? What had she done to me?

There was so much of it with some sort of sticky grey-pink chunks mixed in just under my blouse and hoody, running down my back and shoulder.

My heart rate soared. Had I really messed up this badly? I knew I'd stepped in it last night when I'd pulled that trigger, but surely they wouldn't kill me. Not here! Not in the fucking consolate, right?

And then I realized it. I hadn't showered. I'd scrubbed the blood from last night off my face and hands. Cleaned up and covered any stains on my clothes so that I could walk through the streets without starting a panic or drawing attention, but the blood was old. It wasn't mine. There were still flecks of it in my hair and running down into my blouse. It scraped off with a fingernail.

I let out a deep breath to steady myself. I closed my eyes and controlled my breathing until my hammering heart settled into a dull thud, a flutter, then finally a hardly noticeable pulse.

I opened my eyes and saw that I was leaning against the sink, my arms straight, hands on the rim. My knuckles were just starting to regain their color. I must've been squeezing it pretty hard.

Just as I was turning to leave the small bathroom behind, motion caught my eye on the mirror. I didn't jump, but my brain did interpret the image and swing my head back around to look at those damned old photons scattering in my direction on instinct. I should've been looking behind me. Like I said, your brain lies to you all the time and it makes stupid decisions based on invented detail.

The mirror showed me nothing, but I could've sworn I'd seen the handle on the door behind me turn and the door begin to swing open. When my conscious thought caught up with unconscious reaction, I dragged my eyes from the mirror and turned to leave. Just as the front of my mind remembered, I'd locked the door, just as I always did, even in my own flat. It gave a delicate pop as I turned the slightly curved handle, the small nub now extending out from its little pocket a quarter inch.

Returning to the meeting room, I was surprised to see two new faces already seated at the small black rectangular meeting table. They were sitting next to each other on the left side.

Closer to me was a middle-aged guy in an off-the-rack suit he'd probably had lightly tailored in an effort to look pricier than it was. Graying brown hair. Clean shaven. Faux-gold rimmed glasses from a few cycles of fashion ago. Focused look to him, but trying to appear calm and at ease, hoping I'll mirror him.

Behind him was a woman, roughly my age, maybe a year or two older, but definitely not any older than thirtyfive. Her hair was longer than mine and maybe a shade or two lighter. Her suit was similarly mass produced and I couldn't tell for sure with her legs under the table, but I was pretty sure she'd opted for a skirt. Who wears a skirt these days? She was letting the guy lead here and had the look of inexperience about her. Training to work NOCs maybe?

"Sam," said the guy, "We appreciate you coming in for a debrief so fast. Probably not a surprise, but we'll be sending you home straight afterwards. Situations like these require us to be delicate and move quickly. I promise we'll keep this as brief as possible and get you right back stateside. First thing's first, though. Can I get your ID phrase?"

NOCs like me are kept at arm's length by design. When you leave the Farm, you get a special phrase to memorize so that you can verify your identity to friendlies if you have trouble abroad— more specifically, if you get called in from the cold because you've become a liability.

"The griffin laughed at the yellow eggplant sometime after April thirty first in the fall of fiftytwo."

It sounds dumb as hell, but that's how you make sure nobody but the people who should know it, know it. It'd take a shitload of luck to guess that bad boy.

The guy nodded, accepting that the nonsense I'd just spewed matter-of-factly was a completely normal thing for me to have said.

"I'm Richard Turner. This is Louise Miller," he continued, rolling back his chair so I could see Louise who gave me a polite nod and was clearly concentrating on seeming endlessly professional, "Please, have a seat and we'll get you out of here as soon as possible."

Light, friendly words. He was repeating himself to convince me they were inconveniencing me and not the other way around. It's a tactic to get more information out of someone. You bore them into giving you more than they might want to. He knew what he was doing and if he's in charge of this whole thing, he knows that I know it too.

I sat down and waited. If he wanted to play the game, I'd play too. You don't give them any more than they ask you for. I knew my part. Pleasantries are for people who can't stand silence.

Richard let the silence hang for a few moments longer than most would and then, "Well. Let's start from the beginning. I'm going to review your history with the Agency, so we're all on the same page. We'll talk about your overall remit and the objective last night. Sound good?"

"Yes."

He turned to Louise, "Sound good to you?"

She nodded, "Yes."

He was including her so we all were part of a singular endeavor. It wasn't them versus me on the other side of the table. We were all on the same team.

Turner opened a folder stamped TOP SECRET (just about

the only thing about intelligence work the movies get right) and started summarizing from what must be my service records.

"Washed out of the ROTC at University of Colorado in 2012," Turner was matter of fact, careful not to let in a judgemental lilt to my inauspicious start as an adult. Mercifully, he did not elaborate on that particular incident.

He continued, "Dropped out of school a year later. Traveled to Barcelona for a gap year. Worked odd jobs until you were re-cruited after outrunning the Guàrdia. Seems the local station chief witnessed a shoplifting incident and was impressed with your E&E skills. Got everything right so far?"

"Yes," *let's just get this over with please.*

"What happened when you got recruited?"

Really? "What do you mean?"

"What precipitated the Agency's contact with you and how did that contact get made?"

Is this really relevant right now? I hesitated and Turner gave a faint smile, trying to appear encouraging no doubt. He's really leaning into the this-is-a-safe-space schtick.

"An acquaintance of mine distracted a pharmacist. I jumped the counter to lift some stuff that can make parties more fun. Uppers and things like that. Pharmacist noticed me coming back over the counter and chased us out. Got a couple of beat cops who were nearby to come after us. We split up and I ditched my backpack in a safe space and left my coat in an alley. Stopped at a newsstand and the guy chasing me ran right by me. Station chief saw the whole thing and followed me by chance. He clocked my wardrobe change and stalked me back to my hostel. Said the only test I failed was not picking up my tail, but he gave me the offer anyhow. A week later I was back stateside at Camp Peary."

"And the pills?" Turner's soft assuring smile didn't drop.

Ah. So that's where this is going. Druggy NOC shoots Asset.

Never mind that half the other operators I'd dipped in and out of drug problems. How else do you stay awake watching some guy's second story studio window for sixteen hours straight while he has dinner, watches soccer, jerks off, and falls asleep without even washing his grubby mitts? Turner would be popping pills too.

One question in and I was already losing control here. Part of Agency training is learning that all conversations are adversarial— even the ones with your supposed friends. I'd already fucked up enough. This was about damage control now. I had to make sure I was getting sent home and not to jail. I didn't know Turner from Adam and had no idea if he was looking to hand me over to the Dutch to right some other wrong or score some political points. My past was in my file for sure, but I had to minimize how much of it could get used against me—just in case.

The question was if I should be truthful now to build trust so I could lie about something else later. What all did he have in my file? How many details of my recruitment were written down?

I kept my posture neutral. It's not actually as easy to read people as you might think. You get vibes and you can learn to manipulate people, but you can't instantly know if they're full of shit with any real accuracy. Even if you can guess that they're lying, the why of the lie can be a whole lot more important than the what.

And when people are trying to read you, it's usually best to be careful not to give them any impression at all. I controlled my breathing, my blinking, every twitch and foible had to be tightly held. If he was trained, he'd know I was doing it, but at least he'd get nothing from me without prying it free first.

I met Turner's eyes, planning to hold his gaze while I answered. But then I noticed my reflection in his glasses. It was vague in the dim glow of the yellow daylight bulbs illuminating the conference room. I could see myself in silhouette, the slight suggestion of my own eyes bouncing back from the thin glass focusing his eyesight. I couldn't help but involuntarily flinch at the sight of multiple hazier shadows—blurrier duplicative human forms all cluttered together behind me, one of them reaching for my right shoulder. The spot where I'd felt some jab under Anderson's frisking began to itch.

I blinked and the shadows coalesced like I'd adjusted my eyes and suddenly found the hidden image in one of those old magic eye posters. I realized that each silhouette was just another copy of me—half reflections bouncing off the imperceptible prescription curves of Turner's lenses. More lies concocted by an overtired brain. When you forgo good sleep, your brain becomes even more desperate to interpret information quickly and becomes a world-class liar. It takes one to know one.

But it was too late now to lie. No doubt, Turner and Miller had seen the nervous twitch. Surely they'd braced themselves for a full scale fabrication.

"I kept them. Friend got released the next day and we partied like we'd planned," I shrugged, fighting my composure back into shape, keeping my voice even and matter-of-fact, "Was told I shouldn't just disappear on folks. That leads to more questions. So it was a last hurrah before training."

Turner nodded and dropped his gaze back to the file, his kindly semi-smile never moving.

"You were designated an NOC," he stated the initialism

letter-by-letter instead of the more colloquial phonetic reading, "and returned to Europe nine months later. Specifically, sounds like you started back in Barcelona, bounced around Germany, did some time in the Eastern Bloc and even wound up in Abu Dhabi for a few months, before you came back here to Amsterdam. Which was your favorite?"

"Until last night, I would have said Amsterdam," I hadn't hesitated. The half-joke would set a casual tone and hopefully reset us a bit so that I could wrangle this conversation back under my control. I didn't elaborate beyond that answer. It was honest enough.

Turner's smile grew just a touch and he might have even chuckled lightly. I knew it would sound like a joke, but it was also the truth. Either Turner had slipped in his reaction or he was trying to manipulate me back. Humor keeps the mood lighter—it was kind of a way for me to act like the whole we're-all-friends bit was working for him. I noticed that Miller's face hadn't budged. The work must come naturally to her. It did for me too.

I mirrored Turner, the corners of my lip gently drifting upwards into a half-smile, completing the exchange and hopefully, locking the answer in without diving too deeply into it for now. There was no doubt that most of the questioning would focus around last night, but I wanted to warm up to it a bit more.

This tactic backfired spectacularly as Turner decided to lean into it, "Right. Let's talk about last night. We can go back to the broader context later. What were you there to do? What was your mission as you understood it?"

Damn. I didn't let my face slip, but I dropped the amiable half smile. They'd be expecting serious professionalism now. I reminded myself to just answer the questions asked exactly. *Do not expound.* Everyone talks so much when they get nervous. It wasn't so hard for me, but masking as other versions of myself sometimes built the muscle to try to be overly helpful. Even though I was watching my breathing and wrangling my stress levels, sweat was forming on my brow.

"It was a black bag job. I was there to retrieve all available data sources. Quiet. Copy everything I could get my hands on, take photos, leave a worm the geeks cooked up on any device I could get my hands on. Leave everything I found at my drop."

Turner nodded. Miller had turned her attention to a legal pad. She'd shoved a thick back mat behind the front page to keep her writing from leaving ghostly impressions on the pages behind and was now scribbling notes. They'd get transcribed into the very folder Turner had been reading from later no doubt, and appended to any other mission notes, before the raw notes were incinerated.

"And in your own words, what happened? Start with your intel gathering and infil."

Is it getting hot in here? Why am I sweating? I'm good at keeping my biology in check. It's always come naturally to me, but paired with training at the Farm, I could make the Pope believe I was his wife and almost believe it myself. *Am I getting sick? What is wrong with me?*

I swallowed and answered, falling back to my normal monotone, hoping that if I dropped some of the stress of matching Turner's good guy energy, I'd keep them from reading too much into my physical reactions.

"Target was a single male. He—"

"Sorry," Turner interrupted. Miller stopped scribbling, her

pen hovering over the page. Her eyes flicked back up and met mine briefly, before dropping back to the page, like it was all that mattered here. *Don't worry, girl. You'll realize that getting to the truth is a luxury reserved for those outside our career.*

"I should have been clearer. Let me back up. Who was the target?" Turner continued.

Was he trying to unbalance me more?

"Goswin Vos."

I waited, staring at Turner. He still had that focused look in his eyes, his mouth relaxed, just shy of a smile. Most people made eye contact naturally to indicate they were listening to you. Turner was reading, watching every move I made. He let my answer hang in the air, probably waiting to see if I'd get uncomfortable and carry on.

I was uncomfortable alright, but not socially so. Awkward pauses don't feel all that awkward to me. My body and my brain however, had apparently given up all semblance of composure. I could fight my own complete lack of sleep all I wanted, but my brain could do as it pleased. If you go long enough without good sleep, the fallible three pounds of congealed meat soup kicking around in your head can really go off the deep end. A bead of sweat traced a path down from my forehead and down to the tip of my nose.

At long last, Turner caved, but he surprised me again. I should've known. You win conversations by keeping your opponent off-balance. But his next move was beyond the pale.

"Sam, are you feeling alright?" he met my gaze so thoroughly it was like he could see that I was staring at my own fractally exploding selves vanishing into the infinite, dark pools of his eyes—that *fucking* old light bouncing off me, hitting the lenses of his glasses and scattering in a hundred different directions, half of it pulled into the black holes at the center of his eyes, and half of it coming back at me, forming dozens of shadowy ghosts, all attached to me, waiting for their chance to take over.

"Um," I cringed inwardly as that damned bridge word cleared my lips, but it just snuck up on me. "Sorry," another word that rarely crossed my lips, "I haven't slept in close to forty eight hours. I'm just feeling a little off."

And then Turner hit me with another surprise, "That makes sense. We have to keep this moving, but why don't you take a minute in the bathroom? Splash some cold water on your face. You'll have plenty of time to sleep on the plane home."

He knows I'm vulnerable. Why isn't he keeping the pressure on?

I didn't care. I felt like I was running a marathon in the middle of the summer. It wasn't just my forehead. I was flop sweating under my clothes.

"Yeah. Sorry," that word again. *What am I apologizing for?* "I'll be right back," rushed out of me faster than intended as I stood and moved as quickly as I could without looking like I was losing it to the restroom.

The world was spinning. I was nauseated. My neck ached like I'd been in a car wreck the day before, screaming at me for mercy I couldn't give it. *What the fuck did Anderson do to me?*

My mind was racing, but all I could think to do was follow Turner's suggestion. *Did he know? Was this organized? Fuck!* I grabbed the pristine ceramic of the sink for a moment, then let go to crank the cold water on. I thrust my hands into the stream and felt it sap the heat from my fingers. They went white almost immediately as my blood fled the digits for warmer climes. I splashed the water against my sweating face and felt momentarily better. I repeated the move three more times and on the final time, ran my cold hands back around my chin, over my ears and round to the back of my neck.

The ping-ponging race of my panicky thoughts cleared just long enough and I began to probe my fingers around where Anderson had done . . . whatever she'd done while patting me down. *She must have done something.*

But there was nothing to feel outside the throbbing aching on the back of my neck. I checked my fingers and once again had a moment of vindicated discovery before realizing that the thin red-pink water dripping like violent sunbursts into the sink was, once again, not my blood. I needed a shower. I needed sleep.

But first I had to figure out what was going on with me.

I looked into the mirror again, steeling myself to let my tired brain play catch-up before it landed on what I was actually seeing.

There I was, bags under my eyes, standing in some mock recreation of a bathroom out of time. No sleep-deprived hallucinations. Just a woman in her thirties, dark bags under the flat hazel-eyed glare, brown-black hair in a messy ponytail held together by a hairband rapidly losing its fight for order. I looked like shit.

I had just started to lift my hair to do the awkward look at the back of my neck again when I noticed that the mirror had changed. I had not expected my brain to parse information logically when I'd first hazarded a glance into the glass, but I'd expected it would eventually catch up.

I hadn't expected to see a silhouette—my own miniature doppelgänger—striding forth as if walking down a long hallway running from my heart towards the mirror.

I froze.

I strained to get my mind to stop bullshitting me. This didn't make any sense and I certainly had enough going on without a mental breakdown on my plate. The figure was getting closer to the mirror, despite there certainly not being my own little Mini-Me marching through air in front of me.

Did Anderson dose me with something?

Just as the thought entered my mind, the reflection sped up and charged the mirror, coming at it at a full sprint.

The mirror exploded inward silently, shards not tumbling from the frame as they should, but flying away from me as if there were no wall behind it.

And there he was.

Green eyes. Dark, Mediterranean skin, faded light from lack of sun. Short, hair slicked back with some kind of treatment. Meticulously kept side-burns and beard.

Goswin Vos.

Just staring at me. Glassy eyed. Nobody home. Just a flat, even stare.

I stepped backward and my foot must have caught on the tile and the spot where the mirror had been, Goswin, all of it, dropped from sight like an elevator that had its lines cut. Unconsciously, I braced to hit the floor, but I met no resistance, no sudden stop and aching body. No crash. No blissful blackness to drop all awareness from my mind for a few brief moments of senselessness. Just air rushing by me as I toppled backwards and the world spinning for a moment before my damned tired brain decided to completely lose any ability to process reality.

I felt like I was floating. It was as if some capricious god had turned off physics.

I was spinning, but spinning through nothing—just a never ending whirlwind of off white bathroom tile. No matter how much I blinked or tried to focus on a point, my brain found no detail to cling to. No sink. No anachronistic Dyson hand dryer. No mirror. No Goswin Vos. Just an endless whirling sense of nothing.

The worst part was when it stopped.

At first I thought I was having an out of body experience. When my brain finally settled on something, it was me.

Gray blouse stained with fresh blood up around the right shoulder. Dark athletic slacks. Dead, hazel-eyed stare peeking out from a mass of dishevelled brown-black hair, matted with crimson and flecks of grey-pink tissue. Walther P99Q held firmly in my right hand, red-tinted finger off the trigger.

I realized I could see a bathroom behind me. This one was clearly in a nice flat somewhere. All hypermodern silvers and sharp edges.

I was looking in a mirror hanging on the back of the bathroom door. It was last night. I could feel the gun in my hand, the splatter of blood going tacky on my skin and clothes. But that didn't make sense.

Mirror Me lifted her gun arm and slid her finger into the trigger guard. My hand stayed at my side. I willed it to stay at my side. My nerves. My muscles. Every other signal my body was getting was screaming at me: *your arm is by your side.*

That wasn't me.

It couldn't be.

But that damned old light had bounced off that fucking

mirror, falling into the black holes of my pupils and there I was, pointing a gun right back at me.

I pulled the trigger. Or rather Mirror Me did.

And I was off to spinning ass-over-teakettle again, a kaleidoscopic mess of silvers and blacks and a splash of crimson sliding by with no sensation of motion.

When it finally stopped, it had given way to a smear of black.

What. The fuck. Is happening to me?

My eyes couldn't be trusted. I squeezed them closed and tuned to all my other senses. Trying to make any sense of anything. I needed to find the door to the bathroom. I needed out. I needed a hospital. Worse. I needed Turner. I needed Miller. Hell. I'd take Anderson and her jabbing fingers. Something was seriously wrong. *No way out on my own.*

I listened carefully for any hint of noise. Maybe I could hear Turner and Miller talking about me on the other side of the door or the tap of the bathroom I was surely still in, cold water still *shushing* into the sink.

There! It sounded way too far off, but there it was: the noise of water flowing into the sink from the tap.

I must be on the floor. I must have hit my head. Did Turner and Miller not hear me fall?

Eyes still closed, I felt around.

Smooth, cold tile. Yes. I was on the floor. I gingerly pushed myself up onto my knees and felt my way towards the sound, knowing if I found it, I'd just turn around 180 degrees and carefully step to the door. Shutting out the lying signals my eyes were giving me would prevent me from getting distracted by hallucinations and I could . . .

What? Beg for help? What if this was by design? What if I'd been lured here just to burn me? Was this a trap or was this some mistake? Had they meant to dose me with something just to loosen me up for questioning? Or was I just tired and losing my grip?

It didn't matter. My mind was rapidly drifting off to La La Land and I needed help. Getting out of this bathroom was my best chance. I could deal with what was happening and who had done it to me later.

Squeezing my eyelids shut, I worked my way to standing. I kept my hands out in front of me, swaying them back and forth like I was searching for a light switch in the dark. Fumbling for the sink.

Nothing . . .

Nothing . . .

"AH! SHIT!"

My hands felt like they were suddenly on fire. I couldn't help it. My eyes involuntarily flew open.

My hands were sparkling and dripping bright red. Dozens or hundreds of tiny reflective pieces of glass pricked from my hands like I was gearing up for some deranged post-apocalyptic slap fight.

"What the fuck?"

The light *shushing* I'd heard was not a *shushing* at all. I'd reached into a mound of broken glass pouring forth from an empty frame floating in blank white space before me. A shattered mirror, endlessly pouring out millions of tiny fragments of small, reflective lies, rolling and sliding and bouncing off each other.

I'm a little blond girl, blaming her brother for a broken window.

I'm a pimple-faced mallrat wannabe in some Hot Topic tee,

hair cropped to a bob and died jet black, telling my dickhead manager, Steve, I was late to work the drive-through, not because I was getting high, but because I had to help wrangle my neighbor's dog back into their house.

I'm dressed in a crop top and hip hugging white slacks, jumping a counter to snake as much Adderall as I can grab and tearing out of there like a bat out of hell.

I'm all done up with a blond wig and a black cocktail dress, looking like some rich pervert's wet dream version of that little girl by the broken window, flirting with an ambassador whose name and country I've forgotten so another NOC can go through his shit in his hotel room.

My face, my hair, my clothes, my body kaleidoscope wildly in all the shards of glass. Thousands of different "mes". All women that existed in some other time, some other universe. Each one is me. Each one is not me.

The shards of glass illogically spewing from the mirror like a Swarovski store display concocted by an architect who's done way too much cocaine suddenly stopped, leaving just a thin, silver frame hanging in the void.

Once the shards settled and stopped bouncing and shattering down their chaotic sedimentary pile, things went quiet again. The only noise was the gentle *tap tap* of the blood dropping from my hands, clutched around each other and pulled in tight to my chest, snaking down my arms, and dripping off my elbows to the endless white plane that passed for a floor here. I expected little crimson dots to be littering the ground and desperate scarlet handprints that slid backwards away from the pile, but the endless white seemed to pull in the blood. The droplets splat and vanished instantly as they struck the ground.

There was no door. No sink. No frame of reference, but the now empty silver frame hanging on a wall that wasn't there over an impossible pile of glass it never could have contained.

Now what?

I almost laughed. What the hell was I supposed to do now? I thought my brain was misinterpreting signals from my eyes. The blood running down my arms in large crimson rivulets begged to differ.

I was still working out my next move when I heard a familiar voice. A voice I'd not expected to hear again.

"Wie is daar?" Masculine. Dutch. Strong diction, no word running into the next, giving the voice an air of fine education.

"Who is there?" he tried switching to English. Slight tinge of British to the Dutch accent, with a hard *dz* sound in place of the *th*.

I kept my mouth shut and backed away from the empty mirror frame—no, wait. It was no longer an empty mirror frame. It was now a closed door and I realized I was standing in a darkened room. Keys clattered on some end table, muffled by the door and distance.

I heard a door smack against its stop and it was like someone hit the lights in the void I was in. Gone was the endless blank of white, replaced by light leaking from around the frame of the door where that illogical shattered mirror had hung.

"I know you're here," the voice seemed to be wandering closer and then further from the door, "I always lock my door."

Where are you going? Why does this feel familiar?

"I'll call the police."

He was getting nearer the door. I saw a shadow break up that faint line of light pushing past the door-that-was-formerly-a-mirror.

It was last night. I was in Goswin Vos' home office again. Standing flat-footed like an idiot. This was wrong. I was supposed to be hiding behind the door. I was supposed to jump him and try to choke him out. He was going to reach for me and against all odds, knock the pistol at the small of my back out of the holster. I hadn't known that was possible. I'm still not even sure how he did it. Then he was going to go for the gun. I was going to drop off his back and smack him in the balls before I went for the pistol. He'd grab my leg and drag me towards him. I would pop the safety, kick my free leg out to roll, and put a round into the wall behind him and another just to the right of his nose. Then he'd collapse into my chest like an exhausted lover.

That's what was supposed to happen. That's what had happened.

Instead, he stepped through the door, silhouetted by light behind him, and looked around for a moment before reaching over and tapping the light switch. My eyes adjusted and I was standing in Vos' office, behind his neat, darkly finished oak desk, laptop cocked half open in front of me. I'd been swiping files when he'd unexpectedly arrived home.

"Oh," he sounded disappointed, "it's you."

Vos stood there, hand still on the light switch, looking at me like he'd caught his wife sneaking about.

I didn't know how to respond. This was not how it went.

"S— sorry?" I stammered.

"You shoot me in the face and then you have the nerve to

come back here?"

Sure enough, there was a small round hole on his cheek. The skin was purpled, a nasty bruise running up and around his eye, the wound all puckered in on itself, but there was no blood.

"You're dead," I finally replied weakly, as if stating the obvious would make it true again.

"So it would seem," said Vos, though it certainly didn't.

He stood there at the light switch another moment before crossing the room to me.

"Excuse me," he said as he stepped around his desk, waggling the ends of his fingers on his left hand, shooing me away from his workspace. He had a wedding band on his ring finger and a fat sigil ring of some kind on his pointer.

"You can take the chair over there if you like," it was more instruction than invitation as he indicated a posh black leather number that looked like it belonged in some bougie therapist's office.

Not really sure what else to do when confronted by a dead man, I took a seat, leaving dark crimson handprints on the arms of the chair as I eased myself into it.

"So, what are you doing here?"

"I'm not really sure," was the best I could come up with.

Vos shook his head almost imperceptibly before leaning forward and rolling his chair closer to his desk, leaning forward and staring at me over steepled fingers.

"You murder me and you can't even come up with an excuse?"

"I didn't murder you. I'm not a killer."

"Could have fooled me," Vos pointed to the hole in his face.

"You attacked me. That was self defense."

"Interesting thing for someone who broke into my flat to say. Seems more like you attacked me."

He has a point. I leaned back into the chair, trying to reverse his aggressive energy by looking relaxed and comfortable. I didn't like feeling like I was on the back foot in a conversation for the second time today, "That was an accident."

Goswin Vos fully laughed. This wasn't some mirthless chuckle in the midst of a battle of wits. He kept his eyes on me, but his mouth was open, teeth visible, tongue pressed to the floor of his mouth, rolling upwards just like the corners of his lips as he cackled across the room at me.

"Oh. My mistake," the laughter subsided slightly, "You accidentally made your way into my office without turning on a single light and started fucking with my computer. You accidentally hid behind the door and jumped me when I was calling out to see who had picked my lock. I see now that I was in the wrong here."

"You weren't supposed to be home," tumbled out of my mouth all at once with all of its terrible implications following along. I didn't feel guilty, but I'd come up blank on how to respond to Vos's joking. The other option was to sit here in silence with a dead man taunting me. A base statement of simple fact seemed best—not an admission to anything—just a fact.

There was a pause as Vos finally wrangled his laughter.

"Ah yes. Now we are getting to it. You murdered a man for the crime of returning to his own home sooner than you expected."

"We were both scrambling. I didn't mean to shoot you."

"I might not be American, but even I know you don't point a gun at someone unless you mean to hurt them."

I shrugged. This wasn't personal. This was a job gone wrong. I was only there to copy his files. Take pictures. Leave a virus on his computer. Disappear without a trace that I'd ever broken in in the first place.

"It's not like I can tell anyone. I'm dead, right? So let me ask you again and don't give me any of that evasion shit. What are you doing here?"

"I don't know," I sighed, "I was in the consulate and now I'm here."

Vos' eyes focused when I mentioned the consulate.

"I see. Do you know who I am?"

"Goswin Vos."

"Yes. So you probably know that I'm a businessman."

"Arms dealer."

"That's my primary business, yes. I follow all international regulations and provide a necessary service to many clients."

"Including puppet states in the former bloc, the Middle East, Africa, you name it."

Vos paused with a slight smile on his face. "All under NATO's watchful eye and in line with their goals."

Supposedly. It wasn't my job to judge. It was my job to observe and report back. And sometimes observing meant breaking in to make sure we were seeing the whole picture. I just hadn't had the chance to actually check Vos' office. Gunshots in metropolitan areas tend to draw attention, so the mission had changed from data extraction to rapid cleanup, escape, and evasion until I'd gotten to my emergency drop and the instruction to head to the consulate.

"So who had it out for me then?" he asked.

"Nobody. I don't do wet work."

"Right," Vos shook his head and seemed to hesitate with the

bullet hole angled at me each time, "says the mystery woman wearing my clothes to cover the bloodstains."

He pointed at my chest and I realized I was still wearing the oversized "The Little Dippers" hoodie. I'd raided it from his coat closet on my way out the door.

"Didn't strike me as a local dive bar band kind of guy," I said, nodding at his gray suit.

"I'm allowed to have hobbies," he shrugged this time, "So you won't tell me who sent you to kill me."

"I wasn't here to kill you."

He waved his hand dismissively again, "Right. Who are you then, mystery woman?"

I certainly wasn't going to answer that question, dead, figment of a sick and tired mind, or whatever else this might be. Instead, I tried, "Why did you come home early?"

It was sloppy. An obvious deflection. But I was getting desperate. It's tough to keep control of a conversation with your hands cut to shit and blood pooling everywhere you set them.

"I got a text. A client I'd been waiting on finally got back to me and wanted to have a confidential chat."

A text? I'd watched him for six weeks, every move, and on Thursdays Vos always headed to some posh bar just outside the red light district with what must be his drinking buddies and stayed out well into the early morning hours. I had no idea where his family was, but this had to be a working flat because I'd never spotted them. The place was supposed to have been mine for hours and I got blown by an offhand fucking text.

Unless you got blown on purpose . . .

Whoever my Amsterdam handler was knew I had been

planning to make entry this week. *Fuck.*

Vos smiled at me, "So you weren't here to kill me."

"What?"

"You asked why I had come home early."

Shit. I was off balance. He was right. Questions can tell some-one just as much as answers. My hands were throbbing, blood still oozing between my fingers. My eyes were stinging, feeling simultaneously too wet and too dry. It was clear that I was in no shape to be discussing things with anyone.

And I was lost somewhere in my own mind trying to find a way back to an interrogation room where real live people could end my career. One way or another, I wanted to get back to reality.

I stood, leaving more dark crimson stains on his sleek leather chair.

"Well, talking to a dead man has been fun and all—"

"The man you murdered," Vos amended.

"—but I think it's time I leave."

I basically ran for the door, abandoning all pretense of having my shit pulled together. *No need to impress the dead.*

I left his office and ran face first into myself, careening onto my back with no time to get my arms out behind me. Cold air blasted out of my lungs as my head smacked the floor.

My head pounded and my vision blurred as I lay there for I'm not even sure how long. Everything hurt. The pain at the back of my neck. The throbbing burning of my lacerated hands. My smashed face. I was so tired that all of these signals were colliding into just a mass of pain screaming out of every nerve in my exhausted body.

My hands glided over smooth tile as I pushed myself back up to sitting, letting out a short groan as I did. Looking down, it wasn't tile . . . it was glass. My own weary face looked up at me stupidly.

I scrambled to stand and realizing that I'd not collided with my own doppelgänger, but my reflection. I was surrounded by smooth, reflective glass, no edge or corner in sight. My brain screamed to make sense of it.

I closed my eyes, hoping to reset my vision. A few moments later, I opened them.

And there she was. Dark auburn tresses framing tired hazel eyes. Uncontrolled split ends flying off in all directions. Face dripping cool water, droplets rolling down over slim cheeks, around her chin, and dropping into the sink, her hands braced on either side of the basin. She blinked as one drop of water fell from her eyebrow, swirled into the socket and filled her eye.

She ran her arm across her face to wick away the offending water, straightened herself, and smoothed out her clothes. She shook out her arms, letting the bunched up sleeves of the random indie band's black hoodie unfurl and drop over her hands, still oozing red. She blinked a few more times, turned from the mirror, and took a deep breath.

She pulled the hoodie up over her face and dried it on the inside of the garment before finally reaching for the curved handle and turning it.

A faint pop echoed through the bathroom as the lock came undone and she strode through the door clicking off the bathroom light as she left.

She returned to the meeting room and was greeted by the end of a hushed conversation between Richard Turner and Louise Miller.

"—wrap this up. We can do the report," said Turner.

"But, shouldn't we do the full debrief to decide if she goes home or over to them?"

Turner shushed Miller lightly, holding up his hand to indicate they were done with their discussion as she reentered the meeting room.

"Sam," said Turner, back to his gentle nice-guy routine, "Feeling better?"

She nodded, "Yeah. Thanks."

"No problem."

"Where were we?" she asked.

Turner stood before she could reclaim her seat.

"No. That's okay, Sam," he said sympathetically, "I think we have enough. Things just go wrong sometimes, right? Nature of the job."

He smiled at her reassuringly.

"Why don't you follow me, and let's get you out of here?"

Turner indicated she should follow him. He led her out of the sparsely decorated hyper-modern meeting room and back out into the restored hardwoods and pastel plasters of the rest of the building.

They went down the stairs to the ground level and after a few winding turns, Turner led her to a back entrance. He checked in a guard stationed right next to the door.

"Richard Turner," he said flashing some credentials, "We've got a car waiting."

The guard nodded and waved them out the door, clearly expecting this particular exit already.

Turner led her to a black sedan parked in the small fenced-in lot, which looked back across the park to the strange mirrored cube sitting just outside the Van Gogh Museum.

She kept her eyes focused on her feet as Turner opened the passenger door for her.

"Let's get you out of here," he said again pleasantly as he closed the door behind her.

§

Louise Miller blew out a sigh as the door closed behind Turner. She'd never debriefed a NOC before, but then again, most who slipped up this badly didn't get a chance to come in for a debrief. Sam was lucky she'd shot someone, let alone a citizen of a friendly nation, in Amsterdam instead of Minsk.

All these field agents were the same, NOC or not. They were shameless adrenaline junkies with no notion as to the broader consequences of their actions. Useful tools, but blunt instruments—hammers wishing they were scalpels.

She needed a vacation. She thought this job would be all travel and fancy state dinners, but most of it was dull interviews in boring offices. And when it wasn't that, it was staring at reams of paperwork for hours on end. But a week off was not forthcoming.

Maybe Sam and her ilk were onto something. Hell, Louise would shoot someone right now just to leave this stupid meeting room and head out on a walk through the city. She'd go until her legs ached and her feet refused to carry her any further. The fresh air would remind her that there was more to life than the recycled freshness of AC and cold coffee.

She was just fantasizing now and she'd never be able to pull a trigger. It wasn't why she got into this in the first place. She wondered if that small fridge near the bathroom had something sugary that might smooth out the flagging energy of the afternoon and take her mind off the sheer boredom of her life.

On her way to the fridge, she noticed that the bathroom door was slightly ajar.

Louise gently nudged it open with her knuckles and for just a moment her reflection in the mirror looked all wrong to her: hair a little darker and pulled back in a disheveled pony with split ends flying off in all directions; clothes all bulky and strange like she'd pulled on some outer layer—and what was that written across her chest?

She flipped on the light, and there Louise was in all her suit-jacketed, professional glory, staring uncertainly back at herself. Any suggestion of that strange messy woman her bored mind had conjured in the gloom was obliterated from reality.

GORSE 206

BENDIX ROSS

The desuckering crew trekked home from the Gorse 52 fields without much conversation. After a day of forced labor on Frutex, we were too goddamn tired to talk.

The light was dimming in the planet's oatmeal sky. You'd think I'd have been used to the permanent, cloudless haze that hung in the lower atmosphere. That I'd stop yearning to see my home world's golden dwarf sun. But five years in exile didn't matter; I would always miss the blue and yellow of a hot Earth day.

My back was tight from hours bent low clipping lateral shoots, or suckers, from the root collars of Frutex's shrubby, pale brown plants. Working vineyards in Earth's Willamette Valley got me pegged early on as a skilled pruner, meaning I was assigned to a lot of desuckering.

The dusty path cut through an ocean of shrubbery. There was so much of it, we'd nicknamed the planet "Shrub." Bushes with beige leaves and tan, woody stems grew on either side of me, reaching my waist. A light wind moved through the uppermost leaves, making a whistling sound — the Shrub Squeal.

It was a "Friday." For everyone's sanity, the human colony had started up our seven-day calendar shortly after arriving on the planet. My plan that evening was to clean up for Shabbat services after work and then head to shul.

Like a lot of people in the colony, I wasn't that religious before the Galactic Interventionist Coalition brought us to Shrub. But now, most of us went to synagogue, church, the mosque, or the Buddhist temple. It helped with the massive guilt we carried over losing our home. Five years ago, when the GIC aliens removed every human from Earth and resettled us in small groups on a bunch of different worlds, they made sure we knew it because of how badly we shitted up our planet.

Nobody was outside when we trudged into our townlet. There was no bustle of adults wheeling barrels of gorse bark and carrying buckets of berries. No children darted among them, laughing and squealing when the grownups told them to move. Instead, there was quiet — and a strip of gorse rag tied on the handle of every front door.

Somebody had gone Petrie.

My crew members scattered. I headed straight to the gorse-thatched cottage I shared with my roommate. Wilson had knotted a rag around our front-door handle.

From the combined living and kitchen area of our bungalow, I could hear Wilson crying in his bedroom. My stomach felt like it was dropping into my knees. I watched the empty village road from the window. Wilson would eventually come out and tell me who'd gone Petrie. Until he did, maybe it hadn't happened.

I tried to think of likely Petrie contenders. Frutex sucked as a planet, but most of us had survived our first five years in exile. Who would become violent now? Who would risk the consequence of being taken off-world for experimentation?

Wilson opened his door. His usual greeting was, "Any luck, Elli?"

That's because I was working on fermenting gorseberries, and Wilson really wanted me to bring alcohol back into his life.

Instead, he whispered, "It was Gladys."

Gladys.

My legs gave way and I crumpled. On my knees, I stared at the gorsewood floorboards, buff-colored like the rest of the planet.

Gladys. The information didn't compute. Gladys was the rock of our Shrub colony of 3000 humans. She was also my best friend.

Bent and birdlike, about 85 earth years with wispy, white hair, Gladys' assigned task was watching children at the lower kinder. Along with other adults past farming age, Gladys helped teach, entertain and corral kids while their parents worked in the fields or made stuff out of gorse. But Gladys' unassigned work was much more important.

Wilson helped me up to our kitchen table. He sat his large frame on his bench opposite mine, leaning forward against the gorsewood table top.

"She stabbed Harley."

Grubby tear tracks marked his face and water seeped from his green eyes.

"Harley's okay," Wilson explained. "It was just a surface cut."

"Dementia?" I asked. My chest tightened, like I couldn't

breathe.

"Did you ever see Gladys show signs of cognitive decline?"

I didn't take Wilson's pissed off tone personally. My question was stupid.

He stood up to pace back and forth between his bedroom door and our tiny living area. Wilson was always too big for the space Shrub allotted him.

Gladys was old, but sharp — a former professor of antiquities. When we first got to Shrub, she taught us obscenities in Greek and Latin. My favorite was "Es scortum obscenus vilis." It meant "You're a vile, perverted sex worker." Gladys said this was a serious insult in ancient Rome.

Wilson was snuffling now as he paced, trying to suppress his sobs.

I got up and went to the cooker to boil water for some gorse tea. Not that the tea would do much good. The stuff tasted like oatmeal water, but at least its heat would be soothing.

Wilson came back to the table, put his head down and cried. His big shoulders heaved and joggled his black curls. After a while, he sat up and took a sip of the tea I'd put in front of him.

I patted his arm, not crying myself. That would happen later. Exile on Shrub had warped my emotions and expanded my already robust capacity for denial.

"It happened in the community space," Wilson explained. "Everyone was chilling, joking — the usual," he told me. "I was talking with my forewoman about next week's harvest. Gladys walked right by us. She came up behind Harley and pulled a shelling blade out of her pocket. Stabbed at his lower back."

Wilson and I held hands across the table.

"It didn't seem real, total slo-mo. I couldn't react."

Most adults on Shrub carried their own shelling blade. These small knives were good for husking Gorse 32's pecan-sized fruit. That variety grew everywhere. It was protein-rich and an easy snack.

"Father P. was on the other side of the room, over by the speaker's box. He saw Gladys going for Harley and yelled in time for him to move."

Wilson pulled his hands from mine, standing up and knocking over his bench.

"The Blockheads were there in 30 seconds. They took her away."

The Frutices (aka Blockheads) were the aliens who ran the planet. They always knew when a human did something violent. My guess is they could smell it somehow, even when we didn't draw blood.

Wilson sat back down and cupped the mug in his hand. He sipped a few times and said, "She named the planet, for fuck's sake."

It was true. During our first terrible days on Frutex, Gladys moved us beyond the routines of the agricultural work required by our Blockhead overloads. She started Taverna Nights when, once a week, we'd crowd into the community space to hear stories. In the beginning, only Gladys told them because everyone else was too depressed.

Gladys was an expert in ancient languages like Greek, Latin, Etruscan and Hebrew. Her narratives were usually classical myths. Sometimes we got a tale from world history, like General Hannibal attacking Rome with his elephants. Eventually, Gladys convinced other people to talk, so the stories grew in variety and became something to look forward to.

Her interest in improving life on Shrub made the Frutices approach Gladys early on about human words for everything on our new world, including a name for the planet. We couldn't speak their language or even hear it, since they communicated on too high a frequency. But the Blockheads had the vocal structures to speak at a lower vibration that we could pick up. Their English sounded like an ocean mammal, sort of dolphinesque.

Gladys set up a planet-naming contest, but all our entries ended up being disqualified. She felt we'd regret living on Shit-world, Suicidia or Smegma.

Instead, Gladys chose Frutex. It was Latin for "shrub" and also a Roman insult meaning "blockhead." We were already using both words to describe the planet and its indigenous occupants, so the name was a win-win all around.

Gladys was big on contests. In our first month, she set up a competition to see who was best at lashing gorse bundles. The contest was supposed to be human-judged, but Gladys had to get some Blockheads to officiate, since none of us gave a shit. Even so, she didn't give up. With story events, potlucks, cookoffs and whatnot, she made life on a loathsome world tolerable.

Just last week, Wilson took first prize in the village flatbread baking contest. His bread had a light, chewy consistency. Successful fermentation was rare on Frutex, so our bread didn't generally rise very much. But we were enthusiastic judges of texture. We had to be — food made from gorse had next to no taste.

Now Gladys was gone. We assumed the Blockheads had sent her off world. But we actually didn't know what happened to a human who became violent. Only that we never saw them again.

No one could remember where the idea came from, but the story was that violent humans ended up serving as guinea pigs in some alien lab. Hence the term, "going Petrie."

We'd asked the Frutices about it, but they didn't provide clear answers to questions relating to anything except gorse farming. Maybe they didn't know what happened.

The Blockheads weren't part of the original extraterrestrial coalition that engineered our removal from Earth. It's possible some faction of that group took people off Frutex when they went Petrie. We weren't allowed near Shrub's landing port, so there was no way to know.

Wilson always said, "If the Frutices have any say in it, going Petrie will get you turned into fertilizer."

I think he was wrong about that, but they did care a lot about agriculture.

Wilson and I had finished our tea, so I got up to make more. A squeaky voice called from outside the front door.

"Elli! I'm coming to see how you and Wilson are doing?"

A lot of the Frutices phrased English statements as questions. I recognized the voice as belonging to a Blockhead named Bogus. I could tell by the low chirpiness of their speech. (We still hadn't figured out Frutician gender. The Frutices weren't great at answering non-farming questions.)

"Fuck no," Wilson said, setting his jaw.

Bogus was standing at the door yelling. They wouldn't knock. To a Blockhead, hitting a door was violent.

"Sure, Bogus," I called. "Come on in."

The door creaked open and Bogus entered the bungalow. They had the same body plan as a human — two arms, two legs. But their blocky head was bigger and squarer than ours, kind of like a black wasp's. Bogus' hairless skin was beige, same as the planet.

Wilson's shoulders stiffened. He didn't greet Bogus.

A Blockhead showing up was strange. None of them came to my door the other times someone went Petrie. I motioned Bogus to my bench and offered them some tea.

"No thank you."

I came and sat next to our visitor. It seemed like the polite thing.

"It's good you are together? No suiciding," Bogus said.

"Fuck you," Wilson answered softly. He pushed away from the table, careful to do it slowly this time, so it was clear he wasn't being violent.

"Gladys raised her hand," Bogus answered. I couldn't detect much emotion in Bogus' speech. Just labored breathing as they worked to lower their voice to our frequency. Bogus' two principal eyes were wide open like a small child trying to explain something important to adults who weren't listening.

Was Bogus worried about us? Did they think we didn't understand that Gladys was taken away because she did something violent?

Wilson exhaled, hissing at Bogus.

"You're a leather-sofa-skinned freak who doesn't care about us — or Gladys. Would you like to know how you can help us get through this?"

"Yes?" Bogus asked, eyes still wide, their blocky head angled toward Wilson's taller, larger frame. Bogus really wanted to know.

"Crawl. Into. A. Hole. And. Die."

The words fell from Wilson's mouth like icy drips of poison.

Then he walked to his bedroom, each long step taut with the control required to keep from kicking something.

Because the rule on Frutex was simple: You couldn't attack with your body, but you could say whatever you wanted.

Bogus said nothing. By now, I was pretty sure the Blockheads knew our language well enough to sense an insult. But they never acted like they cared. Maybe they viewed rude remarks from a disgraced species like ours as trivial. We were a galactic pariah, after all.

During our first days on Shrub, I'd insulted them too. But hating the Frutices made my face ache. It took so much energy and got me nothing.

Gladys felt the same. Early on, she tried to persuade Wilson to let go a little.

"I see the honor in your hatred," she told him. "But don't you think the cost to you is pretty high?"

"Happy to pay it," Wilson had responded. About half the village believed hating the Frutices was their duty—the only resistance available. It was one of the few things Wilson and Gladys disagreed on.

Bogus sat quiet and still until my thoughts came back to them. The Frutices were super patient that way.

"No suicide here," I reassured. "Thank you for looking in on us. We're very sad. We all loved Gladys."

"Of course?" Bogus nodded, the lids of their eight eyes closing for a moment. The Frutices' assorted eyeballs had been the hardest thing to adjust to. Wilson said it was a similar setup to a jumping spider: two primary high-resolution eyes at the front for sharp vision and four smaller eyes on each side for catching little details and the surrounding movement.

I suspected Frutician vision was an advantage for farming. The eight eyes would let you gather information about large swaths of plantings and detect the small organisms in the soil that attacked the gorse. The Frutices spent a lot of time looking for these tiny pests, so we could control them with Gorse 585 oil. Protecting the crops was their only justification for the "violent" application of this organic pesticide.

"Gladys raised her hand," Bogus repeated.

"She also did a lot of good things, and you know it," I told them. Bogus had no clue that their English name would have been "Jizzface" if Gladys hadn't reasoned people out of it.

It wasn't that she was worried about offending the Blockheads. Like I've said, we'd already found that impossible. Gladys' concern was for our reputation with the GIC.

"Those GIC bastards have a pretty good handle on human language," Gladys had argued one day as we sat outside the community space munching gorse nuts. "They could show up any time and hear that we named the Blockheads 'Asswipe' and 'Hitler.' Why confirm their belief that we're the worst species in the Milky Way?"

Loud crying noises came from Wilson's room.

"We failed, Elli" Bogus said, with a quick head-tilt toward Wilson's bedroom. Did they always feel like this after someone went Petrie? Or was it because this time, the Petried person was Gladys?

Out of nowhere, Bogus placed their seven-fingered hand over mine, pressing down rhythmically with their wide, muscular thumb. A Blockhead had never touched me before. Weird.

In honor of Gladys, I decided not to be an asshole and placed my free hand over theirs, squeezing back. The leather toughness of Bogus' fingers didn't surprise me. Frutician hands were basically the Swiss-army knife of farm implements.

"I think the Blockheads are in a tough spot," Gladys had said during our conversation about not giving them unreasonably rude names. "Look at their aversion to violence. The GIC must be giving these guys something pretty good in exchange for taking us on."

Bogus got up and walked out. Only a few of the Frutices had mastered the human convention of saying goodbye.

As the door shut behind our visitor, I heard a buzzing sound. Before I could check on it, Wilson stomped back out of his room. The buzzing stopped. Apparently, he hadn't heard it.

"You don't have to be so nice to them."

Wilson's voice was taut. He let his big body down on the bench with a thunk, not having to worry about the force of it triggering Bogus.

"Being civil to them keeps me from going Petrie," I told him, shutting down that line of conversation.

We talked late into the night about Gladys, trying to understand why she would attack Harley. They always got along. Gladys got along with everyone.

The fact we could stay up into the wee hours was because Gladys had worked with the Frutices to implement a weekend. She'd predicted — correctly — that a five-day workweek would lower the Petrie rate. So, no worries for me about showing up for more pruning in the morning. I'd go to shul of course, but that was a lot easier on my back.

§

The next morning at synagogue, the loss of Gladys hit me during the Kaddish portion of the service. That's the part where you recite the names of people who've died recently. The only name we said was Gladys.

I don't recall much except wailing, and my friend Abby leading me outside. The members of Congregation Beth Israel all knew each other pretty well, so I doubt any of them were surprised. Outside the low-slung building, I flung myself down in the dirt and Abby sat on the ground next to me until the end of the service.

I didn't stay for the *oneg* because eating sounded disgusting and I couldn't handle any more talking. I went home and slept for a few hours.

It was still light when I woke up, so I grabbed a shoulder bag and walked to my fermentation shed. The bag's woven gorse fibers scratched my neck as I scanned the road hoping not to meet anyone on the way.

The dusty area around the shed where we kept the Gorse 22 harvest equipment was deserted. The 22 strain stayed dormant for most of the year, making this shed a rarely entered place where I could ferment in private. Today I was testing the Gorse 206 barrel. Aging for seven months wasn't long, but enough time for me to get a sense of the "vintage."

Over the last four years, I'd been experimenting with every gorseberry I could find. Most of them looked something like a garbanzo bean and tasted even blander.

What we called "gorse" was all that grew on Shrub. Obviously, it was neither Earth gorse, nor a monoculture. The planet had thousands of these low-growing, shrubby, camel-colored plants that were clearly different strains and species. I was going to fer-ment them all until I found one that made drinkable wine.

From my early attempts, I'd confirmed Frutex had at least one wild analog to Terran yeast that would break down a gorseberry's sugars, leaving alcohol as a by-product. So far, the wine from those strains had extremely unpleasant notes – think dog piss and vomit.

It was dark inside the shed, but I'd stolen a solar lantern and hidden it there. The Blockheads, like all members of the GIC, were suspicious of humans possessing any kind of technology because of how we used it to cock up the Earth. Even flashlights were treated as a privilege.

I pulled the stopper from the fermentation barrel and filled a cup. I had my secret fermentation log book and gorse pencil ready to make notes.

As a mid-21st century winemaker, I'd always used the latest testing equipment. But forget titrators and pH meters on Shrub. I was lucky to get hold of five gorsemeal barrels just to do the fermentation.

Remembering my oenological mentor back on Earth made me feel better about the lack of proper tools. José was somewhat old school. He always told me, "The best tool a winemaker has is a glass."

"To José," I toasted, raising the cup in his memory.

I swirled the light-brown liquid, aerating it. I stuck my nose in the cup and inhaled. It smelled like apple and walnuts.

My first sip was fruity — as close to fruit as I'd come in five years.

That's because the only "fruits" on Shrub were gorse berries and nuts. Along with the plant's leaves, these insipid balls of bleh met our nutritional needs. But they lacked the joyous sweetness of an Earth grape or peach. Gorse fibers were good for weaving clothes and linens. Its branches provided solid material for housing, furniture and equipment. The plant could do just about everything — except feed your soul.

Until now. It would never be Earth wine, but what I tasted took me back home. After draining the cup, I had a mild buzz. Gorse 206 was wine.

I filled a small jug and stoppered it before hiding it in my bag. Outside, I kissed Shrub's soil. On my knees, I kissed the planet's boring, beige ground under its boring ecru sky, smelling its boring wheaty scent.

This was a moment for saying the *Shehecheyanu*. But instead of the prayer praising Adonai our God for allowing me to live long enough to reach this moment, I stood next to a gnarly gorse clump and poured a little wine from the jug onto the ground. It was an offering to the Elohim. Gladys would approve, and Rabbi Talya didn't need to know.

§

When I got to Beth Israel, the Shul crowd was gone. Rabbi Talya was still in her office, which was more of a shed attached to the side of the one-room synagogue. When she saw me, Talya started making tea on her office cooker.

Gladys had gotten our shul several nice additions by convincing the Blockheads that humans relied on religion to keep people from being violent (or some version of that fairy tale). Thanks to Gladys, we had a *ner tamid* (sanctuary lamp), plus practical lighting and a heater, too. She also hooked up some of the other faith groups, including Father Panganiban over at St. Fiacre's.

Gladys told me Fiacre was a seventh century abbot who became the patron of gardeners and hemorrhoid sufferers — so a totally perfect saint for Shrub.

Talya sat hunched across from me at her desk while our tea steeped. She gripped a gorse hankie in her left hand.

"Fucking why?" she asked me, like I had an answer for why a pillar of the community had suddenly gone crazy.

"Gladys made the difference for our Torah scrolls," Talya said, drying her tears with angry swipes.

As a diaspora people, the portability of the Torah and all the writings was a major reason Jews kept their religion going after the Romans destroyed the temple in 70 AD. But the GIC members wouldn't let humanity take *anything* when they peeled us off the Earth. They viewed all aspects of Terran culture as tainted.

Talya kept herself from going Petrie by trying to reconstruct it all — the Torah, the Talmud, the Mishnah. Beth Israel had three scrolls now.

Gladys and Talya did most of the work. Without books, computers, apps or internet, they drove the endeavor from memory. Plus, Gladys and Talya improved on the original by leaving out the more misogynistic and homophobic parts.

Talya banged her fist on the desk, making our teas slosh in their cups.

"Why would she? Was it the fucking Squeal?"

"I don't think it was the Squeal," I told her, trying to imagine I was picking up floral notes in the tea, just to make it all less depressing. "If Gladys was going to lose it over that, it would have happened years ago."

In the early days of our life sentence on Frutex, a small number of us succumbed to the Shrub Squeal. Shrub had no birds or flying insects to help with pollination. That happened through anemophily, essentially air currents spreading the pollen around.

Like settlers on the North America prairies driven insane by the constant wind, some humans couldn't tolerate the incessant whine of air rushing through the gorse. The Shrub Squeal made them lose it until they hallucinated or became violent. Some took their own lives.

The Squeal never bothered me. Not that ending my life didn't come into my head that first year on Frutex. I couldn't stop thinking about my depressed neighbor back on Earth. He'd made a quick cut to his jugular with a carving knife. I was pretty sure a gorse scythe would do the job.

But farming kept me going. On Earth, growing grapes and making wine was all about staying around to see what your work would yield. It might have been planting Dijon clones or tending a single vineyard designate. You always had some vision and wanted to see it through.

My vision on Shrub became gorse wine. There were endless varieties, and it wasn't that different from other non-green Earth plants. Frutex's bushes had roots. They carried out photosynthesis, producing enough oxygen for us and the Blockheads to breathe. It seemed doable.

Unfortunately, the day before I succeeded, my best friend lost her mind and attacked someone.

"Rabbi," I said, grabbing her hand. "Shabbat is a day for joy, and I have joyous news."

Talya stopped crying. Her dark chocolate hair was thick and shiny, her olive skin luminous. She had those really thick eyelashes that made it look like she was wearing eyeliner even though she wasn't. Nobody on Shrub wore makeup. The planet had no resources for creating dark pigments.

Our adopted beige world totally changed the desirability calculus for the human colony. If you cared about other people finding you attractive on Frutex, hair and skin like Talya's were assets. Same for Wilson, who was already considered hot on Earth. As a Black man on Shrub, people hit him up almost daily.

Not me. My hair, eyes and skin were the same color as the planet. Being long and lean with symmetrical features went a long way on Earth. It didn't on Frutex.

As a 32-year-old woman nearing my sexual peak, the situation would have left me pretty lonely. Luckily, forced exile had destroyed my sex drive. I envied Talya not because I missed sex, but I because I wanted to be desired.

"Tell me, Elli," Talya ordered. "Tell me the good news."

It felt like a dare. What good news could there ever be again?

"I did it."

For some drama, I opened my bag and set the little jug of wine on her desk. Talya stared. Then her eyes flickered. She screamed, jumping up and spilling her tea as she came around to wrap me in a hug. The desk was awash in light brown liquid, my jug of wine an island in the middle.

§

In the midst of my wine success—which we were keeping a secret until Talya could get Blockhead buy-in—we had to plan Gladys' memorial. It's hard to sit shiva for someone when you don't even know if they're dead. So for Petrie situations, we just threw a big, non-denominational party.

"Party" was the polite word. In truth, these events were actually major fuck-a-thons, and we didn't just throw them for Petrie send-offs. With no booze or drugs for the last five years, how else were we supposed to cut loose?

Not that everyone went to every orgy. But a Petrie send-off cut across cultural and religious lines. The whole village showed up—including faith leaders. Even they couldn't judge someone for trying to feel good in this situation. At the last Petrie memorial, I nearly tripped over my rabbi and the pastor of St. Fiacre's banging away in the middle of the festivities.

The Shrub penal colony had just three rules for sex: consensual, age appropriate, and no fucking a Blockhead. This last rule was creating some tension on the day of Gladys' memorial.

Wilson and I argued about it as we walked through Fornication Field, picking up rocks and sticks that might make the festivities uncomfortable.

"No way is Cliff allowed to come," he said, chucking a grapefruit-sized stone to the edge of the field.

Cliff had been caught holding hands with Upchuck, the Blockhead who was in charge of teaching us gorsewood carpentry.

"Holding hands isn't fucking," I argued. "Gladys would say you were being ridiculous."

Poor Cliff was the color of a whole wheat cracker, and ill-favored in the facial department.

"Cliff was probably just lonely," I added. "And who knew what Upchuck was thinking? A Blockhead probably wouldn't even get the intimacy of handholding."

"Cliff's a piece of shit. Traitor trash," Wilson insisted. He and Harley were the authors of the no-sex-with-Blockheads rule. Since the community couldn't kill or imprison you for messing around with one of the Frutices, Wilson and Harley argued the punishment should be shunning. People in the colony were generally on board. I never saw a Blockhead's junk anyway. Who knew how you were supposed to smash them?

More people showed up to prep for Gladys' memorial. Wilson supervised spreading blankets and where to set jugs of water for when people got thirsty. The water bummed me out. If humans knew how to control themselves, we could have toasted Gladys with my wine.

The memorial started in the afternoon. As Gladys' best friend, I stood next to Wilson and others who were close to her. People filed past and said nice things. It all felt far away.

Wilson couldn't stop sobbing, so he didn't notice when Abby quietly brought Cliff in from the edge of the field. Abby was brave that way—not giving a shit what Wilson and Harley thought. Gladys would have been proud.

The Blockheads stood guard at the edge of the field. They were squirming the whole time but couldn't do a thing as long as the festivities stayed consensual.

I remembered Gladys telling me that the GIC had to teach the Frutices about human sexuality. She'd heard it from Bogus who told her the Blockheads were horrified during the training because even our fun, positive sex stuff seemed violent to them.

As Glady's Rabbi, Talya opened the festivities with a eulogy that left everyone weeping. Even me. No more of Gladys' stories, no more of her jokes and no more of her bullshit-free kindness.

How many times had those things helped me survive the day, so I could fall onto my gorse leaf mattress and escape into sleep?

The colorless bushes surrounding the field seemed paler, more devoid of vitality. For the first time since Wilson told me Gladys was gone, I wasn't sure our slice of the galaxy-wide human diaspora was going to make it.

After the eulogy, a small band of musicians began playing horny sounding melodies on their drums and flutes. Everyone started doing it.

For form's sake, I gave Mel Wallach a hand job. I tried to look out for Mel. He was a Beiger, similar to me. That meant he got a lot less action than people like Talya or Wilson.

After Mel, I threaded my way between writhing bodies until I was out of the field. The need to feel closer to Gladys was driving me to the fermentation shed.

When I got there, I found four Frutices stationed around it. That was Talya's doing. It was annoying, but I was grateful. Posting guards was the only way to safeguard winemaking on Shrub.

I waved and they let me in. No verbal greeting. One of them did the Blockhead bow, dropping their head forward, pausing and then bending at their middle. They bowed for Gladys all the time. I also got the bow on occasion, I guess because the Frutices respected my farming acumen.

The bower followed me inside and greeted me.

"Elli."

The voice told me it was Bogus. We all had trouble telling one Blockhead from another by their appearance. It would have made us the ultimate racists, if we'd hadn't already mastered that one.

I took a small jug from a tool shelf and tapped the barrel. Bogus stood there stupidly.

"Es scortum obscenus vilis," I told them, in honor of Gladys.

"Yes?" Bogus answered.

I left the shed and stepped over the dusty kasha-hued ground toward a tall, round clump of gorse. There were three useless varieties that grew in this shape, their stalks reaching over 10 feet. These small thickets reminded me of tree hangars in the Everglades. During carpentry training, Upchuck told us the Frutices never cultivated these places. We couldn't get a straight answer about the reason.

I'd have preferred Bogus leave me alone, but they wouldn't understand what I was doing. Blockheads were sort of like furniture. It didn't really matter if they were there or not.

I stepped inside the hushed wildness of the gorse copse, stopping in the center. Then I took a drink of wine in honor of Gladys and poured the rest over the ground. Inhaling, I began reciting the prayer Gladys and I used to say when we were alone. The prayer to the Elohim.

"B'reshit bara elohim et hashamayim v'et ha'aretz ..."

Elohim is a Hebrew word for God in the first line of Genesis, where it describes God creating the world. Except it means "divine beings" — as in more than one. My first Hebrew teacher said *Elohim* wasn't really plural, just an ancient way of saying God.

Gladys disagreed. She said *Elohim* was plural, and that the word ended up in the Jewish creation story because it came from a much older myth that involved multiple gods.

Jews weren't supposed to pray to the *Elohim*. *Adonai* was our one diety — the singular God who supposedly cared about us. But after a year on Shrub, Gladys and I said fuck that. We started praying to the *Elohim* — as in more than one god.

Because where the fuck was *Adonai* when the humans in

power were ruining Earth? Where was *Adonai* when we all got punished for what the powerful did?

"v'ha'aretz hayeta tohu va</u>ohu vechoshekh 'al-pene tehom veru-ach elohim merachephet 'al-pene hammayim . . ."

As I recited the prayer Gladys' had composed from the first verses of Genesis, there was another voice. Bogus stood behind me . . . also saying the prayer. I kept going, not knowing what else to do. When we were done, I turned around.

Bogus began making an odd buzzing sound — the same one I'd heard outside the door the day Gladys went Petrie. Blockheads didn't cry, but Bogus' droning timbre felt mournful.

"I am sad, Elli?" they said. "Gladys showed me praying. To the *Elohim*?"

Gladys was civil to the Blockheads, but she would never pray with them.

"You're lying," I snapped at Bogus. "You must have spied on us."

Sweat formed on my upper lip. The smothering, grainy smell of the gorse hangar lay over us.

"I don't spy? Gladys taught me when were by ourselves."

In a quiet corner of my mind, I noted Bogus hadn't phrased the second sentence incorrectly as a question. An image flashed across my eyes and I moved back, unsteady.

"Did you and Gladys touch each other?"

"Yes. I wanted to? Also with Harley."

I turned away from the wine offering that was drying on the ground and took a few quivering steps to the edge of the gorse hangar.

The copse was spinning, closing in. I wanted air and tried to push past Bogus. Fast like an insect, Bogus whipped out an arm and wrapped their seven fingers around my wrist.

"You killed her," I responded, trying to tug my arm away, but strangely not revolted by their leathery grip.

"Bogus killed her?" they asked.

"You were with Gladys. And you were with Harley. You. Killed. Her."

The scent of wine and gorse hung between us.

Bogus pulled me close, right up to their big head, so that I was staring into their two black primary eyes.

What happened next was a weird feeling, as if roots were spreading through me. Humans think they understand closeness. But Bogus' touch and stare were taking me way beyond that . . . integrating me with them, the gorse, the whole planet. The experience definitely didn't feel human — because it erased the sense I'd always had of being separate and alone.

§

We spent the night like that in the gorse thicket. It was a relief to be so combined, not to have to talk or worry about my individual thoughts. When we left in the morning to go in separate directions, we didn't say goodbye. It would have been extraneous.

On my walk home, Frutex's sandy brown sunlight warmed the path and the air whistled gently in the surrounding shrub leaves. I wanted to stay wrapped in these soft impressions.

But I couldn't, because my own nasty human separateness wasn't gone. Just hidden, kind of like an eel in a rock that decides to poke its head out.

My skull throbbed with a sudden, grasping conviction. It ripped an angry hole in the sensation of oneness Bogus had left me with.

Fucking Harley. He shouldn't get to feel like that. I would have to kill him.

THE IMMORTAL MONK

NAOMI ARTEMI

They came from far and wide to pay alms to the Immortal Monks, but Tenzo had only to step out the front door of his shack and sit on his stoop. From there he liked to pilgrim-watch, and it was endlessly entertaining, for an endless stream of pilgrims were passing by at any given moment. Some came from out of sight where the beginning of the line of gray statues with painted red robes was said to start, but where Tenzo had never been. All he knew was weathered skulls and carved smiles, far as he could see.

"Why go anywhere," his mother scolded when once he had complained, "when all the world carries itself to your door?"

Tenzo saw the logic, even as a young child, and from then on felt very special and important that he lived along the middle of the line where the whole world passed by. For everyone, at least once in their lives, would "walk with the Immortal Monks" to receive their collective blessings. The statues carried stone alms bowls in stone hands—the greater the offering, the greater the blessing.

Most only walked with them for a little while; they were poor, elderly, they had nothing for which to repent. Those who came from out of sight, those were the ones who really needed blessings; a loved one was seriously ill or they themselves were nearing rebirth. Because Tenzo was a child, he could ask questions like, *Why?*

"Pester them now," his grandmother used to say, "before you have to wait to be my age and then you'll be too tired to be curious."

Where are you from?

What for are you paying alms?

Do your feet hurt? Why suffer when you could have some fresh sandals?

Selling sandals was what Tenzo was supposed to be pestering pilgrims about, but since most said *no* with a swatting look like he was a biting fly, he asked the other questions first.

He learned all sorts of things just outside his own door with the world passing by. He learned that there were great mountains towards the beginning of the line of Immortal Monks where there were birds as big as men. And the men there wore whole animals on their backs to stay warm. He learned that some were from the South even though they walked from the North because they had traveled to start all the way at the first statue. He learned that people from the South thought they were the most pious because they had to travel the furthest from where the monks finally walked into the Infinite Waters. And there were fish the size of houses! He learned that most adults did not know much more about life than a child like he did. That people will walk for days on blisters to try and pray back a love lost. Those inevitably started with a sack almost too heavy to lift and paid one coin and a prayer into each alms bowl they passed. By the time they got to Tenzo's stretch of statues, their backs were twisted and spasming, their legs hobbled, and their feet were bloody. Their sacks were lighter, though.

"Do you think you will get to the end?" Tenzo would ask.

"I hope so. This is all my alms savings. I have nothing more."

"Would you like a fresh pair of sandals then?"

Others did not walk from the beginning but would come from the East or West and make a great show of offering all of their wealth into the bowl of just one statue. They would collapse to the ground and grovel at the stone feet in a spectacle of reverence. These pilgrims Tenzo could not sell sandals to, but the sandals were just the excuse to live beside the Immortal Monks, so selling them did not really matter.

Every day, sun or storm, Tenzo's mother would dress in pilgrim robes with her hair down and hood up so that the neighbors who sold snacks and boiled stream water would not recognize her, slip out of their shack, and into the line. At each alms bowl she put in one coin and palmed two. When she returned, her sack was twice as heavy. This was the real reason they lived there. At night, she would sneak out and empty entire bowls, but only in the rain, because night was the most dangerous: pilgrims returning after they did not get the blessing they had asked for and wanting their alms offerings back, drunks and thieves and gamblers from the nearby shantytown. It was not uncommon to see blood or a dead body in the morning. His mother would drag the body off with some neighbor and Tenzo would be made to wash the statue. Everyone who lived beside the Immortal Monks could agree, murder was not good for business.

Sometimes pilgrims died of natural causes. Heat stroke, relief of offering their last coin, a broken heart (his grandmother had told Tenzo this, though a heart not yet broken cannot comprehend such an invisible injury). Only just the other day, while Tenzo was filling the time by pilgrim-pestering, he spotted a figure in the distance shuffling along the line. At each statue, the figure dropped to the ground and lay, belly down, at the monk's feet. This is what pilgrims would do who had no coins left to give but more blessings still to ask for. As the figure approached, Tenzo saw that it was a man, wearing thick robes that were ripped all along the front from his prostrating and so covered in ochre dust that he could not tell what color they had been. There was a heaviness about him, and though he was not nearly as old as his grandmother had been, he looked it. Fifty pilgrims must have passed in the time it took the man to reach his statue.

Tenzo had been waiting for him. "Where are you from?" he pestered.

"You are asking," the man rasped, "the wrong question."

"What should I ask you, then?" *Forget sandals.*

"Ask this: 'What horrible acts did you commit to earn the coin with which you are trying to buy redemption?'"

Tenzo was surprised to hear a pilgrim admit that they had been horrible. But he was not about to give up the opportunity to hear the answer. "What horrible acts did you commit?"

It had been one of those adult answers that sounded like a riddle. A riddle that would never be solved, since the man had collapsed, right there, at Tenzo's feet.

His mother had rushed over. But it was not to come to Tenzo's aid, or the pilgrim's, though he reached out to her with his dying breath. It was to slip a ruby ring off his pinky finger before the body was carted away. This was nearly as shocking as a man speaking his last words to Tenzo. Not that his mother pocketed the ring, but that it had been a ruby ring. Everyone knew that because the Immortal Monks wore red robes, that no one was allowed to wear that blessed color in their presence. But it did not matter because his mother would not wear it. She would hide it along with the rest of their riches. For what, Tenzo did not know.

Tenzo's mother had so much gold that they did not have to live in a shack, but she said: "No one will rob a shack," and buried the coins in the dirt floor and covered the stash with a simple grass mat. Tenzo had no real concept of how much she had buried until one morning he went outside and found that one of the dead bodies was hers.

The ground was foggy with evaporating dew. Perhaps it had rained in the night and she thought it safe to empty a bowl or two. Perhaps the fog was too thick to see that there was already somebody there, doing just that.

Tenzo was an orphan now.

His father had died when he was very young, though it occurred to him that he did not know how, and his grandmother had died sitting in her chair out front of their shack, jubilantly criticizing the passing pilgrims two summers past. Tenzo could only remember her gap-toothed smile and that she smelled of incense ash and fried sweet dumplings.

Tenzo was too small to lift his mother from the base of the statue, but a kind neighbor offered. They had moved in next door because they wanted to lead a more pious life in the shadow of the Immortal Monks. His mother had said, "More for me." There were no valuables to remove from her body before they took it away. No earrings, no bangles, no silks, though she could have afforded them all. She had not wanted to draw any attention to her wealth.

"You can pray over her if you want," the pious neighbor said, "but this body is only a husk. Your mother lived her life so reverently, she is sure to have an esteemed rebirth. She is very fortunate, for there is no holier place to die than at the feet of an Immortal Monk."

Tenzo thought that this was a curious thing to say as his mother had always called the bodies bleeding at the monk's feet "fools."

Tenzo went back inside and peeked through the crack between two of the shack's slats. He watched as the neighbors put his mother's body in their body-removing-wheelbarrow and carted her out of sight. All of a sudden, he felt the need to sit down on the worn grass mat.

It started with curiosity. Tenzo peeled the mat up, just a corner, and brushed the dirt away until he saw the glint of a coin. There beside it, another. He had no trowel, so he used the wooden sole of a sandal to dig. He dug for what felt like hours, stopping only for a snack of dried fruit and rice sticks and then digging again. Whenever he thought, "Just one more," he'd find two. He dug until he fell asleep digging. When he woke, it was beside a pile of coins nearly as large as him.

Orange light flickered through the peek-crack. There was a knock at the door—what must have woken him.

"Tenzo?" It was the voice of the pious neighbor. "Would you like to join us for moonrise meal?"

There was no hiding a pile of coins nearly as large as him.

"I am still praying for my mother!" he called out. "I will come later."

The neighbor left and Tenzo started digging with more purpose. He was only a child, and some other adult would come and take his shack and all the wealth buried in its floor. His mother would not have wanted that. He would not be able to live with his pious neighbor because, if he did, he would be made to give it all back to the monks. His mother would not have wanted that, either.

He found jewels along with the coins, including the ruby pinky ring, which he slipped on his thumb.

By the time he had dug up every coin, Tenzo's hands were blistered and filled with splinters, his arms shook weakly, and the entire floor was a dirt pit. The pile of coins was taller than he was, standing.

The dusty light of dawn sliced through the peek-crack and across the dirt pit of the floor, and with it a dawning awareness that he would not be able to carry such quantity of coin. Even their rice sack would be much too small, and he too small to carry even that.

He covered the pile as well as he could with the grass mat and went out to his stoop. There were his neighbors, already offering blessed water to the first customers of the day. They looked at Tenzo like he was a pilgrim with bloody feet.

"I have decided to go live with my uncle," Tenzo said. He had no uncle, but this is what the child of the last neighbors had told him before he walked into the distance of the East with his family, carrying everything they owned strapped to their backs because they had no mule. But they had not had a pile of coins taller than Tenzo was standing to carry. "Only, I do not have any way to carry my belongings. Could I buy your wheelbarrow?" He held up a single coin. "My mother left me this."

"Keep your coin," the pious neighbor said. "You can have our wheelbarrow. We can build another."

The neighbor went behind his hut and returned with the bamboo wheelbarrow, empty of his mother's body.

Tenzo spent the day holding sandals out to passing pilgrims because he did not know what else he should be doing. He did not ask any questions. He did not want to know *"Why?"*

That night Tenzo ate with his neighbors under the rising moon—leaf steamed sticky rice and green curry—then went back to his shack to "sleep at home one last time." He waited until he could hear the tree frogs telling each other to come out and play, then Tenzo began to fill the wheelbarrow. This took him a long while, as he filled it one coin at a time so that they would not clink. Coin by coin the pile grew, by coin, by coin, by— bamboo splinters went flying as the wheelbarrow collapsed in a pile of coins and kindling.

There was no chance the neighbors three shacks over would not have heard such a noise!

Tenzo had only just covered the remains of the wheelbarrow with the grass mat when, sure enough, the pious neighbor called through the door: "Tenzo, are you alright?!"

"Yes! It was only the . . . the wheelbarrow broke. I . . . over-packed it. I am sorry for the noise."

"Let me enter so that I may help you."

"No!" Tenzo panicked. "I am sorry I woke you. I will be quieter."

"You don't have to do this by yourself, Tenzo." The neighbor's voice was tender. More tender than his mother's had ever been. He did not trust it.

"You bless me. I may ask for help tomorrow. But now I think I will sleep."

"Blessed dreams, then," said the pious neighbor and went away.

Tenzo would need something sturdier than a bamboo wheelbarrow. He wanted to go to the West where there was the shantytown that the thieves who came in the middle of the night snuck from but, for that reason, he also knew that he must wait until dawn.

Suddenly, there was a *snap* at the door as the bamboo closure sliced into two pieces. The neighbor entered. Machete in hand.

"This was my mother's. You can't take it!" Tenzo tried, almost comically, to block the pile of treasure with his scrawny body and outstretched arms.

But the neighbor did not advance.

"Long ago, I promised everything I had to the Immortal Monks. It is a way of life: giving so much to the needy that you become needy yourself. You always need more to give, because you are so desperate to prove yourself as pious enough to be in their presence. All that I would take from you, I would give to them."

Exactly as he had feared! Tenzo stretched his arms wider but only succeeded in stretching himself thinner.

The neighbor could have easily shoved him aside, but he only clasped his hands behind his back. The machete too. "Although, if I give it to the monks, another needy person will take it."

"You know that the monks don't take the coins?" (His mother had told him that the pious 'are so blinded by their faith that they can't see their own foolishness.')

"The Immortal Monks are not so greedy that they would keep wealth for themselves when others are in need." The neighbor smiled, knowingly. Tenzo usually hated when adults smiled at him that way, as if there were a secret he was too simpleminded to understand, and this time was no exception. He was about to argue, when the neighbor reasoned, "An orphaned boy, what more needy a person could there be?"

Tenzo dropped his arms. "You're letting me keep it? All of it?"

"Use your wealth to help others like yourself, and you will have a blessed life indeed."

Tenzo was shocked into silence.

The neighbor grinned like a monk with a secret. "Do you really have an uncle you are going to live with?"

Tenzo did not want to lie, but he also did not want to say the truth, so he only looked at his blistered hands.

"You can stay here, you know." Then, as if hearing Tenzo's thoughts, "But if you cannot, you will need something more than a bamboo wagon to carry such a heavy load."

Tenzo felt angry again. *Of course he knew that!* "I was going to buy a cart and ox at sunrise. From the West."

"I think it will be safer for me to go to the West. Why don't you give me the coin and I will get what you need."

Tenzo's first reaction was to think, *a trick!* But he quickly realized that the neighbor could have taken all of his coins if he wanted, easily.

"You bless me." Tenzo handed over a handful, which was really only a few coins because his hands were child's hands.

"I will need a little more than that."

So Tenzo gave him a little more. But no more than a little.

After the neighbor left, there was nothing for Tenzo to do but sleep. But sleep does not come peacefully to a recently orphaned child. When the sun arrived with the first pilgrim's prayers, Tenzo was still awake. He heard the pious neighbor say blessings to his family and leave.

Tenzo spent the day sitting on his stoop, too dazed and weary to do anything but pilgrim-watch (not even pilgrim-pester). As the sun floated higher in the sky, the monks' shadows grew shorter. Tenzo stopped watching the people and started watching their shadows. He imagined that there was a shadow world with shadow monks and shadow pilgrims and coins made of pure light. The shadow of his mother was there, still walking the line, trying to palm coins that burned through shade hands. The more her shadow shrank, the more wildly she snatched at the alms bowls— dusk desperately trying to hold onto daylight. She grew shorter and shorter as the sun reached its pinnacle in the sky—grabbing faster and faster—until she nearly disappeared, her hands but wisps of shadow clinging to the coins.

A voice hollered at her. It was a neighbor, selling sugarcane.

Tenzo turned back and saw that the shadow world had grown in the other direction, the statue's silhouettes now long as men. He must have dozed off. Tenzo searched the shadows for his mother, but she was not among them.

At moonrise meal, the pious neighbor returned with a cart and ox, as promised. The ox was a dirty white with bony haunches and had large watery eyes. Tenzo decided to name it Hempato after the name of a king one of the pilgrims from the North had told him about. That night the neighbor even helped him load the coins into sacks and sacks into the wagon.

They had only just heaved in the last sack and covered the haul with a burlap tarp, when the monkeys called forth the sun. Tenzo was very tired and very much wanted to sleep, but now that the wagon was full, he was afraid to leave it.

He decided to steer Hempato in the direction of the South because he wanted to see the monks walk into the Infinite Waters. Tenzo surprised himself by telling his pious neighbor this.

"I came from the East so I do not know how many monks it is to reach the South, but your mother had so much alms savings that I imagine you could walk with them to the Infinite Waters then throw the rest to the waves. You will be the most pious of men then. You will become holy yourself." His neighbor then handed Tenzo a small but weighty pouch. "Put your first coin in this one."

It was the statue at which his mother's body had been found. The blood was gone but Tenzo still saw it.

The neighbor smiled encouragingly.

The monk smiled serenely.

Tenzo took a coin from the pouch. It was silver, but sunlight flashed it gold. He did not want to give it away to some statue's bowl that a thief would steal from later. Tenzo's mother had always thought the pilgrims foolish that they gave their fortunes away, and Tenzo found he agreed. But the neighbor was watching and would never let him leave if he thought Tenzo would keep all his wealth for himself.

He put the silver coin in the stone bowl that held a number of copper coins and one other silver, praying what he had heard a thousand thousand times before, "I pay reverence to you, oh, venerable Immortal Monk. Bless me with this offering."

As soon as his cart was out of sight, Tenzo stopped putting coins in bowls. Yet he sulked for some time about the thirty or so he'd had to give away. His hands were too small to palm coins as his mother had but he resolved, bitterly, to get them back somehow.

The wagon was so heavy and the ox so slow, that the pilgrims paying alms all passed him, even though they stopped to pray at each statue. Tenzo started to play a game, see if he could move fast enough to keep a pilgrim in sight. One with a grass woven sunhat gave alms and prayers at the statue beside him. Though Tenzo tried to keep up, he watched the sunhat grow smaller and smaller until eventually it disappeared into the distance along with the prodigious procession.

There were shacks all along the path and at each one someone offering to sell him everything from rice balls to souvenirs to holy water collected from the bowls of the monks after a rain. Tenzo now understood why the pilgrims had looked at him like he was a biting fly. He soon felt that if he gave them all a bite, he'd be devoured alive long before he reached the end.

"What do you have in the wagon?"

It was a girl around his age, but a least a monk-step taller than him.

"Yams," Tenzo said because it was the first thing he could think of.

"Can I have one?" asked the girl.

"No," said Tenzo.

"I'll trade you. I have fruit." She held up a melon the size of her head. Tenzo suddenly wanted nothing more but to sit and rest and eat a melon the size of a girl's head.

"How much does it cost?"

"Three yams."

Tenzo did not really have any yams, and so he had to ask: "How much in coin?"

The girl laughed. "*You* have coin?"

"Forget it. I will buy fruit from someone else," said Tenzo. He was tired and sore and his mother had just died; he had no patience. Tenzo put his weight into yanking the yoke rope again.

"Just one copper!" the girl called out.

Tenzo reached into the pouch of coins and felt for the smallest. He handed it to the girl and received the fruit.

He could not carry the melon and guide Hempato at the same time, so he had no choice but to sit down right there and start to eat it. It was slightly overripe. Sticky juice ran down his blistered hands.

The girl sat beside him.

"What's really in the cart?" she asked.

Tenzo assessed the girl. In his weakened state, she would easily be able to overpower him.

He stood up and dropped the rest of the melon even though he would like to have eaten more. It cracked apart and splattered their dusty feet—his sandaled, hers bare.

"It is overripe," he said. "I don't want the same for my yams." Then he pushed onwards without looking back.

It was clear that Hempato was as weary as he. The ox's bony haunches quivered with every step. And Tenzo found himself struggling even to keep up their labored pace. They needed a place to rest, but also to put the sacks while they rested or they would surely be stolen—even yams had worth to a hungry thief. Some of the shacks along the path offered lodging. He waited until he was out of sight of the girl selling melons bigger than her head, and then took the first one offered.

It was a simple one-room shack that reminded Tenzo of home. He unloaded his sacks of "yams" and dragged them inside one at a time. Blisters tore open. The bow-legged elder who had sold him the night of lodging, only watched.

"That's a lot of yams," he remarked. Tenzo could not tell if the tone was mocking or disapproving. He only hoped it was not suspicious.

A spindly stick secured the shack door, a door that could easily be broken open by a well-aimed overripe melon. So Tenzo shoved and shimmied a sack right up against it. Then he cried. He cried until he cried himself to sleep.

When he woke, it was with eyelids crusted closed and a tight belly. For a brief moment, he thought he would go sit on his stoop and see what his mother had made for sunrise meal. But then Tenzo remembered how he would have to find his own meals from now on.

Tenzo did not want to leave his sacks but he also needed another ox to be able to drive them any further. Hempato needed help. He took just three coins—one copper, one silver, one gold—then he shimmied and shoved and pushed the sack away from the door just enough so he could slip his thin-as-bones body through the gap. He pulled the door closed.

The sun had already risen above the trees and was casting short shadows from the Immortal Monks. His shadow mother would soon disappear along with the coins of light.

"You slept long time," said the bow-legged elder. "The sun will think you believe yourself better than him."

Tenzo wanted to say that he never slept that late, that his mother already had him out distracting pilgrims with sandals, but that she died and so he had no one to wake him anymore and also that her coins were too heavy for him and that his arms shook even to lift them to dry his tears. But he only said, "You are right," because he had been taught not to contradict elders. "I will try to wake up earlier tomorrow. If you will sell me the room for one more night?"

"Will your uncle not worry if you are delayed?"

"You are right," agreed Tenzo again. "Would you mind if I leave my yams here—just a short while—so that I might get some supplies for the journey ahead?"

"You can pay me not to mind."

Tenzo knew that he was being *played like a songster's lute,*' as his grandmother used to say, which made him angry because he was just a child and this coin was his mother's who had died for it. But he said, "You are right," and paid the bow-legged elder one of his three coins. The copper one. With the other two he walked quickly towards the West.

As he turned his back on the Immortal Monks, his stomach squirmed like a pinned snake. With every step he took away from the statues, it tried to twist free. If ever Tenzo had ventured to the North or the South along the line, he knew he could always retrace his steps to find his way home. This was the first time he had ever strayed from their straight and true path. *You will never find your way back,* the snake in his stomach warned. Tenzo tried to ignore it as he scanned the tree line. There was a shantytown hidden along his stretch of monks, why should it be any different here? Almost as soon as he finished the thought, he saw a figure emerge from the trees.

The shantytown was not hard to find. An ochre path had been worn through the tangle of forest and faded strips of prayer cloth hung from nearly every branch along it, some tied so heavily that there were more knots than leaves. There were also remnants of fire rings and charred debris. Splintered spokes and shattered pots.

He heard the town before he saw it. Shouting and clanging. He smelled it too. Smoke and manure. Then he emerged from the forest path, and he saw it. No two structures looked the same. Some shacks were built right up against one another, as if propping themselves up. Others were made from clay, same as the ochre muck which oozed through the cracks of haphazard boardwalks. Tenzo noticed wagon wheels used both as windows and planters. Grass mats as awnings. Stacked doors as walls. The more he absorbed the details, the more it seemed that every piece of building material had been repurposed from something else. Something broken.

Tenzo was afraid to enter but he was more afraid of losing his mother's coin if he could not find a way to carry it.

The shantytown was all corners and alleyways and soon Tenzo was turned completely around.

"Need help?" A woman with one tooth was leaning against a door frame that looked like it really should not be leaned against.

Tenzo took a sharp turn in the other direction.

"You lost?" A man with all his teeth, which seemed suspicious in a place such as this.

"No," Tenzo assured, hurrying away.

He needed to get ox and get out. The snake coiled around his intestines. *You will never find your way back.*

After a few more wrong turns (were there any right turns here?), Tenzo found a family selling animals for work, slaughter, or ritual—they did not seem to care what for, as long as they were paid. Tenzo had prepared a lie. If asked where the coin came from, he would say, "I found it on the trail, a pilgrim must have dropped it." But they did not ask.

With the gold coin Tenzo bought another ox, though it was not yet broken in. He asked what her name was. One of the children, younger than Tenzo, said an unblessed word. Tenzo decided that a more appropriate name would be Madu.

With the silver coin he bought a large bag of perfectly ripe melons. He ended up having to hold a melon in front of Madu to get her to move. She took a bite for every step. Half his supply was gone by the time he got back to the Immortal Monks.

At the sight of their uniform red robes and serene smiles, Tenzo vowed never to stray from the straight and true path of the monks again. The snake uncoiled . . . then constricted tighter than ever. The door to the shack was open.

Tenzo entered to find the elder standing bow-legged over his mound of sacks. Many had been opened, and coins were spilled on the dirt floor like recently unearthed treasure.

"That's mine!" shouted Tenzo.

But the elder said, "This cannot be yours. Where did you get it from? Was it from the person who wore that ring?"

"It was my father's," Tenzo lied. He turned the ruby ring inward to hide the red, cursing himself for not doing so to begin with. "So is the coin."

"Well now it is mine." The elder reached out and picked up one of the gold coins.

Tenzo did not say "you are right" this time. Tenzo ran over to the old man with rage in his belly (along with many sloshing melons) and pushed him away from the sacks of coins. His bow-legs cracked as he hit the floor. Tenzo did not know if he was dead or collapsed from pain, but he did not wait to find out. He took the coin from the elder's cramped hand—his skin was like cooked fish skin, thin and flaky—and shoved it back into an open sack. He reloaded the rest of the sacks into the wagon with a sort of strength typically reserved fighting off tiger attacks. He did not even notice his blisters.

Tenzo hitched the new ox alongside the old one. Gave the command to move. Tugged the yoke. Tugged the yoke. Tuuuuuug-gged the yoke. But Madu refused to budge with this new weight, even when bribed with a melon. Tenzo stood behind the stubborn ox and began to push.

Slowly, begrudgingly, Madu began to move.

He heard plenty of pilgrims laugh as they passed him by. But this only made Tenzo push harder. His grief had turned fury.

How *dare* that elder try to take from him? He'd had a full life and a place to live alongside the Immortal Monks with coin from selling lodging, whereas Tenzo had no home and no mother. All he had was what coin she had left him. He needed it more. The pious neighbor had even said so.

Outrage fueled him onward until, before he knew it, he had reached a town *(he never knew he lived so near!)*.

The road was smoothed with packed dirt and wide enough to accommodate two carts at once. The buildings that lined it all had windows, some with ornate wooden screens, some even with glass! Some even had windows on top of windows with roofs that towered taller than any person could reach.

The wide road opened up even wider into a center marketplace. There, they sold all the things Tenzo had ever wanted—prepared foods, shiny leather sandals, clothing of every conceivable cut and color (but red, of course)—and many things he did not even know were things he could want—flowers, vases for flowers, feathered caps, bundles of silks, even people.

They were in a cage at the edge of the market square. As he looked them over, Tenzo found that he could look at every part of them but their eyes. What had these people done to end up like this? There was a man who sat limply in his own filth. A woman who stood at the locked gate like a tiger poised to pounce. And a boy, about Tenzo's size, only skinnier (if that were possible), looking like he was doing his best not to cry. He lifted his chin as if to say, *You may be out there and me in here, but that doesn't mean you are better than me.*

Tenzo moved on to the next stall. Fruits and sweet sticky rice. And the next. Boots and belts. And the next. Incense and works of art. Tools. Toys. Ornaments. He wanted it all! But he also did not want to draw too much attention to himself. After his encounter with the bowlegged elder, he was now terrified of his fortune being forcibly taken from him. He needed a protector, like those who escorted the pilgrims with the finest robes. But what protector would not protect their own needs first?

Tenzo found himself circling back to the cages of people at the edge of the square.

The man looked like he couldn't fight off the biting flies on his face, how would he fight off a thief? The tiger-woman looked like she would fight a thief, and Tenzo, not necessarily in that order.

Then there was the boy. He stared at Tenzo on the other side of the cage. *You may be out there and me in here, but that doesn't mean I'll look away first.*

"If you want to talk to your little friend, there's plenty of room in there with him."

Tenzo was suddenly in shade. The slaver grabbed him by the back of the neck. His grip was a blister beetle's pincer.

"Oh no, sir, he is buying me for his master." The boy in the cage had spoken.

The slave owner laughed. "This rat?"

The snake in Tenzo's belly arched to strike, and he found himself spitting back, "I am so here to buy him." Then, "For my master."

More coin than he suspected he should have spent later, Tenzo walked off the square with the boy from the cage. He smelled of rancid meat and Tenzo was torn between giving himself more breathing room or keeping his eye on his purchase. He was also torn between being angry that the boy had tricked him into buying his way out, or thankful that he had saved him from a similar fate.

"I'm Senu."

"Tenzo."

"Bless for getting me out of there," Senu said.

"Bless for keeping me out of there," Tenzo replied, deciding in that moment it was easier to be friends than fight. "I'm eleven," he offered.

"Twelve."

"Eleven and a half, really," Tenzo amended.

"Your master must be nice? To let you spend his coin this way."

"He is." Tenzo felt he was not really lying because he *was* nice and, technically, he *was* this boy's Master. And someone who knew this unfamiliar environment *was* useful to have around. "He sent me ahead to set up lodgings for him."

Senu livened. "I know a place!"

Now Tenzo had another choice: accept this slave boy's help but risk him stealing his coin or try to figure out what to do on his own and risk someone else stealing it.

Senu was clearly in a weakened state. Tenzo would win the fight, should it come to that (though he hoped it wouldn't because he did not want to get any nearer to Senu than he needed to).

"He also needs to board his oxen and a safe place to keep his—" Friendly or not, Tenzo was not foolish enough to tell some boy he did not even know about his fortune. "—yams."

"I don't know about storing yams," Senu shrugged, "but I know of a safe place for coin."

He knew.

"Why do you say that?" If a slave boy could figure out that he was not carrying yams, who else would?

"Your cart is about to crack apart. And that one ox of yours looks close to collapse."

The snake wound so tightly that Tenzo's stomach cramped. Would he be able to fight him off, after all? Now he wasn't so sure.

But then Senu whispered the most incredible thing, "Our master must be extravagantly wealthy to have so much coin to send ahead of him!"

"He is the richest person I know!" Tenzo laughed shakily. "So, you know a place where he could keep his—sacks—safe?"

Senu frowned slightly, twisted his hands together. "Do . . . do you think he would spare me some new garments? I am afraid no merchant would want to deal with me in this state."

"Yes," said Tenzo at once; new garments might help the stench. Then, with a flash of inspiration like a coin dropped into a sunlit alms bowl, he added, "He told me to get some for myself when I got here anyway, after such a long journey."

Senu proved to be quite useful. He first took them to the shop that sold garments. Tenzo was tempted to buy himself a set of fine robes (he was particularly enchanted with one that was embroidered with colorful silk birds), but as he was pretending to be a servant himself, he had to stick to necessities. Nice necessities.

Senu then took them to something called a "depository" to keep his sacks secure. But Tenzo would only leave one. He wanted to see if they would give it back when he asked.

Next, Senu took Tenzo to their lodgings. The building was one of those impossibly tall ones with high windows, but no nearby trees to shimmy up to reach them. When Tenzo followed Senu inside, he was met with a hill of steps that climbed to another room above his head! Senu started walking up them without even using his hands for balance, stepping each leg up one at a time. Tenzo followed, feeling that he was very high and did not like to be very high. He tensed his leg muscles with every cautious step, a monkey preparing to leap to safety.

At the top of the steps was a long thin room of doorways, a different symbol marking each one. Senu seemed to know what the symbols meant because he led them confidently over to one of the doors. Tenzo was impressed but tried not to show it.

This up high room was also like no room he had ever been in. The walls were the color and texture of mashed taro root and there was a plant *inside* next to a window—of glass! He could see the top of a tree through it. Tenzo told Senu to close the screens.

There was also a sleeping mat that was lifted off the floor. But only one. At the base of the lifted mat was a floor mat such as Tenzo's. He wanted very much to lie down on it. But once they had settled in for the night, it was Senu who stretched out at the base of the lifted mat, presumably where Tenzo was meant to sleep.

It was suffocatingly soft. Tenzo began to sink into it— to drown in it— but he dared not move or risk falling— crashing to the floor like a branch in a monsoon— breaking— splintering—

"You've been sleeping in that cage; you deserve the good mat," Tenzo told Senu, "Let's switch."

Senu thanked him so many times that Tenzo would have become annoyed, if it did not make him feel so pious.

§

When Tenzo had lived along the middle of the line of Immortal Monks, he'd seen the whole world pass by his front door, but no one ever stayed, and now he understood why. He had lived between. Between places worth stopping at. Between comforts. Between culture. Here was music he had never heard a lute master play, stories he had never seen a storyteller enact, foods he had never smelled his mother prepare.

Their days were filled with exploring the town to stock up on supplies, and exploring the town to explore it. Tenzo was content to try every new thing (even the bed, which he was determined to get used to). But Senu was less content. Every few days, he would ask: "Have you heard word from your master yet, when he is coming?"

One day Senu came to Tenzo and said, "You don't have a master, do you?"

Tenzo answered by not answering.

"Where did you get your coin?"

"It was my mother's. She died." It was perhaps the first truthful thing Tenzo had said to Senu, though he wished it were a lie.

"My mother is dead too," Senu related.

Senu's mother had died and he'd ended up in a cage. If Tenzo had not had his mother's wealth, he might have too. How close they were to walking the same path.

"Then *you* are my master?" Senu asked, rescuing Tenzo from his imagination. He was grinning.

It seemed surreal that Tenzo could own a servant, when he himself had been living in a shack selling sandals to pilgrims not three weeks before. But he was also quickly coming to rely on Senu's resourcefulness.

"I need the coin back I spent on you. But once you work off the debt, you will be free."

As a joke, Senu started calling him "Master Tenzo" and Tenzo did not stop him.

The very next day, he bought the robes with the embroidered birds.

§

Tenzo had Senu arrange transport to the South.

Senu traded Hempato and Madu for two much healthier looking oxen. Tenzo secretly missed them (he resolved not to name any more of his work animals). Senu also purchased them a new wagon for the long journey ahead. It had a bench seat. Tenzo had not asked Senu to do either of these things and so mentally added the cost of the oxen and the wagon to what he owed.

On their way out of town, they went to retrieve the sack

of coins from the depository and Tenzo was pleased that they returned it without hassle, but could also not be sure that they had not slipped out a coin or two. He wished he had counted.

§

After many more towns, each making the one before it seem primitive by comparison, Tenzo began to see signs that the monks were nearing the Infinite Waters. Salt from the tangy air dusted the folds of their red robes. Sparkling grains of sand settled between their stone toes. Though he knew their smiles carved, they seemed to be enjoying the warm breeze. The sounds of gulls echoed in their alms bowls and the coins reflected the strength of the sun. *Coins of pure light.* Then, at last, he saw the line where sky and water touched. Tenzo thought of two shantytown shacks holding each other up. Only the sky was a palace of infinite space and the water a palace of infinite depth. And into that infinite depth walked the Immortal Monks. Pale green waves lapped at the ankles of one statue, the shins of another, the knees, the torso, the chest, the neck, the eyes, until only the very top of the head of the statue was above water. But the water was so clear that Tenzo could see the stone monks that continued to walk beneath it. Stripped fish nibbled algae off their flaking robes. So far and so deep they walked, that Tenzo could not tell where the line ended.

There was a strip of beach that stretched like a bridge to a large island, thick with vegetation, just offshore. A few smaller islands dotted the distance. Tenzo wanted to walk across the land bridge to follow the monks further and see if he could find the very last one, but Senu said, "It is best to wait until after the tide or we will be stuck there with the fishers."

Tenzo did not know what a tide was and was about to ask,

when he was interrupted by the sound of wailing.

Nearby, a pilgrim was walking into the Infinite Waters, tossing handfuls of coins and prayers to the surf. With her last coin offered, she fell to her knees and cried tears of release. Tenzo cried too, but for the opposite reason. Before they'd even secured lodging, Tenzo had Senu hire a night fisher to dredge the treasure out of the waves.

The next morning (having learned what the tide was), Tenzo was able to explore the island. There was a shanty of fisher shacks jumbled amongst the jungle trees. The smaller islands, though, seemed uninhabited but for sea birds, streaking the rocks white with droppings and fish bones.

"I would like to live on one of those islands." Then he turned to Senu, "I want glass windows."

§

They lodged in a large room with a view looking out at the East. Tenzo had become used to being up high and now quite enjoyed looking down at the people below. It reminded him of pilgrim watching. Except that almost no one ever glanced up so he could stare at them all he wanted without any swatting looks.

Every sunrise, Tenzo was awoken by the shrill alarm of gulls fighting over fish guts. And every sunrise, Tenzo nearly leapt out of bed to see what his night fishers, who had no fish to gut in the morning, had hauled up. Mostly, it would be green coins which he gave to Senu to trade in for gold, but sometimes there were silver cups, sand-worn rings, parts of incense holders, altar candlesticks and icons. Senu was often out tending to the building of their house, so Tenzo could take his time. He would turn each piece over in his hands. Polish each jewel, each coin. He liked running his fingers across the ridges of a cut gemstone, around the curved edge of a coin, over the features of an icon.

Some time later, when the room was shadows, Senu would return (he had to take a roundabout route back to avoid being followed.) Then the two boys would share moonrise meal together. With the rich foods he ate, Tenzo soon fleshed out into a very healthy-looking young man and Senu had to have grown half a monk's step already. As they ate as much as they could manage to fit in their unstretched stomachs, Senu would tell about his day with this builder and that gardener and Tenzo would show the best finds from the day's catch. Then they would spend hours dreaming up plans for the house and teaching each other the different games they knew until the moon was too high in the sky to ignore.

Reaping Festival came, marking Tenzo's twelfth year since rebirth.

Senu had a surprise for him. "Your house is complete."

Tenzo looked up from his inventory.

"Then we will sleep there tonight!"

"You can sleep there tonight."

"And where will you be?"

"I will be here. I have worked for you for many moons. Surely, I have earned back the coin you paid for me."

Tenzo had thought Senu was his friend. But evidently, he was not spending time with him by choice.

"I have housed you for just as many moons," Tenzo refuted. "I have fed you sunrise and moonrise meals, have bought you new robes and fresh sandals. You have not paid back your debt yet."

That night they both slept on the island.

§

Tenzo decorated the house in red. Red tapestries and red

cushions and red bedspreads from the red silks and linens and satins that Senu had imported. Nothing along the blessed path could be red but the statue's painted robes, so red became Tenzo's favorite color. He turned the ruby on his ring to face outward again.

Senu had made sure that the house had a glass window with a view of the Immortal Monks. On a clear day, you could see the line of red robes walking into the Infinite Waters, past his island, and off into the distance of the horizon. Sometimes Tenzo saw pilgrims in the water, so pious that they tried to complete their pilgrimage by swimming out to the last monk, but all either turned back or dipped under the waves and did not resurface. Tenzo could also see fishers hauling up writhing silver nets. It struck Tenzo that the night fishers they hired were probably putting most of their catch of coin into their own pockets. He had Senu buy more slaves. "Instead of languishing in a cage, they will be fishing under moonlight in the fresh breeze," Tenzo reasoned.

"And you will let them buy their freedom?"

"I promise."

Senu dutifully did as he was instructed, telling each slave he obtained that they could buy their freedom with their catch (after they paid off their purchase cost and fees for room and board). Senu made sure that Tenzo kept his promise. To every slave but Senu himself, who had to let others free when he could not be.

Tenzo came to expect that if he needed Senu, he would be found in the gardens.

Whereas Tenzo spent his time spending his coin.

He commissioned elaborate décor: an ebony chest set with pearls, a vase of inlaid marble in the motif of parrots and persimmons, a silver tureen that looked like a conch shell, candelabras draped with real snakes that had been encased in wax then cast in gold, ceilings carved with fruit bats, a grand bloodwood and ruby incense burner set on a matching pedestal, and a board game with jasper and lapis pieces for him and Senu to play.

They still spent their evenings eating moonrise meal together, but the tone had shifted. Friends catching up to slave reporting to Master. Friends playing games to slave entertaining Master. "Master Tenzo" had lost the joking tone. For every ten bites Tenzo took, Senu would take one. With the rich foods he ate, Tenzo soon fleshed out more than a healthy amount. One day, he was counting the most recent fisher haul and realized that his thumb felt stiff and unable to bend. He barely got the ruby ring off over his knuckle. Tenzo slid it onto his pointer finger. It fit.

As Tenzo grew wider, Senu grew taller. By the time the ring transferred to Tenzo's middle finger, Senu had grown so tall that he had to bend through doorways.

He started to wear other jewels beside the ring. Gold cuffs set with emeralds and peridot, a brooch of citrine in the shape of a bird (with a sapphire eye!), rings on every finger—coral, amber, carnelian. A medallion of jade, vibrant green. He had a dagger fashioned which he wore at all times, its gem-crusted hilt commanding notice. He celebrated his thirteenth year since rebirth with a chain of thirteen ruby teardrops, each one bezel-set in buttery gold. Each year thereafter, he added a pendant to the necklace.

Tenzo had Senu buy land along the southern shore and then charge dues for its use.

§

A gate was erected around the whole of the island. Though

ornate, it was not gilded; Tenzo didn't want to any night thieves to chisel parts off. Still fearful of his wealth being stolen, he had Senu sew coins into the lining of his robes. The weight was comforting. This limited the extent of his outings, but staying away from others was more secure anyway.

The ruby ring was tightening around Tenzo's middle finger now, or rather, his middle finger had outgrown the ring. Tenzo finally moved it to his ring finger.

Tenzo stayed on the island for longer and longer periods of time. Merchants had to come to him, should they want his business. He began to command.

"Senu, fetch me my seamster."

"Senu, fetch me my decorator."

"Senu, fetch me my blacksmith."

He would greet them in his Receiving Room, a room whose sole purpose was to astound. The summoned would have to walk across the long, high-ceilinged room, lined with grand tapestries and great gilded pillars, to Tenzo's chair at the other end.

"Senu, fetch me my jeweler," commanded Tenzo one day. He wanted to commission a new ruby pendant to mark the upcoming Reaping Festival and, with it, his entering the age of adulthood. Ten and seven years.

But when his jeweler came, he brought with him an uninvited guest. "This is my daughter, Kho."

Kho smiled sweetly until her father looked back at Tenzo, then the corners of her lips fell flat.

"She is learning the trade."

She glowered at Tenzo.

"Is that so?"

The jeweler, whose name Tenzo was desperately trying to remember (Senu would know), presented him with rings and pendants, glancing at his daughter with regularity, who smiled when he looked and glowered when he looked away.

Tenzo tried not to pay her any notice, but he couldn't help himself. Her skin was the shade and smoothness of caramel jasper. Her lips were rose gold. Her hair reflected the light like a dark star sapphire. And her eyes, her eyes shone like rare black pearls.

Every so often, those black pearl eyes met his and Tenzo would feel a shock like he'd been stung by a jellyfish.

"Senu, fetch me my jeweler," commanded Tenzo the next day. "I am not satisfied with the setting of this ring."

But the jeweler answered his summons without the company of his daughter. Tenzo had no choice but to ask why not.

"I apologize, sir, but my daughter has decided she is not interested in the family trade."

"What *is* she interested in, then?"

Tenzo gifted Kho the most expensive horse he could find. A rare purebred, with muscles like coiling watersnakes beneath its sea-foam white hide.

Kho sent it back.

"Senu, fetch me my jeweler," commanded Tenzo.

"She prefers a wild horse, not one too tame. I am afraid she is not too tame either." The jeweler hung his head. "But I'm sure she can be, with the right touch," he added encouragingly.

Tenzo had Senu see to the capture of a wild horse. It was a rich brown and had eyes that made him want to take a step back.

After two days of not receiving so much as a "bless," Tenzo called out: "Senu, fetch me—"

"—your jeweler," Senu finished.

This time Kho accompanied him.

Tenzo liked to think that her glowering had softened to suspicion.

"With blessing, I would like to take your daughter riding."

The jeweler nearly choked on his delight. "Yes! Yes! Yes, certainly. You have my blessing."

Tenzo rode the white horse—he had kept it; it offered a certain prestige to own the most expensive horse, after all. Kho rode the wild one. She rode it without saddle or reins. She caressed its wild body with hers, and Tenzo felt, for the first time, envious of an animal.

"Why did you give me this horse?" she confronted as soon as they stopped to let the steeds replenish by one of Tenzo's many garden ponds. "What do you want in return?"

"Whatever you are willing to give," Tenzo heard himself saying.

Kho frowned. A single disapproving line appeared between her brows. "What if I don't want to give you anything?"

Tenzo could show indifference, remorse, pleasure. Which would she find the most attractive? He thought of his grandmother and his mother. They would not have wanted to be told what to do.

"Then you do not have to."

"You will not try and command me?" She pulled a leaf off a perfectly pruned bush and began shredding it.

Tenzo decided that he liked her wildness. "I will not."

"You command my father like he is a mule." Kho threw her shreds of leaf to the ground. She was clearly testing his reaction.

"You are right. I should not treat him that way." Tenzo suddenly wanted real connection, like with the pilgrims when he asked them *why*. "I am only trying to demand respect because I am too young to have earned it."

"Isn't it lonely to be someone who commands respect?"

Because he could not meet her black pearl eyes, Tenzo looked out at the line of statues walking into the waters.

"Yes. It is."

"Why do you care so much about the Immortal Monks?" Kho asked. "Everyone says you are obsessed with finding the last one."

Tenzo quickly looked away from the statues. "Is that what they say?"

"Well, is it true? Do you want to be a monk or something?" She gestured to his red robes. "Because you don't act very monk like." Her arms crossed.

Tenzo could not admit that he did not care about the Immortal Monks, only finding all of their treasure, so he said: "Only curiosity," and then instructed Senu to recall the night fishers the moment Kho departed.

§

Tenzo hired pearl divers to find rare black pearls to match Kho's eyes. Enough to make her a long strand.

"I know you cannot be bought," Tenzo said when he gave the pearl necklace to her, "Please, consider this a gift. Every pearl on his strand represents a thought I've had about you." He pretended to study the necklace. "About kissing you."

"Then I should kiss you once for every pearl." She held the pearl nearest the clasp between her fingertips. Then she put her rose gold lips to his. But they were not cool and hard like metal, they were wonderfully warm and oh-so-supple. With every pearl she thumbed, Kho gave him another kiss, until passion made her lose count.

§

Morning of the Reaping Festival, Kho delivered Tenzo's ruby teardrop to him personally. She added it to his chain, her caramel jasper fingers brushing against his collarbone.

They attended the festival together, Tenzo even leaving his red robes with the coins sewn into the lining at home so that he could enjoy the frivolities longer.

He felt lighter, and not only because of the change of robes.

Tenzo found himself looking more often at Kho than at the monks. His love seemed more immortal than any stone statue.

§

One day the jeweler came to the island unbidden.

"I did not summon you," Tenzo said. He was being fitted for new, looser, robes.

The seamster continued the fitting, though he conveniently angled himself to get a better view.

"I have been expecting you to."

"Why is that?"

"I thought you might ask me to make you a ring."

"I have many of your fine rings. I do not need another presently."

"I thought you might ask me to make you a ring to give to Kho. I know the size of her finger, after all." At this the seamster stopped all pretense of work and looked up at Tenzo to see what his reaction would be.

"Don't you want me to ask for her hand first?"

"You have had her hand from the day I first brought her here."

The snake in Tenzo's stomach woke. Kho's father clearly wanted them to be married. You could see it in his thirsty eyes! How he ogled Tenzo like he was a pitcher of blessed water. This had clearly been his plan all along. It could have been hers as well.

The snake hissed, *They will kill you to inherit your riches.*

Tenzo's mother would not have wanted that.

"No, I do not think I want a new ring."

§

"Kho is here for you, Master," said Senu.

Tenzo was seated by the window overlooking the harbor, eating a large plate of fried sweet dumplings, watching the fishers pulling up nets. He owned almost all of them now, but still worried that they were keeping some of their catch for themselves. Tenzo had told Senu many times that he found it suspicious how quickly his slaves could buy their freedom. But Senu always replied that Tenzo's generous offer only motivated them to work that much harder. But they would have had to work that much harder regardless—with Kho gone, Tenzo's obsession to find the last monk's treasure returned with vehemence.

"Kho is here for you, Master," Senu repeated. He did not raise his voice, correctly presuming that Tenzo had heard him the first time.

"Send her away."

But Senu did not excuse himself.

"She will want to know why."

"Tell her to ask her father."

"She cannot control what her father does."

"Exactly."

Senu hovered like he did when he had an opinion to express. "Yes?"

"I think she is good for you."

"And I think she is a gold miner."

§

Kho sent back the horse. And the pearls.

"If she was a gold miner, she would have kept the pearls," reasoned Senu. "I'm sure if you apologize, she will forgive you."

But Tenzo had her horse tamed so that she would never forgive him.

He finally understood what his grandmother meant when she said that someone could die of a broken heart.

§

Tenzo bought a mine so that he would not have to use the jeweler's gems any longer. The mine came with more slaves. Senu came to him with one of them.

"This is Paak. He was a respected merchant before he fell on hard times."

"Why are you showing me this man?"

"I believe he would be an excellent replacement for me."

"Replace you? But you are irreplaceable to me, Senu."

When Tenzo had outgrown his Receiving Room chair, the one that replaced it could have been mistaken for a throne. This is where he sat now.

"I have worked for you for many years. I have eaten as little as I can and fashioned my own sandals so that you would not have to purchase them for me. I have earned my freedom."

"I cannot trust this man like I can trust you."

"You now have many slaves," Senu pleaded. "Surely one of

them can take my role."

"As I said, Senu, you are irreplaceable." He set his arms on red velvet armrests. "Now, do you have yesterday's yield yet?" Tenzo asked, the matter closed.

A small calfskin pouch hit Tenzo like a punch in the chest, then dropped into his large lap.

Senu left the room. The slave named Paak bowed awkwardly and hastened to follow. Tenzo would have felt guilty if he didn't depend on Senu so. And whatever guilt lingered, he now had a welcome distraction from.

Tenzo had taken it upon himself to price the rubies from the mine, for he trusted no one else to judge their quality. He also felt such a thrill every time he saw Senu enter the room with the calfskin pouch in hand. He picked it up from his lap. Heaved himself out of his red velvet chair and over to his red velvet stool. The sorting table was made from sunbleached ivory and inlaid with white seashell and bone.

Tenzo poured the stones out slowly, as if from a broken hourglass, until they formed an ant-hill-sized mound. He set the empty pouch aside. Then he slithered his finger through the rubies like a snake through red sand. Closed his eyes to listen to them clink softly, then opened them to marvel at all the little glints of light. Picked some up, poured them back into the pile.

Then, he sorted.

He lined them up by color. By clarity. By size. Then by how they should be cut. Round. Marquis. Emerald. Oval. Square. Cushion. Pear. It was an art, he found, choosing the right shape. It was about extracting the greatest beauty from the stone. Highlighting its attributes while whittling away its flaws. Scratches could be polished off. Inclusions could be hidden in the prism of cuts. A well-cut gemstone could be the difference between pretty and captivating. It could draw you in like a tranquil pond, the kind so pristine you almost expect to see something magical below its glassy surface. When Tenzo would hold such a specimen up to candlelight, sometimes he imagined he could.

The very finest one from every pouch, Tenzo always kept for himself. The deepest purple red, clear as a cloudless sky, large enough to be fashioned into a teardrop. When Reaping Festival came, marking the day of his rebirth, he would select the finest of the finest. By the time he turned twenty-five, the necklace of bloodred tears wrapped around his neck twice. By the time he turned forty, it wrapped around several times. This was also the year that Tenzo moved the ruby from his ring finger to his pinky.

He had a fleet of fishers now. But word had spread to the North that pilgrims should no longer through the last of their alms to the waves. Tenzo's boats were pushed out further.

He had the black pearl divers try and find the last Immortal Monk, but they reported back to Senu that they could not dive deep enough. To make certain they were not lying, Tenzo began to accompany the boats out in his own, resplendent with all of the comforts of home and a flag of monk robe red.

In the belly of his ship, he had a storeroom crafted to house all of his favorite treasures. The marble vase of parrots and persimmons, the jasper and lapis game board, the incense pedestal, even a pair of the candelabras modeled with real snakes. And an exact replica of his Receiving Room chair.

Tenzo commanded that the divers bring up a handful of sand to prove that they touched the bottom, or a finger would get cut off. With every handful of sand, he sent the diving boats further out. Most divers had missing fingers. Some would float up dead.

When he ran out of pearl divers, he moved on to miners. They had been told what all the others had been told: that if they could find the last monk, they would be set free with a handful of rubies. He heard that many of his men practiced holding their breath in the silty puddles beside the mine.

Many times, Senu would try to convince Tenzo that he had amassed enough riches.

But these were his alms savings, Tenzo would argue.

He deserved his wealth, his pious neighbor had said so.

§

Tenzo no longer left the ship. He barely left his chair. His meals were brought to him, as were his earnings. The water level around the ship rose. The size of his robes grew. The ruby ring tightened on his pinky until he could no longer remove it. The gold band grew into his flesh like a tree growing into a fence. But he would not have it cut off.

His necklace now cried almost fifty bezel-set tears.

§

It was ideal weather conditions. Tenzo had excavated a new stock of divers from his mines, the ones so eager to earn their freedom that they stuck their heads in puddles. Perhaps they would have more success than the last stock. The surface of the Infinite Waters was so calm and clear that he could see all the way down to where the water shifted from aquamarine to sapphire. Tenzo leaned over his gold-lacquered railing. He thought he could just make out nebulous shapes within the deep. Seaweed, no doubt. But walking through it? He squinted. Only as his body hit the water below the boat, did his mind register that he had fallen overboard.

Tenzo sputtered and gasped trying to catch his breath, but even though he flailed toward the surface, he kept sinking beneath it. The coins sewn into his robes were dragging him down like a hundred gilt anchors. But he did not want to offer them to the monks below. Above him—*there!*—the tall and slender figure of Senu at the railing. He was saved! Tenzo called out for help, seawater frothing from his mouth, but his trusted servant only turned away from him.

Tenzo had been pushed.

He looked up through salt-blurred eyes at the bottom of the ship, receding from view. At last, he tried to remove his robes, but his fingers only slipped over the carved ruby buttons. Soon the ship was but a dark blot above him.

Tenzo sank deeper and deeper until he felt seaweed ticking his ankles. And there, an Immortal Monk in the murk, smiling serenely despite the man drowning beside him. Then, as if tied to a yoke, Tenzo was yanked by a strong undercurrent. It rushed him along a line of algae and coral-covered stone statues, brushing past seaweed and shipwrecks and heaps of treasure paid as alms to the deep. The current increased, ripping the inner lining of his robes and freeing coins like a hive of swarming bees slashed open by a moon bear hunting for honey. Tenzo desperately tried to catch them, but he might as well have been trying to catch water. Rings dropped off his fingers—more were lost as he tried to snatch at them. Clasps snapped. Ruby droplets bled into the current. He grasped at his robes. Felt a single coin still sewn against his chest. He clutched his hand over his heart. Noticing the flash of ruby embedded in his pinky finger, he felt relief that he at least still had that.

Though his lungs burned, Tenzo felt a coldness seep into him, as if his skin were dissolving into the Infinite Waters. His vision blackened just as he glimpsed the last in the line of the Immortal Monks, walking into a temple. Under the ocean. Shining solid gold.

Tenzo was spit out of the current and onto a waterless floor. He sputtered bile and brine. His heart pounded—waves smashing to shore. Wave after wave. Even though he was no longer being swept along by the current, the sound of blood rushed in his ears like saltwater froth fizzing into sand. He was a beached jellyfish, suffocating in the salty air. Yet, he was alive! But *how* was he alive? What was this place?

He peeled himself off the floor with the sound of a conch being pulled from its shell. He had been face down on a mosaic mandala made up of thousands upon thousands of inlaid gemstones. But the floor was only the foundation upon which unimaginable riches rested. Tenzo swayed as his eyes moved upward. The room that he found himself in made his Receiving Room look like the one-roomed shack that he'd grown up in. The walls were encrusted with coins and jewelry and goblets and pitchers and statuettes. It was as if Tenzo were standing inside a pile of treasure. Gold bracketed torches made it all glimmer like sunset rippling across the surface of the Infinite Waters. Tenzo looked back at the entryway and saw the last Immortal Monk statue standing just on the other side. The ocean simply didn't enter the temple. The walls had no windows, only the impossible doorway of water and an archway across the vestibule that led into a flickering passage beyond.

When a pilgrim tried to swim to the last monk and did not

resurface, it was assumed that they had drowned or been eaten by a fish the size of a house. Had they instead made it to this temple hidden under the waves? Had any of *his* slaves made it here?

All of a sudden, treasure started to pour through the impossible barrier between the temple and the ocean, and clattering onto the floor at his feet.

"My ship!" cried Tenzo as he looked down at the growing pile of treasure. He recognized it at once as his own. Tenzo knew every coin, every gem-encrusted hand mirror, every silver cup, intimately, as only a man who spends more time with his riches than his friends ever could. His riches *were* his friends. And here they were returned to him!

"Your slave sank your ship."

Tenzo started. Beside him stood an Immortal Monk—he recognized him by the red robes, the shaved head—only this one was not made of stone. Instead of an alms bowl, he carried a gold candlestick with a curved base.

"You are not a statue," Tenzo said stupidly.

"I am not." And there was the serene smile.

"But— you— you are an Immortal Monk?" he asked over the echoing racket.

"You have discovered the monastery of the Immortal Monks. Only the most giving, or greedy, ever find their way here."

As Tenzo's treasure continued pouring in through the ocean door, he understood which one he was without having to ask.

The treasure— "Senu didn't want the treasure for himself?"

The Immortal Monk smiled pityingly. "No."

"But Senu was *on* that ship. What happened to him?"

"He drowned."

"Why would he do that? He was finally a free man!"

"He was free of his enslavement, but he would never be free of his remorse."

"How do you know this? Will he be coming here too?" Tenzo looked at the barrier where the stream of treasure was still trickling through, as if his servant's body was about to be deposited atop the pile like a fish flopping on the deck of a boat.

"Yes. He will be reborn as one of us."

"You're making my murderer an Immortal Monk?!" Tenzo coughed up some more water.

"If that is how you see it," the Immortal Monk conceded, "yes."

Tenzo could not believe that a slave would be honored above him. "What about me? What will happen to me?"

"You, will follow." The monk turned toward the archway that led out of the vestibule and, presumably, to the rest of the monastery.

Tenzo eyed the pile of treasure, now nearly blocking the temple entrance, and thought, *How will I get it out of here with me?*

"Let me just gather my belongings first—"

"Your 'belongings' will stay here."

Tenzo instinctively clasped his hand over the remaining coin in his robes. The ruby ring he did not have to hide, so buried was it in the flesh of his finger.

The monk walked through archway opposite the ocean. Tenzo was tempted to grab as much treasure as he could carry, but to what end? He did not even know where he could stash it, yet.

Tenzo followed the monk, hand over his heart.

The hallway was equally splendorous as the vestibule, torches every few paces illuminating a trove of treasure set into the walls.

Vase stems. Chain links. Trunk lids. Tenzo noticed a small Immortal Monk icon stuck out at an angle that he might be able to pull free; he would try to find it again later. The monk took him through a series of hallways and rooms. With no windows and the overwhelm of treasure, Tenzo was soon lost. He saw more living Immortal Monks, many cupping "alms bowl" candles. Some sat together on silk meditation cushions. All wore red robes and that same serene smile of the statues. But the patient smile of Senu was not among them.

Tenzo's tour guide stopped. They were in a hallway with solid gold doors all along it.

"This will be your room." He gestured for Tenzo to open a golden door.

Tenzo did so enthusiastically. If his room was anything like the rest of the monastery, there would be plenty of treasure for him to pry out of the walls, but no watchful eyes to stop him.

It was not. His room had walls of plain sandstone and only a simple mat on which to sleep. A plain grey robe hung from a peg on the wall—the only decoration. Unless you counted the tin bucket in the corner.

Tenzo turned to argue, but the monk guide was gone.

Tenzo left the room and wandered until he wandered his way back to the vestibule, only to find that his pile of treasure was already gone. He looked all around, as if it were hiding in the corner. A ring in the wall captured his attention. It looked a lot like the one he usually wore on his middle finger. And another that was distinctly familiar as the one he wore on his left thumb.

Tenzo clutched at his ruby ring as if it could have been magically slipped off his pinky without him noticing. It was still there, burrowed into his puffy flesh.

Tenzo spent a few minutes attempting to pry his belongings out of the wall but soon gave up; they had been fused with the rest of the treasure.

He walked over to the impossible ocean door. Put his palm up to it and skimmed the surface of water. The last statue was there, just on the other side. Smiling at him. Or perhaps he was smiling because his bowl was full of alms. Tentatively, Tenzo pressed his hand through the barrier. It was spit back at him with the force of an ocean and he fell to the floor for the second time. Without the initial shock of where he was landing, the landing hit harder.

He groaned onto his stomach. The mosaic mandala gleamed. He ran his hands across the footstep-smoothed tiles, feeling for any that might be coming loose.

"It is time to eat the ocean."

Tenzo looked up from the floor to see his monk guide standing over him, serene as ever.

"Eat the ocean?"

But his guide was already drifting away.

Long lines of shaved heads in red robes sat on long lines of cushions. Tenzo was the only one not wearing the robes of a monk as he still had not changed out of his own. A bell chimed, echoing off the treasure-laden walls. In silence, the monks began to eat.

The meal was seaweed salad (hardly "the ocean") and a glass of fresh water. Tenzo drained his glass in several large gulps. He looked for a carafe on the table from which to refill it. There was none. The air was salt.

Tenzo leaned over to the Immortal Monk beside him, chewing with his eyes closed. He softly cleared his throat. The monk did not open his eyes.

"Pardon, uh, Venerable One" Tenzo whispered. "Where might I get more water?"

"No more water," the monk said in a perfectly loud voice. All of the other shaved heads turned in their direction. Tenzo looked for Senu's face among them, but there were too many to focus on any one. The heads turned back to their silent chewing.

Tenzo ate the seaweed because he was hungry, but very much wished he had saved a sip of water for the end of the meal. Instead, he had to make do with lifting his glass up and shaking it until a single sweet drop spread across his tongue.

The bell chimed once more. The monks rose and filed out. Tenzo followed them back to the hallway with golden doors. The monks entered the doors one by one.

"It is time for deep relaxation," Tenzo's guide said, materializing once again beside him.

"You mean sleep?"

"If you must."

"I need more water first."

"There will be water with the next meal."

Tenzo tried to sleep on the mat, but his soft body had grown too accustomed to soft beds. He tossed and turned, trying to get comfortable. But how could he be comfortable with all these coins under his mat? He was in his old shack, trying to sleep on the pile of his mother's treasure that he had just unearthed from the dirt floor. He had to keep it safe! For the bow-legged elder was standing over him, his cooked fish skin flaking. Flaying. Tenzo contorted his body around the mound of coins.

He did not know what came first, the wakefulness or the bell, but he felt like he had barely slept. For all he knew, he hadn't; with no windows, it was impossible to tell the time of day.

"Sunrise" meal was the same as moonrise meal: seaweed salad and a glass of water. This time Tenzo forced himself to take only a tiny sip between each well-chewed bite, saving a nice big gulp to wash down the meal. When the bell rang and the monks rose, Tenzo thought he caught a glimpse of Senu. But the monk had already filed out with the rest.

His guide sat beside him.

"What will happen to me?" Tenzo asked.

"You will take the coin out of your robes."

Though they were stiff with dried salt water and torn all along the inside, Tenzo had still not changed out of his robes. He felt the comfort of the coin next to his heart. But Tenzo thought better than to lie to an Immortal Monk. He reached in and ripped the last remaining coin out of his lining. Regretfully, he held it out to the monk to confiscate.

"Come back when you can see the clouds in this coin." The monk stood up, the lesson apparently over.

Tenzo was left to himself for the rest of the day. He wandered the halls. He tested the treasure in the walls. He sat on meditation cushions and stared at the coin. He turned it over in his hand. Found the angle that best reflected the torch light. Ran his finger around the ridges along its edge. But no matter how long he stared at it, how blurry his vision became, he could not see any clouds in it. What would it matter if he did? Clouds could not buy him new robes. Clouds could not return him to his riches.

After moonrise meal, Tenzo went to his room and stared at the coin until he fell asleep. But all he managed to see in it was the things he could buy with it. You could not buy a cloud. If one could, Tenzo already would have.

At the sound of the bell, he went to dress. But with the coin removed from his salt-stiff robes there was no reason to wear them any longer. He changed into plain grey.

When he returned to his room after the last chime of the day, his old robes had been taken away.

§

Time passed. Weeks? Months? The same routine. Seaweed salad and a glass of water. Wandering the halls alone with his thoughts and his coin. Seaweed salad and a glass of water. Sitting in his room alone with his thoughts and his coin.

From time to time he would think he saw the lanky figure of Senu amongst the monk's robes. His own robes were fitting looser. For the first time in many years, he was able to flex his pinky.

His guide did not check on him. The other monks only smiled at him.

"What will happen to me?" Tenzo would ask one of them from time to time.

"Come back when you see the clouds in the coin," their only reply.

"How do I see the clouds in the coin?"

"Come back when you see the clouds in the coin."

Finally, Senu came to Tenzo's room. He looked like every other Immortal Monk. Shaved head, red robes, serene smile. For all Tenzo knew, he could have seen him a hundred times but not recognized him from the back.

"You look well, Master."

"You would still call me Master?"

"Would you have me call you anything else?"

He was ashamed that he had ever let him call him anything other than— "Tenzo."

"Then you look well, Tenzo."

To Tenzo this felt as though he had finally set Senu free. "I'm sorry I never freed you."

Senu only smiled that monk's smile. "I cannot find fault in the path that led me here. You were that path."

"You are happy then? As an Immortal Monk?"

"I am not an Immortal Monk yet, but I am learning to be. And, bless, I am very content."

Senu was still standing on the other side of the door. The side that was gold.

"Would you— like to sit?" asked Tenzo, moving to make space on his simple mat.

Senu sat beside him.

"I have heard that you are struggling with your lesson."

Tenzo at once determined that the monk's serene smiles had all been smirks. They thought him a fool, that he could not even understand his first lesson! But there was no denying it.

"I'm supposed to look at this coin," he flicked it across the mat, "and see clouds in it. But no matter how long I stare—"

Senu reached out and picked up the coin. Tenzo resisted the urge to snatch it back.

"What is this coin made of?" he asked.

Was this a trick question? "It is made of gold?"

"It is made of gold." Senu repeated, but as a statement of fact. Somehow it was comforting to hear him call the coin what it was. "Where did the gold come from?"

Tenzo knew this answer. "A mine."

"And who mined it?"

"There is no way to know," Tenzo despaired.

"But *someone* mined it?"

"Yes, *someone* mined it."

"How did that *someone* have energy to mine?"

Tenzo couldn't help but feel like he was being led to the answer by blindfold. "Do you have a point to these questions?"

"I can leave you to find the answer for yourself, if you would prefer." Senu set the coin down as if readying to leave.

"The miner would have energy from eating," Tenzo hastily answered.

"Eating what?"

Tenzo knew that his mineworkers were fed only gruel, but he said, "Rice and curry."

"And where does rice and curry come from?"

Tenzo had to think about this. "Animals. Plants."

"And what do plants need to grow?"

"Soil. Rain."

"And where does rain come from?"

"The—" the blindfold was suddenly lifted.

§

"The clouds are in the coin because without clouds there could be no rain and without rain there could be no food and without food the miner who mined this gold and the blacksmith who minted this coin would not have energy," Tenzo said triumphantly.

His monk guide definitely smirked. Tenzo was reminded of how he had hated when adults smiled at him in that way when he was a child, as if there were a secret he was too simpleminded to understand, and this time was, still, no exception.

"Come back to us when you can see the clouds in this coin," said the monk.

"But I just told you!"

"You told us that Senu can see the clouds in this coin. Now you must see what he sees."

§

More time passed, Tenzo's loosening robes the only way to tell its passing.

He sat with Senu when he could, but his former servant was often occupied with Immortal Monk training or sitting with other students. Often Tenzo would have to eat alone. He had discovered that the more slowly he ate, the more satisfied he felt. Even full. He began to savor his seaweed salad and glass of water. Sometimes Senu would join him, and they would savor their food side-by-side, in comforting silence. He'd had Senu explain it so many times that there was no point repeating words which he had already committed to memory: "You need to *be* the miner who dug the gold, you need to *be* the farmer who harvested his food, you need to *be* the plants that thirst. You need to *be* the rain, to see the clouds."

But even though he understood *how* the clouds could be in the coin, he could not see them for himself.

Tenzo had tried saying that he finally did, but the Immortal Monks still refused to accept his answer. They could see through more than just the coin.

§

More time passed, still. He stopped wondering how much. He had also stopped noticing the treasure in the walls. He saw the floor for the mandala mosaic, not the gemstone tiles. Tenzo only noticed the coin and his ruby ring. He removed the ring. It was only a distraction.

One day Tenzo woke and took the familiar coin in his hands. It was becoming worn from the restless turning of it through his fingers. He could not know where this particular coin had come from, but it could have very well been one from an alms bowl. It could very well have passed from the hands of a pilgrim into the palm of his mother. Or it could have been a fisher or diver that he had forced to retrieve it. But some human had touched it before. And that human had experienced hunger. As had the coin minter, and the miner who had chiseled its ore from veins of rock with the strength of the blood in his own. When the bell rang, Tenzo did not rise. He would sit here until he saw the clouds.

Many more bells echoed through the monastery. He heard his door open and close once or twice, but he did not look to see if it was Senu checking on him or his guide. Whoever it was, they understood and left again.

The coin could not be without the hands of countless humans and the humans could not be without the nutrients of the soil and the sky and the rain. He let himself travel each manifestation of its being. He was the soil, he was the root, the flower, the bee, the rain, the puddle, the miner who stuck his head in the puddle and drowned his dignity. Everything that existed, present and past and future, existed in this coin because this coin could not exist without them. The coin in his hand was condensed water vapor, was a ball of rice, was the gentle kiss from a mother to a child.

§

"The clouds are in this coin because everything is in this coin."

His guide nodded.

"What will happen to me?"

"We are sending you back to the clouds."

"I am being reborn?"

"No, you are being returned."

The monk held out a cupped hand, resting in his palm was the ruby ring. Tenzo found he did not want to take it. That he did not want to return to his old life, his old desires. "But Senu is allowed to be an Immortal Monk, why not me?"

"Receiving requires offering. Only the most generous can receive the blessing of immortal life."

Tenzo suddenly thought of his pious neighbor. He hoped that he had been rewarded for his generosity to him—such spiritual discipline to not take from a defenseless child!

"As you must see the clouds in the coin to learn interdependence, so must you see the monk in the man to learn why he must be one, but you cannot," his guide continued. "While you were counting your earnings, Senu was giving his to your slaves so they might buy their freedom. While you were decorating your manor, he was tending to the gardens so that he could deliver fresh fruits and vegetables to your mines. When you began to punish your pearl divers, he saved them from further torment by ending the life of his dearest friend. While you were trying to swim to the surface, he sacrificed himself to the Infinite Waters as atonement for his immoral action."

The long-dormant snake in Tenzo's stomach struggled to break free, to slither away from him. He understood why he could not be a monk, and why Senu must be.

He took the ring.

Tenzo's old robes were returned to him. The lining had been

repaired, coins sewn back in. The robes felt much heavier (and much larger) than he remembered. They fit like a burden. How had he shouldered such a load for so long?

Senu came to say farewell.

"Thank you for helping me, after how I was to you," Tenzo said, his guide's words still crisp in his conscience. "I am glad we could become friends."

"You have always been my friend," Senu said.

When it was time, Tenzo walked willingly into the ocean.

§

The current rushed him along at inhuman speeds, past seaweed and stone monks. But instead of being swept to the surface and spit out on the sand like a beached dolphin, Tenzo felt the current suck him *down,* into the abyss. The warm water turned cold as suddenly as if he'd jumped into an ice bath on a summer afternoon. The current cut like diamond-sharpened knives.

Tenzo wanted to scream but could not open his mouth to let out his last breath of air. He could see sunnier water above him, but the coins in his robes, once again, anchored him from the light.

He tried to fight against the flow, maneuver his arms to remove the robes, but it was too strong a force. He should not have accepted them in the monastery. It had been a test. He had failed.

Tenzo felt his body yield. Muscles that had been straining against the cold, slackened. Lungs that had been burning, sighed out a stream of bubbles. His last breath—greater a treasure than any his fishers had ever dredged up—lost to the deep.

This was the price for his greed.

Tenzo stopped fighting the flow and surrendered himself to the current. The current that took a sudden sharp turn to the surface and regurgitated him out of a waterfall.

Tenzo tumbled into a white pool where he was plunged under once again by the force of the falling water. He flailed until his hand found a solid pillar of rock. Clinging his way up the pillar, Tenzo managed to pull himself to the surface. He gasped. Sputtered. Chunks of ice churned around him.

Tenzo sloshed his way out of the pool at the base of the waterfall and fell onto the bank of the stream that ran from it. He lay there retching. Shivering. Shivering and retching.

"What were you in there for?" asked a voice from above him.

Tenzo opened his eyes and saw a stone foot. He scrambled to a seat and realized that several onlookers cloaked in furs were standing around him.

"He wanted to start at the beginning, the fool."

The beginning— Tenzo looked back at the waterfall and saw that the stone pillar he had climbed his way out on, was, in fact, the very first Immortal Monk in the line that walked out of the waterfall and into the distance of the Infinite Waters and (he now knew) the hidden temple beneath it. As he watched, the falling water turned gold. Coins were pouring out along with shattered icicles. Jewels and goblets and decorative objects. The monks had sent his treasure back to him.

Those who had just been mocking him for being in the water, leapt in without hesitation. Soon pilgrims were flopping around in the icy pool like breeding fish. Tenzo let them. Anyone who jumped into frozen water to wrestle for riches needed them far more than he. Besides, he was wearing wealth enough. For it was clear to Tenzo what he must do. He had been returned to the beginning of the line. He was meant to walk it.

His robes hung wet and heavy off his shrunken body. It was with relief, not regret, that he ripped the first coin from its lining and offered it into the first bowl.

"I pay reverence to you, oh, venerable Immortal Monk. Bless me with this offering." Tenzo thought of Senu as he said this.

Tenzo continued to walk the line and put a coin and a prayer into each alms bowl he passed.

For every bowl, there was a hand. Biting fly children hovering around the pilgrims like they were walking carcasses. He gave them each a gold coin and told them to keep their wares.

For every statue, there was a shack. None were larger than Tenzo's smallest closet had been.

By moonrise meal, he had ripped the last coin from his robes. With no coin for food or lodging, Tenzo slept against the base of a statue. He could only hope that should a thief find him there, they would realize that he was not worth killing.

When the monkeys called forth the sun, he continued walking the line of monks. With no coins left to give but more blessings still to ask for, he prostrated himself at each pair of stone feet, like he had seen such pilgrims do, so long ago. Then again, those pilgrims had prepared by wearing leather aprons and wrapping their knees and hands in prayer scarves.

"I pay reverence to you, oh, venerable Immortal Monk. Bless me with this offering."

Tenzo's knees soon bruised from kneeling.

"I pay reverence to you, oh, venerable Immortal Monk. Bless me with this offering."

The muscles along his ribs trembled.

"I pay reverence to you, oh, venerable Immortal Monk. Bless

me with this offering."

The front of his robes ripped and hung in dusty tatters.

A scrawny boy ran up to him from a nearby shack and asked, "Where are you from?"

It was a question he himself had— Tenzo understood then that he had not only been sent back to the beginning of the line, he had been sent back to before he'd ever walked it!

"You are asking," Tenzo replied to himself, "the wrong question."

"What should I ask you then?" His younger self was so curious, so uncorrupted.

"Ask this: 'What horrible acts did you commit to earn the coin with which you are trying to buy redemption?'"

The boy's eyes got wide. "What horrible act did you commit?"

"Not seeing the clouds in the coin."

Then he was looking up at the clouds from his back. Then he was looking up at a woman crouched over him.

Here was a woman who cared more about gold than caring for her own son. Here was a woman who cared more about gold than living a life of comfort. Here was his mother.

Tenzo reached out to her. She took his hand. And slipped the ruby ring off his pinky finger.

The clouds came back into view.

Tenzo's last thought was of his pious neighbor telling him that his mother was fortunate to die where she did, where he now would, *for there is no holier place to die than at the feet of an Immortal Monk.*

ACKNOWLEDGMENTS

Thank you to Lix North for the original oil painting cover art. To all our advanced readers for their kind reviews. And to the numerous writers who submitted stories to this anthology, thank you for putting a little more imagination out into the world. Stay weird.

§